ST

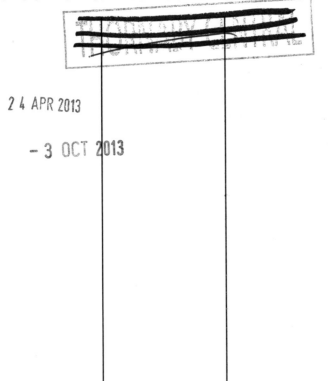

SANTA'S HOT SECRETS

A collection of twenty erotic festive stories

Edited by Antonia Adams

Published by Xcite Books Ltd – 2012
ISBN 9781908086709

Printed and bound in the UK

Cover design by Madamadari

Contents

Chills and Thrills
by Celia Montgomery

Lily drove the car through the open gates of Dìomhairich Forest Park, skidded slightly on the icy stones of the driveway and killed the engine. It was easy to locate her destination – only one building had any lights on, a welcoming glow in the otherwise empty holiday park. From the outside, the lodges were small and simply constructed wooden structures, with slate roofs and plain box windows.

The roof, decking and surrounding grounds were covered in a deep layer of powdery snow, glittering beautifully in her headlights. Why had she decided to come out to the middle of nowhere, in the middle of the worst winter in living memory?

A sudden mental picture flashed into her memory and she shut her eyes in an effort to stop it. Too late! It burned into her mind afresh, as though the image was imprinted on the inside of her eyelids. Steve; his head thrown back with a smug smile on his relaxed face. Georgina; the neat blonde ponytail bobbing into view from under his desk. Lily rubbed her fingers over her eyes to disperse it, her skin tight with dried tears. So much for "the most wonderful time of the year" … Anger and hurt had replaced those tears on the road through the darkness. Added to that, she was now tired, stiff and grumpy from the long drive.

She got out of the car, shivering in the biting wind, and began walking towards the well-lit cabin. She had set out straight from work, so she was wearing black high heels. Her feet were instantly soaked and freezing cold. Before she reached the steps up to the decking a figure emerged from inside, his impressive silhouette filling the doorway.

'Stop.'

It was an order, not a request, so Lily automatically halted dead in her tracks. Only when the chill from the frigid air nipped at her bare arms did her brain consider his command a little cheeky, given that she was paying him. She jabbed her fists onto her hips and opened her mouth to answer him back, but he continued, 'There are big icicles hanging from the gutter and I don't want you walking under them. It's a bitch to clean blood off the decking.'

Though she couldn't see his eyes because of the light behind him, she could feel them travelling over her body and it unnerved her. She suddenly became painfully aware of her nipples standing to chilled attention through her thin blouse. His voice sounded again from the shadows of his face. 'Where's your coat?

Lily gritted her teeth to stop herself from snapping at him. The last thing she needed right now was a lecture from a stranger. Bloody men!

'I don't intend to be outside much while I'm here so I didn't bring one,' she muttered, peering up at him, trying to make out his features.

He stepped forward and spoke again, but the words were lost on her. She was momentarily mesmerised, taking in his long legs, snugly clad in an ancient pair of jeans, faded by years of wear and washing. He wore a red-plaid flannel shirt that could have aged other men, but it was both adorable and sexy on him. His sleeves were rolled up to reveal muscular forearms and his top two buttons were undone, showing just a hint of dark hair. Hair a lot darker than that on his head, which was the colour of caramel and looked just as soft as it curled around his ears; too long to be tidy, too short to be unkempt. However, it was his eyes that stunned her and chilled her blood like the snow at her feet. They were a clear, pale blue and studied her with such interest and, if she was not mistaken, a trace of disappointment.

'I said, when will your friend be joining you? So I know when to lock the gate,' he explained. She stared at him in confusion.

'Friend?' she managed to articulate.

'You paid with a man's credit card – I assume it was your boyfriend's? Or husband's?' His question would have seemed much more innocent if his eyes hadn't been watching her so intently. As a result, her reply was both flustered and embarrassed.

'Oh, yes, hmm ... Well, ex-boyfriend. He owes me,' she answered as way of explanation.

At this, a slight smile flitted across his mouth, drawing her attention to his full lips. He had such a sensual mouth that she found she was distracted again and mentally shook herself. Meanwhile, he "tsked" at her, but she found her annoyance dissipating.

'I should report you for fraud, you naughty woman.' His voice was quiet and low, barely audible in the surrounding silence. They stared at each other for a moment before he broke the spell. 'Anyway ... you should come inside and get warmed up. Just let me clear this gutter.'

He lifted a long-handled broom and stretched up to knock the icicles off the lip of the guttering, his shirt riding up slightly as he did so. Lily's eyes were drawn to his waist, the firm skin of his stomach level with her eyes. The heat of desire suddenly unfurled in her belly and her mouth twitched with unconscious want.

Just at that moment, there was dull creak overhead and the huge layer of snow that had collected on the roof began to move. It rushed off like a smooth, white liquid and Lily's world suddenly went dark.

She tried to take a deep breath and assess her situation, but the snow lay heavy on her crumpled limbs, restricting all movement and soaking into her thin clothing. She began to struggle against it, panic and claustrophobia threatening to grip her mind, but she quickly realised it was hopeless and forced herself to stop wriggling. She could hear the blood pounding in her ears, louder because of the compacted snow cocooning her.

But there was another sound, a voice shouting from far away. Though it seemed like she had lain still for an age, suddenly the snow seemed to be shifting and that handsome face appeared above her.

'Are you hurt?' the man yelled, his face showing a mixture of concern and mild panic, his clear eyes wide.

'No,' she managed to whisper. The skin on her face was ice cold, her lips numb and rubbery. She felt his hands frantically pushing snow off her chest and then his strong arms were lifting her, hauling her upright and pulling her towards the cabin. He slammed the door quickly behind them and leaned her against it, putting his cold hands on both sides of her face. For a split second her disorientated brain thought he would kiss her and she leaned into him, closing her eyes. Instead, he gently pressed all around her skull, obviously checking for injuries. She opened her eyes to stare into his. There was a conflict in those blue pools as he stared down at her lips and involuntarily licked his own.

Lily's legs buckled and she slumped to the wooden floor. She knew things were happening around her but felt removed from it all, as if she were hearing and watching it through a dull mist. She was aware of being carried across the room and placed in front of a huge fire, of him stripping off his wet clothes and then doing the same to her, of being wrapped in a duvet and his arms circling her. They lay still for a long while, waiting for the shivers to subside and warmth to slowly return to their bodies.

'I hate to sound like an old cliché, but I needed to get you out of those wet clothes.' He spoke softly, his breath drifting over her ear. She smiled, the fog in her brain beginning to clear. She was aware of the heat of him, of his steady heartbeat against her shoulder, of his hands placed carefully on her midriff. She felt safe yet she suddenly realised she didn't even know his name. Embarrassment flooded through her and she couldn't turn to face him. She cleared her throat and whispered through a small cringe.

'I'm Lily, by the way. Lily Reynolds.'

He chuckled softly, the laugh vibrating through his chest and into her back, causing her to join in his laughter.

'Jacob Dean Anderson-Cupar, at your service, m'lady. My friends call me Coop and since we are on such … intimate terms now, I think you should too.' At the word "intimate", Lily tensed slightly, glancing around at their discarded clothes. As if reading her thoughts, he continued flippantly, 'Loving the little frogs on your knickers.'

They laughed together and he propped himself up on his lower arm, allowing her to roll onto her back underneath him. Their eyes locked and the laughter stilled. He stared down at her, completely at ease but his eyes seemed to darken to a deeper blue. Understanding the desire on his face, Lily involuntarily parted her lips. He dipped his head, paused to search her eyes and receiving no objection, lowered his mouth to hers. The kiss was soft and almost tender in its initial contact, but he tilted his head to gain better access, easing his tongue into her mouth and deepening the intensity.

Lily responded without thought, her body reacting to his every touch, her back arching to press her chest against his. His hands travelled up over her stomach and cupped her breasts. Lust surged through her, her nipples tingling under his palms, sending a shock of desire rolling over her and causing heat to unfold between her legs. Passion fused with need and their caresses became urgent. The kisses were now frantic, tongues exploring each other, teeth sweetly grazing against lips.

She raked her hands through his soft hair, scored her nails down his back and gripped his hips. He read her directions well and shifted his weight, allowing her to spread her legs and wrap them around his waist. His body moulded against hers, his weight providing a delicious pressure against her pelvis. She tilted her hips, bringing her pussy into contact with his firm stomach, letting him feel the warmth and moisture there. He released her mouth with a low groan and branded a trail of hot kisses over her throat. Then with great effort, he raised himself out of her tight embrace and dragged in a deep breath. She looked up at him, anxious and puzzled at the interruption.

He slipped his hands around her waist and rolled onto his back, pulling her over him, keeping their bodies entwined together. He stretched over his head and grabbed his jeans from where they had been discarded, rummaged in the pocket and removed his wallet, extracting a condom with a relieved grin. Her smile matched his and she propped herself up, sitting back onto his thighs.

Now free of the duvet, she ran her eyes greedily over his naked body, admiring his lean torso and firm flesh. As he rolled the condom down his impressive cock, she scraped her nails lightly over his balls, causing his breath to hitch. He reached between her legs and slipped a finger easily inside her, finding her wet and ready, then rubbed his thumb over her clit making her shudder in pleasure.

She rocked forward, locked her legs back beneath his and hooked her hands under his big shoulders, rolling over onto her back again. He slid his body up against hers, the tip of his erection pressing against her pussy. She stared into his eyes, her breath ragged with anticipation, her hips moving against his, urging him on. Still he paused, the dark fire of lust in his clear eyes while he teased her nipples with his fingers. Frustration tore through her and she pressed her feet under the muscles of his bum, pushing him inside.

He entered her and covered her mouth with his, stealing her gasp of pleasure and replacing it with his own groan. With no pretence of lovemaking, they thrust against each other wildly, the friction delicious against her clit. They quickly found a rhythm and she felt her orgasm beginning to build immediately, so turned on by their actions that her mind struggled to focus. She lifted her head, her mouth latching on to his collarbone and grazing it with her teeth as the vigorous delight gained momentum. She wriggled beneath him, providing new sensations for both of them and dug her fingernails sharply into his firm arse.

Lily glanced up and caught that faraway look in his eyes, the one that could only mean he was concentrating on delaying his release. She felt a flash of pride tinted with disbelief that she was causing this and bucked her hips against him in glee. The slight change in angle was all she needed and her body tensed and seemed to crack open.

She cried out, blinded with the intensity of it and shocked as its power rolled over her in waves. Coop continued thrusting throughout, and each time sent shockwaves repeating through her, until his own body tensed suddenly and he groaned with happiness. A deep shudder ran through him and his arms gave out, causing him to drop on top of her, his face buried in her hair. After a few seconds he raised himself onto his elbows, still panting, and looked down into her face. She forced her eyelids open and smiled up at him, languid and sated.

'Nice to meet you, Coop,' she said, running her fingers down his back which was slick with sweat. He laughed and withdrew from her body, rolling onto his side and pulling her against the full length of him. He dipped his head and kissed her, this time gentle and content, soft and soothing on her swollen lips.

'Just so you know, I don't do this for all my guests,' he murmured, gazing down at her.

Lily gave a sly smile and answered with a cheery quip. 'I'd say your customer service deserves a five-star review!'

Rogue Red Suit
by Lynn Lake

I clasped Bevin's pointed ears, pressed his elfin face into my chest. His hot little eager hands tried to clutch my ample breasts, his adorable pink tongue squirming all over my jutting nipples, all around my pebbled areolas. He couldn't quite grasp all my shimmering breast-flesh, however, shoving my tits up more than squeezing them, but he sure could latch his red lips onto my nipples, suck tight and terrific as any regular man.

Bevin was only four-feet eleven-inches tall, lofty by elf standards, diminutive by any full-sized woman's standards. But, as I well knew from excessive experience, while the little guys aren't going to dong your depths to any great extent, they sure try hard to please. And usually always accomplish their combustible task.

Bevin was pleasing me; groping my tits with gusto, licking and sucking and nipping like a filthy Jack Frost at my nipples. The pair of us were naked, laid out on Santa's velvet sleigh cover in the big guy's garage, hot horny Bevin on top of me. I pinched his ears and lifted his head up, kissed him hard and appreciatively on the mouth. His tongue jumped inside, twisted around my own, the guy eloquent in lust like his squeaky elf voice never allowed him to be in life.

It was December 4th. We were all just gearing up for

the busy season.

Bevin broke the tongue-and-tit grapple and yelped in my face, 'Let me eat you, Trixen!' His own face beamed like a certain reindeer's red nose when aroused by the elements.

'Down the chimney, then,' I breathed, smiling at him.

He rapidly scaled lower, over my Alpine-like breasts, in between my spread legs. His little fingers bit into my fleshy thighs, and he quickly took the plunge, diving his mouth and nose against my ginger pussy.

I sang the *Hallelujah Chorus*, Bevin hitting my hot spot.

Elves are first-rate workmen, that's a known fact. They're also first-rate lovers, that's a personally proven fact. Bevin's luscious tongue and sensuous lips were his tools here, down in my lovebox. He worked them in a masterly fashion, teasing my clit to throbbing tautness with the tip of his tongue, then sealing his lips around the buzzing button and tugging on it with impish enthusiasm. Then, after taking one last tingling pull, he started licking my pussy lips, stroking my brimming slit with that talented tongue of his.

'Oh, Bevin!' I moaned, shoving my breasts together and kneading, rolling the spit-shone tips with my fingers. I undulated my hips, thrusting my sodden mound up against Bevin's deliciously dragging tongue. He painted me with pure pleasure.

Until Santa suddenly opened the side-door to the garage and said, 'We've got a rogue, Trixen. I need you.'

Bevin lifted his head. I grabbed onto his sandy curls and planted his face back into my cunt, locking his neck between my thighs. 'I'll get right on it, Santa!' I gasped. 'Just as soon as Bevin gets me off!'

The big boss nodded and closed the door. He's a jolly good fellow for sure when it comes to letting his employees blow off some steam.

'Eat me! Eat me!' I pleaded to Bevin.

He dove back to his task, with relish. His head bobbed briskly, tongue striping my pussy. He nipped at my clit, sucked on it, chewed over my flaps, pulled on them. Then he formed his erotic mouth-organ into a rigid member as long as the real one and thrust it back and forth in my pussy, fucking me.

I shrieked and shuddered, repeatedly, coming on the end of Bevin's pumping tongue, gushing all around it, the guy's buffing fingertips on my blown-up clit adding to my ecstasy in heavy, heated waves.

I kissed his smeared face afterwards, and left him gasping for air and gulping my juices. I wish I could've thanked him more intimately, but I had a job to do. There was a rogue Santa out there, and I had to hunt him down.

His name was Glen Cardinal. He'd been Santa-certified at the North Pole campus three years previously, graduating in the middle of his class. He'd worked a storefront sidewalk his first year out, special events at community and senior centres his second year, before moving all the way up the candy-chain to mall Santa in his third seasonal year. And that's when he'd gone rogue, one week into the job.

'You're *who* again?' Dan Sigurdson, the mall manager, asked me, a frown furling his florid face.

I handed him my card.

He read it. 'Trixen, Santa's Helper.' He studied the embossed crossed Christmas trees, turned the card over, looked back up at me. Only his eyes didn't make it all the way to my face. They met my breasts.

I was dressed in my red coat trimmed with white fur, red leotard, and black boots, black belt cinching the whole arrangement together. My work clothes.

'He stole Santa's Playhouse admission and picture

11

money, that right?'

'Huh? Oh, yes, yes.' Sigurdson's glazed brown eyes refocused behind his refracting lenses. 'And all of the money out of the Salvation Army kettle at the front doors of the mall on his way out. He'd been doing a good job up until that point, got along well with the kids, was moving a lot of merchandise.'

'Santa'll be glad to hear that part, at least.'

'Huh?'

'He can't have gotten far.'

'No. I just called the police five minutes ago, when our accountant told me about the missing funds. He's only been gone ten minutes or so – right after the mall closed. How did *you* get here so–'

'You have an address for him?'

Sigurdson's face got even more flustered. 'Well, um, maybe I'd better wait for the police to arrive … to officially take care of the matter.'

I strolled up to his desk, my breasts bobbing under the tight red velvet. 'We like to take care of our own,' I husked. 'Santa's got a reputation to protect, you know.'

His widened eyes bobbed right along, and so did his head. 'Oh, yes … of course. Glen Cardinal lives at Broxton Manor, the corner of Second and Third.'

It was a fleabag hotel unfit for the dignity of a centre-court Santa. I soon found out the reason for the scuzzy digs from the sleazy front desk clerk. Glen Cardinal liked his liquor, straight without eggnog, and his strip clubs, where he regularly made it "snow" for the dancers. The guy was dragging the goodwill name of Kris Kringle right through the mucky slush, a disgrace to his ceremonial red suit and white beard. According to the clerk, Cardinal's favourite hangouts were on Johnson Avenue, a half-mile of nightclubs, restaurants and sex shops that paralleled Main Street. And so that's where I flew, parking the sleigh and the reindeer in an alley off Fifth.

I had multiple pictures of Cardinal in my Santaphone, along with a complete list of his dimensions, distinguishing features and mannerisms. But it was dark in the strip clubs, deliberately so, of course, and my Santavision glasses would've stood out like a set of antlers come bow-hunting season. So I couldn't very well just spot the Yuletide bandit. I had to get down and dirty, to clean up this egregious stain on Santa's image.

I started riding the pole, stripping up onstage. While the other girls didn't particularly like me barging in on their dance parties, the guys who paid the bills and stuffed the g-strings loved my Christmas-themed costume and the way I filled it out, and took it off. They were more than happy to get a jump on season's greetings.

I pranced up and down runways like a reindeer at take-off, swung and scissored around silver poles like a firewoman come the alarm bell. My plan was to draw Cardinal out, make him come to *me* with his blizzard of ill-gotten bills, so I could positively identify the rogue, arrest him and then later indemnify the mall and the Army.

But after four fruitless frenetic performances at different clubs, all I had were blisters on my bum and burn marks on my thighs, a bra-full of singles. It was 1:45 in the morning, and I was getting discouraged, getting more propositions than during a Santa parade. So, when I strutted out onto the stage at Pleasers, I was just about ready to throw in the garter and call it a night.

And then it was Christmas joy! From my perspective, at least. Because Santa came ambling right through the metal door of the strip joint and announced his presence to one and all with a bellowed, 'Ho! Ho! Ho!' aimed at us three girls onstage. It got a big laugh from the crowd, drew a wide smile from me. I watched as the imitation Claus sat down, spraddle-legged, at a table at a ringside.

The beard and the pillow were gone, but he was wearing all the rest of the costume – cap, coat, gloves, pants, boots and oversized belt buckle. He'd obviously had a few, was full of himself.

I elbowed Athena, the blonde goddess in the see-through Greek toga, aside and jumped down off the stage and into Glen Cardinal's lap. His chiselled face lit up like Mount Rushmore at night time. His hand dove down into his Santa pants and pulled out a twenty. He held it up, shouted, 'Merry Christmas!' And then stuffed the bill into my bulging red satin bra.

I was down to my lingerie-like underwear. But Glen had me covered, his rugged hands mapping out my contours with no regard to club rules and even less for decorum. I was a freelancer anyway, so no bouncers intervened. And whereas I'd thought at first of just initiating a takedown and taking the guy out of there as quickly and discreetly as possible, now I warmed up to another idea. A naughty lap-dancing idea. Glen Cardinal was one good-looking fake Santa, with a pair of big, white-gloved hands that rubbed me just right.

'Niiice!' I enthused, spinning around and sitting back to his front in the guy's lap.

His hands wrapped my buzzing breasts, slid down my stomach, plunged in between my legs. He nuzzled my neck and petted my pussy through my red silk panties. I rubbed my bum against the hardening length in his pants, raising my arms and running my fingers through my long, ginger hair.

It was dark, it was delirious, it was delectably dirty. I had a job to do, but the way I figured it, a disarmed rogue

Santa, one who'd just fired off his rod and was spent of bullets, was a whole lot easier to handle than one who was fully cocked and loaded. Call it prerogative or professional judgement, a heady mixture of business and pleasure, but I resolved to take this perverted *Père Noel* perp down easy and ecstatic for the both of us.

Glen slid a hand right into my panties and rubbed my bare pussy. His fingers found wet fur and swollen lips. His stroke warmed my cunt like a Christmas fire.

His other hand uncupped a breast, spilling mamm and money. He squeezed my shimmering tit, slid his fingers out to the tip and pinched buzzing nipple. I undulated in his lap, in his hands; me rubbing his cock with my bottom, he fondling my breasts and pussy with his fingers. We were putting the X into Xmas, really getting into the erotic spirit.

The crowd was almost completely oblivious to us, focused upon the girls onstage. We were staging our own private Christmas party, undressed for the occasion, Glen stroking my cunt to wet smouldering, mauling my tits and nipples so that my whole chest burned. Then I lifted up off his red tented lap and unzipped his Santa pants with practised skill. I pulled his throbbing erection out, poked its mushroomed hood against my pussy.

Glen gallantly yanked my panties to one side. His cockhead blossomed my lips, his shaft bulged my tunnel. I sat down in his lap again, on top of his studly stocking-stuffer, burying the Pole King-wannabe inside of me.

He groaned. I moaned. The pair of us basking in full-bodied pleasure.

He gripped my bared breasts and bit into my neck. I grasped his thick thighs and moved up and down on his cock. It was wicked, wanton, winter wonderful. We were fucking right there by the side of the stage, music thumping and lights strobing, men yelling and women stripping. We were giddy with delight like on Christmas morning, unwrapped and presented.

I wanted to see his handsome face again, kiss his full lips, get really and totally personal. So, without letting his prick out of my pussy, I spun around and scissored my legs, wound up face-to-face with the rogue once more.

He grinned, his teeth as white as his cap fur, his dark eyes sparkling. We kissed, our lips meeting by urgent agreement. He clutched my breasts and pumped my pussy. I shot my fingers under his cap and into his glossy black hair, riding his hot pink cock, welcoming his thrashing tongue into my mouth, twisting mine against it.

He pumped faster, gripped me tighter. I bounded higher, crowding my chest into his face. The music blared and lights flashed, men and women shouting. Glen and I cried out together, stud Santa bucking, blasting hot liquid lust into my cunt. This Santa's Helper shuddered and squirted, sleighing skyward at warp orgasm speed.

I took his hand and led him out of the bar and into a back room. He was as docile as a turkey-stuffed elf, expecting more good cheer which he was more than willing and able to pay for with his illegally-obtained funds. Glen lost his look of obliging bliss, however, when I suddenly spun him around and handcuffed him, shoved him through a back door and out into the alley.

'What took you so long?' Blitzen groused. 'We're freezing our antlers off out here.'

'I had to sedu– I mean, subdue him. Things got pretty physical.'

It was the "cooler" up north for Glen Cardinal. Hot flashes of memory for yours truly. And to all, a good-night!

Santa Maybe
by Marlene Yong

'But I look ridiculous!' Melanie protested.

'You look fantastic. Enough to give a bishop a stiffy,' Rob said. He had that familiar look on his long, lean face.

She glared into the mirror again. 'No way am I going out into the street like this. It's starting to snow.'

'Er ... OK,' Rob conceded. 'It's too cold. But at the party ...'

'I'll still feel fucking embarrassed.' Against her will, though, Melanie was already experiencing little thrills of anticipation.

Rob had brought it back to their flat – a distortion of the traditional Santa outfit. The red jacket barely reached past her hips and couldn't be fastened in front, the shiny black boots had six-inch spiky heels, and the excuse for Santa's pants amounted to little more than skimpy red furry knickers which would have embarrassed a bikini bottom. Rob had chosen the remainder of the costume to complete her exposure – a black basque with suspenders and semi-transparent fully fashioned black stockings. As a sop to modesty, the costume included a capelet for her shoulders and the traditional red hat with a pompom.

Melanie had never viewed herself as sexy before but whoever had designed the costume aimed to accentuate a woman's curves and even supply a few where none had previously existed. She'd thought of her shape as pretty average but the basque emphasised her cleavage, pushing her boobs up and together in a way which made her blush. Lower down her bum curved impossibly, so that her buttocks looked like two perfect hemispheres.

In spite of all this, the outfit proved unexpectedly comfortable and the knickers fitted so snugly that each time she moved a leg they sent an eerie erotic signal through her crotch.

'Seriously, Melanie.' Rob grunted, as if he thought it would reassure her. 'You look so shaggable I could bend you over the table and screw you from behind if it wouldn't make us late for the party. Anyway, you can wear your overcoat on the way there and I've booked a taxi.'

The very suggestion of wasting their Christmas Eve by going to Rob's office party outside his working hours had struck her as naff in the extreme. But, as Rob explained it, every year the CEO of the investment company where he worked opened his country house to staff and supplied a slap-up buffet and gallons of drink.

'It gets … er … a little out of hand, a bit raunchy,' Rob confessed, then added that the men were permitted to bring along their WAGs and the women their partners. The upper age limit was 45 and anyone who suspected that his or her significant other might be too uptight to join in the fun was gently encouraged to leave the other at home.

It seemed to Melanie that Rob was describing some kind of orgy. He'd gone the previous year, before they'd met, but clammed up whenever she tried to probe for details. She had, however, winkled from him that the CEO topped up the numbers with escorts, male and female.

That had made up her mind for her. Melanie didn't fancy the idea of the guy she'd been fucking for the past six months spending an evening with some nubile slag paid to ensure he left the party satisfied. But she needn't have worried. From the start, Rob had begged her to accompany him – though she still couldn't be sure if he wanted her as a buffer to protect himself from trouble or whether he was intending to land her in it.

The cab deposited them at a big set of iron gates. A manor house stood on the far side of a circular gravel drive, looking spectacular in the snow which was now falling heavily. Dozens of cars were parked haphazardly on the drive and even on the lawn. The massive wooden doors of the building stood slightly ajar and they walked straight in. About 60 men and women of various ages swarmed around the enormous, warm and carpeted entrance hall, where settees, armchairs and also tables laden with food and booze were scattered.

At the far end of this vast room, a sweeping flight of stairs led up to a gallery, off which Melanie suspected that the bedrooms lay. Everyone wore party costumes. To her relief, most of the women were displaying at least as much cleavage and thigh as she herself was. Nevertheless, as soon as she removed her long overcoat, she attracted a number of appreciative glances, from the women as well as the men, including more than a few unrestrained leers. Heat welled up inside her.

Melanie already knew a few of Rob's workmates and others quickly began to take an interest in her. She soon realised why Rob had bought her the scanty costume. She was his trophy squeeze. Everyone could spot the CEO's escorts, so Melanie, a virtual stranger, stood out as a novelty, even though plenty of the girls she could see might have been rated as shapelier or prettier. The basque, stockings and knickers didn't do her any harm either.

Within seconds a six foot-tall hunk with a fixed, licentious smirk sauntered up and said, 'Well, Rob, where have you been hiding this … lovely specimen?' He stared down her cleavage as if he'd dropped his fountain pen into it. 'Please introduce me before I spill my –' he paused suggestively, then waved the wine glass he was clutching '– drink.'

When Rob didn't answer, the man bent down to murmur in Melanie's ear. 'I'm Burt. Can I get you anything? Maybe a salami?' He smacked his lips, his nose hovering only inches from the bodice of her basque. She decided she didn't like Burt.

Several more of Rob's colleagues buzzed around for a while and Melanie soon started to feel more at ease. But there was no indication of the orgy at which Rob had hinted. Not that she intended to participate. But she wouldn't have minded a good ogle – and then, later, Rob could take care of her needs.

Finally, at about ten o'clock, Melanie noticed a flurry of activity in a dimly lit corner of the room. About a dozen guests stood in a semi-circle, watching something hidden from her view. She drifted across to see what was going on. Through the crowd she recognised Zane, one of the colleagues to whom Rob had introduced her earlier. He was pressing the wife of another of Rob's acquaintances up against the wall. Burning with curiosity, Melanie edged closer. Zane had levered the woman's generous breasts over the neck of her dress and was tonguing her nipples like he hadn't eaten in weeks. As Melanie watched, he lifted the hem of the dress to her waist and delved his fingers into her panties. She parted her legs and appeared to be enjoying his ministrations. She closed her eyes and her jaw was clenched in a risus of pleasure. The sight stirred an unexpectedly thrilling vibration between Melanie's thighs.

The cluster of onlookers were nodding their heads and

murmuring their approval. Melanie noticed the woman's husband nearby, his hand clutched to his crotch as if to debar his cock from escaping. She glanced around and other spectacles, blurred by the dim lighting, came into focus. One man, at the edge of the semi-circle of kibitzers, was stroking the buttocks of a girl through her silky skirt. He pushed the thin material into the crevice between them until his fingers disappeared from view. She made no objection – indeed, she wriggled her bottom to allow him access.

Like a slow contagion, the sexual activity spread. Within half an hour, armchairs, sofas, table tops, rugs and areas of the carpet were commandeered to accommodate the participants. No one displayed the slightest sign of reticence. It was as if everyone took it for granted that all bets were off and they had authority to indulge in whatever sexual practices they chose and with whoever showed a willingness to join in. Duos slipped into adjoining rooms off the hall. Scattered around, males paired up with males, females with females, trios fused together wherever they could find spaces. A quartet even attempted a clumsy daisy chain. A girl – unmistakeably one of the escorts – fell to her knees in front of a guy whose prick juddered from his flies in front of her face. She swallowed it in one slurp, pumping the bottom few inches of it in her hand as if she were milking a cow.

Melanie's own juices were running wild by now. Her red knickers felt damp against her pussy. She peered around, trying to spot Rob. She desperately wanted his cock inside her. He would ensure she got her oats. No one else would do – certainly not a total stranger. She'd always remained faithful to her lover of the moment. But Rob was nowhere to be seen.

The flickering in her vagina peaked. She desperately

21

needed release.

Where the hell had Rob gone? She meandered around the room trying to pick him out from the tangled bodies. No such luck. She'd noticed couples disappearing through a door leading into a room off the hall. Perhaps he had gone in there, though she couldn't imagine why.

She drifted across to the door and entered. The room was in semi-darkness but she could not mistake Rob's lean body covering a redhead's, his pants around his ankles, her bare knees gripping his thighs. Melanie felt as if she had suddenly plunged into a bath full of ice cubes. Every nerve in her body twitched in shock. Sickened, she fled from the room.

Tears of fury, disappointment and – most of all – sexual frustration stung her eyes. Curiously, in spite of the orgiastic shenanigans, no one even glanced at her. Maybe she just didn't look ready for action. Not that she wanted any. All the same, she'd never felt so rejected. She'd become the wallflower at the ball.

She stumbled across the hall trying to remember where she had left her overcoat.

'Lost lamb?' a plummy voice enquired. Startled, Melanie jumped. The speaker wasn't much taller than herself, though at least thirty years older, stocky, even a little on the plump side, with sandy hair and green eyes. He was not good-looking by any benchmark, but exuded a strange, voluptuous charisma. His round face was a little blotchy as if he'd been exerting himself, though he was not perspiring. He looked as though he had recently shaved.

He seemed so out of place among the writhing flesh that it struck her abruptly that she'd come face to face with the CEO of Rob's company, whom she had never met. He took her arm and she felt a sudden warmth, both from him and towards him. 'You look upset. Can I be of service?'

His slightly affected courtliness in this sex-permeated environment was both calming and, somehow, erotically stimulating. Melanie got the impression that her nipples were tingling so much they had risen over the top of her bodice. Even though he was only touching her elbow, her labia felt as if they were on fire.

'I … I just need to get away. From all … this,' she said waving her hand vaguely at the undulating mass of unclothed torsos.

He pondered. 'There's no need to leave,' he said. 'Come with me.' Meekly, Melanie followed him up the sweeping staircase which led to the gallery. At the top, he stopped before a big oak door, extracted a brass key from his waistcoat and guided her into a large, comfortable room. She stared around. The walls were panelled and a log fire in a massive fireplace afforded warmth and cosiness. An ancient oil lamp provided illumination and revealed a resplendent four-poster bed. At the far end of the room, a small leadlight window lay within an alcove.

'I want this evening to be perfect for everyone,' he said. 'Rest here for a while, Melanie.' He turned to leave. 'Now, unless there's anything else I can do …'

Later, Melanie realised it never even crossed her mind as to how he knew her name. She'd been observing him keenly. Age indeterminate, possibly over 50, though his smooth cheeks looked so youthful. He was well preserved and had beautifully groomed hands. She became aware of an animal magnetism at odds with his suave appearance. She speculated what it would be like to shag him.

She came to a decision. Her determination to remain faithful to Rob crumbled. She would have her revenge – in spades. The very thought of seducing his CEO made her shiver. Fear? Or pleasurable anticipation?

'No, wait! Keep me company,' she said, 'just for a

while.' Provocatively, she shrugged the capelet and short red jacket from her shoulders and let them slip to the ground. She faced him in just the basque, black stockings and stiletto heels. She inhaled gently forcing her breasts to ride up to the rim of the bodice.

He hesitated.

'I don't even know who you are,' Melanie said.

'Christopher. My friends call me Chris.'

'I don't want to be on my own, Chris. Not tonight. Not Christmas Eve.' She glided over to him. 'Stay with me.' Amazed at her own daring, she placed the tips of her fingers against his cheek and tilted her face towards him. When he did not respond, she pressed her lips against his, coaxed his mouth open and flicked her tongue against his palate. His body arched involuntarily against hers. Her bare thighs were conscious of the stirring hardness in the front of his trousers.

'But I have to …' he began as they broke apart. But Melanie placed a forefinger against his lips to silence him, then ran her palm languorously up the crotch of his pants. The stirring within had become a palpable throb. The rigidity and size of what her palm encountered sent darts of desire through her cunt.

Christopher still clutched the key. Melanie prised it from his unresisting hand and walked unhurriedly to the door, which she locked from inside the room. 'To ensure we won't be disturbed.'

She took his hand and, as she led him towards the bed, she tugged the basque surreptitiously down so that her breasts, hot and swollen, sprang up from the bodice.

Suddenly, whatever his reservations, Christopher appeared to cave in. 'Christmas,' he whispered. 'A time for giving. Let this be my gift to you.' His cool hands caressed her breasts. He pulled hard at one nipple. Then he bent his head to frott the other between his teeth and lower lip.

'Not yet,' Melanie gasped and sat at the side of the bed. This was one CEO who was going to have a Christmas he'd never forget, she thought. And Rob would learn all about it too, she'd make sure of that. Purposefully, she unbuckled Christopher's belt, unzipped his fly and pulled down his pants. He remained standing next to the bed, his expression impassive. His erection jutted out in front of him, pointing slightly upwards from his groin like a thick, cylindrical bracket from which the flower basket has been temporarily removed.

Dreamily, Melanie took hold of it and ran her fingers beneath it until she reached his balls. Power seethed from them, an electric current flowing up her arm to her breasts and down her belly to galvanize her pussy. Christopher hesitated, not touching her, then muttered, 'I'm not supposed to be here. I have work to do ...' His voice faded as Melanie's lips engulfed his organ and began an inexorable glide up the shaft.

Rob had always praised her oral skills and now she employed them to the utmost advantage. As she slid her mouth back along the shaft to Christopher's knob, she took care to concentrate her tongue on his frenum, scarcely brushing the underside of his cock which she knew would be particularly responsive. Then, grasping the stem in both hands, she opened her mouth wide so he could see her rotating her tongue round his glans. At the same time, she tilted her head up to stare up into his eyes so that their gazes locked. Without warning, she clamped her lips once again round his erection and jerked her head fiercely forward until her nose pressed against his pubis.

Meanwhile, she was walking her fingers round his thighs to the backs of his legs and up to his buttocks. She tugged these apart and wormed her fingertips between them. She vaguely recalled reading that a man could be brought to a longer-lasting intense orgasm by stimulating his prostate. She had never tried it with Rob. But this was a stranger and … she threw caution to the winds and wriggled her forefinger into the quivering crevice.

It didn't take long. Less than a minute. Christopher pumped his hips back and forth as if to force his cock down her throat. Just as she was sliding her lips backwards along his shaft, the thick, warm liquid filled her mouth and overflowed onto her chin and breasts. Christopher emitted a long deep sigh of satisfaction and Melanie wanted to cry out in triumph.

'That was the first,' she rasped. Her throat felt clogged. Nevertheless, she clamped her mouth around the knob and was rewarded by the gradual hardening of his tool.

Much later, after her mouth had sucked him dry, Melanie stretched out on the four-poster. After scanning her body, Christopher leaned forward and eased her knickers down her legs. He pressed his palms against the insides of her stockinged thighs and spread them wide. 'I want to look at your cunt,' he said, his voice thick. 'To see it open like a flower, to see your juices glisten at the lips.' Involuntarily, as if hypnotised, her labia responded and moisture oozed out. 'Stockings have a magic of their own,' he went on wistfully. He caressed one suspender strap and fondled the dark welt where it met her thigh.

His hand meandered up to her outcurled lips and gave her distended clitoris a tender nip between two knuckles. He turned it to slip two digits into her, then curled up his middle finger to press against her mons from the inside, seeking her g-spot. Melanie moaned, twisting against them. I'm meant to be seducing *him*, her mind protested. But she had never felt so horny before. Christopher knew exactly what he was doing. She was loving every second, so why not just lie back for the moment and think of Christmas?

To her frustration, he withdrew his fingers entirely and stood stock still. The tension within her pussy gradually built up until she wanted to scream at him to ram them back inside her again. After what seemed like aeons of waiting, he touched the tip of her clitoris with the pad of one finger, then pulled it away. He did this again. And again. Soon he was beating an agonising tattoo on Melanie's clitoris and she was jerking convulsively.

Eventually, the tautness in her clit became so overpowering that she envisaged it as elastic stretched so tightly that it was ready to snap. Her breaths were panting and shallow, her throat rasping.

Abruptly, Christopher turned his attention from her cunt back to her breasts. Lingeringly, he ran his tongue along and up them and, as he did so, coaxed her to lift an arm until he could reach the hollow of her armpit, which he nonchalantly licked. With each sweep of his tongue Melanie felt her secretions welling up and flowing, thick and hot, down her thighs.

She ached for the softness of his tongue to flick around the mound of flesh poking out from within her labia. As if reading her thoughts, Christopher obligingly grasped both her knees and spread her legs as wide as he could manage then bent and blew warm breath directly onto her clit.

Melanie writhed. Carnal grunts tore from her throat. She knew deep down that the lascivious impulses tormenting her vagina derived from something more than mere physical caresses. There was something … well, unearthly … about Christopher. An instinctive animal recognition of her needs and how to fulfil them.

Now his tongue had descended on her pussy and thrust far into her vaginal channel while a finger insinuated itself into her lower orifice. Teasing, he rubbed his nostrils against her clitoris, breathing in the fragrance of her quim. Melanie thrust her hips up to meet his mouth and rotate her labia against it, which pressed her clitoris on to the tip of his nose. But she continued to hold back, unwilling to abandon herself fully. She had never experienced a real, no-holds-barred orgasm before. The thought that she was about to lose control totally terrified her but swept her along in an irresistible vice.

And then, like reaching the top of a helter-skelter and being ripped downwards by the force of gravity, Melanie climaxed. Her head swung from side to side, her teeth chattered, her lips trembled and the room blazed with light and colour.

She lost track of time. When the world swung back into focus, the light in the room was perceptibly brighter. The first rays of a December dawn were filtering through the little leadlight window. Christopher rose from the bed and adjusted his clothes. 'I must go, Melanie,' he said softly. 'You stay and rest as long as you wish.' He smiled, bent and kissed her. 'You tempted me away from some vital work I had to do. But it was worth every second ...'

Melanie must have closed her eyes for some minutes because when she looked, he was gone. She hadn't heard the door open or close. A distant noise, tantalisingly familiar but not one she could immediately identify, reached her ears.

She shivered. The log fire had died down completely. There weren't even sparks in the great fireplace.

Time to go and find Rob. She no longer yearned for revenge. Just to return to their flat and demand his promise never to cheat on her again. She swung off the bed, smoothed down the basque and tugged on the red panties.

With her stilettos in one hand, she padded over to the door and tried the handle. The door didn't budge. The key was still in the keyhole, though. She turned it. A click and it opened. She frowned. It just wasn't possible for Christopher to have relocked the door on the inside after leaving the room. But if not, how did he get out?

She shuffled back to the window in her stockinged feet. Peering down, she saw there was a drop of about 40 feet outside. And the window didn't open. It was sealed.

As she stood, puzzled, the door burst open. She saw Rob in the doorway and behind him, a tall, elegant man in an evening suit.

'What are you doing in here, Melanie? We've been searching for you all over. Everyone left hours ago.' And then, as if by way of an afterthought, Rob introduced his companion. 'Oh, by the way, this is my CEO, the owner of this house ...'

Melanie went cold. If this was the CEO, then who was Christopher? And where had he gone? Not through the door, that was certain. Nor the window. The only other way out of the room was ... impossibly ... through the fireplace ...

And ... of course! *The chimney*!

Abruptly it all came eerily together like a piece slotting into an otherworldly jigsaw. Christopher ... Chris ... Kris. And that familiar noise she'd heard just after he'd disappeared. She recalled it now from years before when, as a child, she'd played in the snow.

The jingling of the bells on her sleigh ...

Christmas Lights
by Elizabeth Coldwell

When I pulled up in my driveway, Trent was putting up his Christmas lights, shirtless in the late-afternoon heat. Two of the houses across the way already had strings of lights decorating every shingle and window frame, their roofs adorned with illuminated reindeer, and fir wreaths hanging on their front doors, so I'd known it wouldn't be long before Trent followed. In the three years I'd been living on this street, the displays had been getting ever bigger and more ostentatious, and Trent Maisner always produced the biggest of the lot.

Me, I'd never quite seen the point, maybe because it never really felt like Christmas here. Back in Montana, where I'd grown up, it got properly cold in the winter, and all my memories of Christmas involved snowball fights, carol concerts, and mugs of hot chocolate, topped with cream and marshmallows, drunk in front of a roaring fire. It felt like the right surroundings for snowmen and sleighs and footprints on the roof tiles that might, just might, have been left there by Santa. Here in Southern California, where the temperature barely dipped below the high 60s, even in mid-December, it was a lot harder to get into a festive mood. As a result, my home always remained undecorated, apart from a small, artificial tree in one corner of my living room. Though he'd never said as much, I always got the impression Trent felt I was letting the rest of our little corner of the street down.

I should have gone inside the house. I had groceries to stow, and a half-finished article about one of Hollywood's hottest young directors on my PC that wasn't going to write itself. Instead, I stood watching Trent, admiring the way the well-defined muscles in his back and shoulders flexed as he worked.

Not that I didn't get plenty of opportunities to do just that. The guy, a builder by trade, spent most of his free time remodelling his own home, the quality of his work a perfect advertisement for his professional services. And he seemed positively allergic to wearing anything on his upper torso. Many was the time when the words just weren't flowing, and I'd step away from my desk to brew myself some coffee and sip it in the kitchen. As I did, I'd watch Trent hammering and sawing, his skin shining with sweat, and imagine how it would feel to lick those salty droplets from his skin. A delicious fantasy, and one I'd jerked myself off to on any number of occasions, but just that. Every impression I'd gained of Trent was that he was as straight as they came; once married, but now divorced, with women seemingly queuing up to become the next Mrs Maisner.

Trent climbed down the ladder propped against his front wall, stretched, and pushed his dark-chestnut fringe out of his eyes. He caught me looking in his direction, and wandered over. I hoped he had no idea of the kind of thoughts I'd been having about him.

'Hey, Andy, looking for some tips on how a pro decorates his home?' The man's self-confidence bordered on arrogance at times. It should have made him less attractive in my eyes, but it didn't.

'I would be, if I had any intention at all of decorating

my own,' I told him. I knew it wasn't what he wanted to hear, but I continued, 'I'm sorry, Trent, but I just don't see the point in wasting all that time and money, just to treat the neighbours to a free light show.'

'You're a regular old Scrooge, you know that?' Trent sounded as though he was only half joking.

'Hey, it's not that I don't like Christmas,' I protested. 'It's just not so much fun when you spend it on your own, that's all.'

When he looked at me, I couldn't tell whether his expression was one of sympathy or pity. It suddenly occurred to me I didn't actually know how Trent passed the holidays, or who with. I tended to shut myself in with a turkey dinner for one and some cheesy old film or other on cable; until now, I'd never really given a thought to my nearest neighbour's arrangements. He probably invited a couple of hot blondes round for a sex marathon, I thought enviously, sharing the kind of Christmas with him that part of me so badly longed to.

He sighed. 'Isn't there any way I could persuade you to put a few lights up for once?'

I shook my head, beginning to get a real thrill from our verbal sparring. 'Do you really think this street needs any more lights? Hell, there are so many up already I bet the whole place is visible from space come nightfall.'

Trent grinned at the image my words created, but he didn't back down from his position. 'Andy, what's it going to take to get you to change your mind?'

With a shrug, wondering just how far he was prepared to push this, I said, 'I don't know. Maybe you'll just have to make me.'

'Oh, really?' He took a couple of paces forward, right into my personal space. So close to him, I could smell the unadorned, masculine aroma of a man who'd been putting in a good few hours of hard, manual work. My cock gave an involuntary twitch in reaction.

'Yeah, really.' This was all kind of foolish, facing off against Trent on my own driveway, but somehow I couldn't help but feel the tension between us was more than just that of two men who were contemplating settling a meaningless argument in a physical fashion.

'OK, but I don't think you quite know what you're letting yourself in for ...' With that, he launched himself at me, reaching for my shoulders and spinning me round, off balance. Until that moment, I hadn't seriously believed Trent was spoiling for a fight, and from the strength of his grip I knew I'd underestimated him as any kind of opponent. I wasn't in bad shape; I regularly went jogging and lifted a few weights, in an attempt to counteract the effects of my sedentary writing job, but Trent was up and down ladders all day, hefting bricks and building supplies, and he had the muscular strength to prove it. In any kind of fight, we both knew he had the better of me.

I looked round to see if anyone was passing, in the moment before he kicked my legs from under me and I went sprawling to the ground. Maybe someone would come to my aid, or at least shame Trent into getting up and going about his business once more. But the street was deserted for once, not even Mrs Waterman from the house across the way out walking her pet Chihuahua, and as Trent half-dragged me round to the side of the house, I wondered what kind of beating I'd let myself in for.

This is stupid, I wanted to protest. We're friends – or at least I thought we were. So why are you intending to give me a licking, and all over a few lousy Christmas lights?

But as Trent crouched over me, straddling my hips with his thick, jeans-clad thighs, I felt the hard length of his cock poking at my leg, and realised I'd been correct in my first assumption. This was about something very different than a fist fight.

'God, you're easy, Andy,' Trent murmured, his breath warm against my ear. 'I've wondered for so long what it would take to have you at my mercy. I just didn't realise which button I needed to push.'

'But …' I looked up, meeting his brilliant blue gaze. His fingers crept under the edge of my T-shirt, tracing slow, sensual circles on my skin. 'I had no idea you were into guys.'

'Why do you think my marriage broke up?' He shook his head, but his fingers never stilled in their teasing progress up my chest. 'I've always liked guys, just as much as I do girls. Gina knew that when we got married, and I hoped that one day she might be open to the idea of a threeway, but she wanted me to be faithful to her, and only her. Well, I managed that for as long as I could, but I always felt like I was shutting a part of myself off. A part that will always respond to a hot guy like you …'

Never had I imagined that one day Trent would be calling me hot, or that when it happened, he'd have me pinned to the lawn at the side of his house, where I could breathe in his heady, male aroma, mixed with sweet overtones of freshly cut grass. Sure now that Trent wanted me in the same way as I wanted him, I felt my cock surge in my pants.

His finger brushed over my nipple, making it spring up hard. He laughed at the strength of my response, then pinched the tight bud painfully between his finger and thumb.

'But that's enough about me,' he said. 'Don't forget, I've still got to do whatever it takes to make you see the benefits of decorating your house for the holiday season …'

As he spoke, he reached over to a box that stood just a few inches away from us, at the foot of the ladder still propped against the side of his house. With a wicked smile on his face, he pulled out a string of Christmas lights in rainbow shades. 'These don't work any more,' he said. 'I was going to throw them out, but now I see a better use for them.'

Too fast for me to react, he pinned both of my wrists together above my head, and started winding the cord of the lights around them, before tying it off. He hadn't fastened the knot too tight, and I reckoned if I really wanted to, I might be able to wriggle free of my bonds, but I found I didn't want to. As I lay on Trent's lawn, tied up with Christmas lights and awaiting his next move, my cock was as hard as it had ever been. When he reached for the zipper of my pants and undid it, hauling them and my shorts down in the same movement, I made a half-hearted protest.

'Hey, man, what if someone sees us?'

'Relax, my truck's blocking the view from the road …'

And what if someone does see you? a little voice asked in the back of my mind. Doesn't it just add to the thrill of being out in public, half-naked and about to let your horny neighbour do whatever he wants to you? In Montana, outdoor sex was reserved only for the high days of summer; there was no way I'd think of even venturing outside in December without dressing in a thick coat, scarf and gloves. Maybe Christmas in this part of the country had some compensating factors, after all.

Trent wrapped his fingers around my shaft, holding it steady, then bobbed his head down, engulfing me in the slick furnace of his mouth. For a moment I couldn't speak, couldn't think, just butted the head of my dick up against his palate, blindly seeking release.

35

He released his grip, and withdrew his mouth with a chuckle. 'Hey, slow down. This isn't a race, you know.'

I mumbled something about it having been a while, the words trailing off as he took an alternative tack, licking up and down my length with smooth, languorous strokes.

'Oh, that's good.' I sighed, no longer trying to force the pace, just happy to let Trent use his mouth to give me pleasure.

His tongue made its wet, slithery way along the seam between my balls, over my taint, and lapped for just the briefest moment at my arsehole. Trying my best not to lose my load, I thought of all the work I'd have to do when I got in the house just to meet the deadline on my article, never mind doing something about the quart of ice cream that was very likely melting in the trunk of my car right at this moment. It didn't help; I couldn't dream up anything boring and mundane enough to distract me from the sensations Trent's wickedly licking tongue was creating in my groin.

He must have sensed how close I was, because abruptly he stopped, and rolled me over on to my front. Crouching over me, he worked to undo the knots in the string of lights binding my wrists.

'You look so hot all tied up like that,' he told me, 'but I want you to be comfortable when I take your arse.'

A shiver went through me. I hadn't seen Trent's cock yet, only felt it nudging urgently at me when we'd been wrestling, but still I hungered to have it deep in my back door. Raising myself up on my knees and elbows, giving Trent an enticing view of my spit-slick arsehole and low-hanging balls, I looked over my shoulder to see him stripping off the jeans that were all he'd been wearing on his lower half. This obviously wasn't the first time he'd been outdoors in the altogether; no tan lines marked the even caramel tone of his skin. I didn't have too long to dwell on the gorgeous image of my neighbour sunbathing naked, because the next thing I knew he'd spit on his palm and used it to give his cock the lubrication it would need to aid its entry into my arse.

'Why don't you open yourself up for me?' Trent asked, giving his length a few lazy tugs. He didn't really need anything more in the way of visual stimulation – his cock stood at full attention, shining with spit and precome – and I suspected he just got off on giving me orders. Orders I was only too happy to obey, reaching behind myself and easing a finger into my hole. While he watched, I worked it in and out, mimicking and anticipating what it would be like when his cock took its place.

When he ordered me to stop, I did so with no little reluctance. But the truth was I needed to be fucked; I'd been on the verge since Trent had first pinned me to the ground, and now I was desperate for release.

He got behind me, running a hand over the curve of my arse before giving it a resounding slap. 'Man, you've got one hell of a cute butt,' he said. 'Why did we never think of doing this before?'

You might not have, I wanted to tell him, but his cockhead pressed hard against the lip of my hole, and then it was sliding inside, slowly but remorselessly filling my chute.

'You like that, huh?' he asked, and all I could do in reply was nod, and grunt, and will him to push harder, deeper, and really give me the fucking I craved.

No longer caring that we were out on Trent's lawn in the middle of the afternoon, with the possibility that someone might spot us naked and rutting like beasts, I gave in to my basest needs. I thrust back, meeting every one of his strokes and then some, driving him on. Our sweating, heaving bodies slapped together, and our gasps and moans of pleasure grew ever louder and more frantic. My arse gripped tightly at Trent's invading shaft, and his calloused workman's hands raked my flanks as his thrusts speeded up. So close to coming, I grasped my cock and gave it a series of short, furious tugs. My head swam, nostrils full of the scents of sex and grass and Trent, and I cried out his name as the spunk rose from my balls and sprayed out on to the turf beneath me.

Muttering words that made no sense, my name the only thing comprehensible among them, Trent filled my bowels with his seed. We collapsed together in a tangle of limbs as he slowly eased his cock out of my arse, sharing a moment of genuine affection.

At last, Trent rolled to one side, normality reasserting itself. 'So,' he said with a grin, 'has that persuaded you you need to get some lights up on your house?'

The following day, I made a small concession to Trent's demand. I went down to the local hardware store and bought a single string of white LED lights. I thought they'd look classy woven into the vine that surrounded my front door; my little tribute to the holiday season. And if that wasn't enough in the way of decoration for Trent – well, I was sure he'd find some way of persuading me to make more of an effort.

Snowball
by Sam Stewart

Amanda watched Bobby, her four-year-old son, eagerly scanning the rooftops for signs of Father Christmas as they walked together up the dark, snow-covered path to her parents' house. She couldn't help having a look herself – just in case. She laughed. Santa and his reindeer, knights on white chargers, fairies at the bottom of the garden ... it's sad, she thought, the way growing up strips away our childhood dreams.

Amanda's dad opened the door, lighting up the night-time garden, and grinned enthusiastically as they approached. Somehow Mum and Dad always managed to hang on to the magic of Christmas and Amanda thought wistfully of Christmases growing up.

'Have you sent your letter to Santa yet?' her dad asked Bobby.

'Not yet, Granddad.'

'Oh come on, then. We haven't a moment to lose.'

'Mummy, you've got to write one too,' Bobby cried, bubbling with excitement.

'Oh, I don't know,' said Amanda. 'I'm sure Santa will be too busy to bring me anything.'

'Nonsense,' laughed her father. 'I'm sure Santa can find time for my little girl.'

Amanda grimaced at her dad and allowed Bobby to

drag her into the house.

As Bobby and his granddad worked on their letter, Amanda looked thoughtfully at her blank paper, wondering what she could possibly write. Her dad looked up at her.

'Come on, angel,' he said. 'There must be something you wish Santa would bring you.'

Amanda picked up her pen and after a moment's thought, she grinned and wrote, 'Dear Santa, Please send me a handsome knight to sweep me off my feet and fulfil my wildest dreams.' She wanted to write "naughtiest dreams" but she was conscious that her dad or Bobby might ask her what she meant.

Christmas morning brought more snow and lots of presents. Amanda and her son headed outside to play with Bobby's new sledge while her mum and dad set to work on the Christmas dinner. Sledging gave way to snowman building and that descended into snowball fighting. Bobby scurried behind the snowman, giggling as Amanda smiled menacingly and scooped snow into her hands.

'Now you're going to get it!' she laughed. She made an exaggerated performance of preparing to throw the snowball and hurled it into the air. She deliberately missed Bobby by a mile but was much less careful about which direction the snowball did take.

At the precise moment she let fly, the next-door neighbour stepped unwittingly out into the fresh morning air. Amanda's laughter turned to horror as she watched her snowball fly with unerring accuracy and then explode a second later into the neighbour's astonished face.

'Hey, you kids!' he shouted, angrily brushing snow off his hair and jumper. 'Watch what you're doing or I'll come round and tell your parents.'

Amanda snatched off her woolly hat and shook her long brown hair free. She stepped forward nervously. 'I ...

I'm terribly sorry,' she stuttered. 'It was an accident.'

The neighbour came to meet her and held out his hand, grinning. 'I'm sorry,' he said. 'I didn't realise you were an adult.' He gave Amanda an admiring look, taking in her slim, five-foot-two frame and the delightful curves that were now evident beneath her quilted jacket. Amanda was equally appraising of him. He was a similar age to her, about 25, athletic, handsome – delicious, she thought.

She shook his hand. 'I'm Amanda Brook,' she said. 'This is my son, Bobby. We're just visiting my parents for Christmas.'

'Mark Knight,' said the neighbour. 'I just moved in a few days ago.'

'Pleased to meet you,' said Amanda, giggling. 'I'm terribly sorry about the snowball but I don't think it would do much good telling my parents. I think I'm a bit too old to be spanked.' She immediately cringed and regretted her words as an embarrassed silence hung in the air. What on earth had possessed her to make such an intimate remark – one that gave such a telling insight into her personal desires? To her relief, however, Mark seemed happy to resume the conversation – and he appeared to have at least some interest in her private life.

'Are you here with your husband?' he asked.

'No, no, free and single,' said Amanda with a shy smile. 'How about you? Er, wife, I mean.'

'No, there's just me. My company has just moved me out here and rented this house until I can find somewhere more permanent.'

The conversation came to an abrupt end when Bobby, suddenly bored, dragged on his mother's sleeve.

'I … I'll see you around?' said Amanda, hopefully. 'Merry Christmas.'

The rest of Christmas Day passed with the usual

41

traditional festivities, but as the evening drew in, there was a rattle at the letterbox and an envelope dropped onto the mat, addressed to Amanda. She ripped it open and pulled out a comical Christmas card showing a mischievous reindeer throwing a snowball at Santa. It was from Mark. It wished her and Bobby a merry Christmas and there was a little message added at the end, which read, 'Amanda – You're never too old.' Amanda blushed.

'What's that, love?' asked Amanda's mum coming up to her side.

'Oh, its just a Christmas card from Mark, the guy next door.'

'That's nice,' said her mum. 'What's that bit? Never too old – what does that mean?'

Amanda knew exactly what Mark meant – never too old to be spanked! She swallowed nervously. 'Oh, I expect he just means no one is too old to enjoy Christmas. Or to throw snowballs – I hit him with one earlier on!'

Mum could tell that Amanda was hiding something but she decided discretion was the best policy. She just smiled and nodded.

Boyfriends had always proved a major disappointment to Amanda. Unreliable, untrustworthy, wanting nothing more than a quick tumble in the sack, or running away when they found she was a single mum. But there was something different about Mark – there had been an instant rapport as though she had known him for years. She felt relaxed and comfortable with him. But did he feel the same way? Was he a potential soulmate or was she kidding herself and seeing him through the rose-tinted spectacles of wishful thinking? There was only one way for her to find out.

Early on Boxing Day morning, Amanda awoke with mischief on her mind. With her parents watching Bobby, she pulled on leggings and a chunky jumper and wandered around to Mark's house. It was crunch time – either she was going to meet her match or else make the most embarrassing mistake of her life. Cautiously, she approached the front door and then, after a moment's hesitation, knocked quickly before she could change her mind. She backed away a few feet and scooped up a handful of fresh snow. When Mark opened the door wearing a bathrobe, he was greeted for the second time that Christmas by an icy snowball exploding in his face.

Amanda could not have delivered her message more clearly if she had hung a sign around her neck saying "I'm a brat. Spank me!"

'What the …?' spluttered Mark. He wiped his eyes with his sleeve and, as his vision cleared, he saw Amanda laughing at him. 'Right!' he said. Ignoring the icy snow biting at his bare toes, he strode out into the garden. Amanda backed away. Her emotions tumbled through a complex mixture of fear and excitement.

'A snowball? Again?' grinned Mark. 'Didn't I warn you you're not too old to be spanked?

'Brave words for a man in his pyjamas,' said Amanda, stooping to scoop up more snow.

Mark rushed towards her and she squealed and dropped the snow. Before she could turn and run, he caught her wrist and bent to wrap an arm around her legs. In a second she was hauled kicking over his shoulder.

'Put me down! Put me down!' she yelled in between squeals and giggles. 'Someone will see us.'

He ignored her protests and carried her into the house. He kicked the door shut and then dropped her, squirming, onto the couch.

'Are you really going to spank me?' asked Amanda.

'I think we both know the answer to that,' Mark

replied. He sat on the couch next to her and patted his knees. Amanda's eyes sparkled excitedly and with a mischievous grin, she crawled happily over his lap.

Mark took hold of her waist with his left hand, then slid his right hand along her thigh and over the perfect rounds of her toned bottom, pushing her jumper up out of the way. He paused to enjoy the moment. Amanda looked back over her shoulder.

'Well? Are you going to smack it or just stare at it?'

'OK,' said Mark. 'You asked for it.' He delivered a tentative smack to Amanda's right cheek and matched it quickly with one to the left. She shuffled a little on his lap. The next smack was delivered harder and the next harder still. A fifth smack was laid on with force and Amanda gave a little cry and fluttered her feet. Mark started spanking in a regular rhythm, alternating cheeks and building up an excruciating fire.

'Mmm ... spank me harder,' mumbled Amanda.

Mark raised his hand higher and obliged.

'No! Harder!' said Amanda.

Mark picked up the pace and really started to whack his hand down, powering from the shoulder and stinging his palm. Amanda started to writhe around on his lap.

'Harder!' she screamed. 'Really hard!'

Mark took a tighter grip on her waist and started to deliver a furious attack on her upturned bottom. Amanda grabbed a cushion and buried her face into it. She raised her bottom, angling her hips to ensure each smack of Mark's hand delivered a pleasure-filled thrill to the erogenous lower half of her cheeks.

Suddenly, with three final hard smacks, the spanking stopped. Amanda lay still, breathing heavily, allowing the pleasure to flood through her as her bottom burned. Mark shook his hand and blew cool air against it. His engorged manhood was hot and hard, pressing into Amanda's belly.

Amanda climbed unsteadily to her feet, turned and eased herself down to sit on Mark's knee, her flushed face inches away from his and her eyes damp with tears.

'Thank you,' she whispered. Her lips parted slightly and her eyes closed. Mark pulled her to him and they kissed.

'Bed?' he said.

She smiled nervously. 'You … you're going to hate me,' she said, 'but I have to get back and see to Bobby.'

Mark smiled understandingly and gave her a squeeze. 'How about dinner,' he said, 'tonight?'

Amanda grinned. 'Love to,' she replied.

At seven that evening, Amanda returned once again to Mark's house. Now wearing a little black dress, favouring style and sex appeal over protection from the bitter night air, she shivered as she approached the door. Mark greeted her with a smile, and perhaps a little relief that her arrival wasn't preceded by yet another snowball attack.

Dinner was fantastic, convincing Amanda even more that he really was her dream man. He poured a couple of generous brandies and they sank onto the couch together.

'I see you can still sit down,' he said, 'after this morning's little adventure.'

Amanda smiled naughtily. She put down her brandy and ran a finger down Mark's chest. 'That was a pretty good spanking,' she said. 'Good enough for accidentally hitting you with a snowball yesterday. But this morning was no accident. I was a very bad girl so what are you going to do about that?'

Mark put down his brandy and gently kissed her. 'What do you think I should do?'

Amanda reached down into the shoulder bag by her feet and pulled out a large wooden hairbrush. She offered it to Mark. 'This is what Santa brought for me this Christmas. I guess I'm on the naughty list.'

Mark laughed. 'Well,' he said, 'I'm not going to argue with Santa.' He accepted the brush and tapped it against his hand. 'Looks like you're going back over my knee.'

He put aside the hairbrush and with Amanda once again face down across his lap, he ran his hand over the soft curves where her short black dress clung to the contours of her waist and bottom. Slipping his hand under the hem of it, he started to gently push the material up and out of the way. Amanda lifted her hips a little, allowing him to uncover her bottom and slide the fabric up to her waist. She felt cool air caress her cheeks where her flesh peeked out from either side of her white silk panties, especially chosen for tonight.

Mark stroked her round buttocks in light, circular movements before moving to the waistband of her panties. She lifted her hips again, allowing the flimsy material to be slipped sensuously over her bottom and down her thighs. She trembled with the anticipation of what was to come.

Now he picked up the hairbrush in one hand and took a firm hold of her waist with the other. She flinched and a thrill ran through her body as he stroked the hard wood over her bare cheeks. There was a momentary pause as he raised the brush, one second, two seconds, heightening her anticipation … then, without warning, fire exploded across her right cheek. A second later, an equally delicious sting blasted her left cheek. Amanda squeezed her thighs together and curled her legs, allowing the rich pleasure-pain to wash over her. She raised her hips and three more smacks landed in quick succession, causing her hand to fly back, an instinctive reaction to protect her bottom. Mark put down the brush. He moved her hand aside and tenderly stroked the hot flesh where her cheeks were starting to blush. Amanda moaned softly and writhed a little. He slipped his hands under her arms and reached around to cup her breasts through the thin material of her dress, squeezing and stimulating her.

Straightening up, Mark ran his fingers along her spine, returning once again to her naked bottom. Amanda parted her legs a little, allowing him to stroke and probe her most intimate charms, feeling the wetness of her excitement. She moaned again and pushed back against his hand, forcing a deeper penetration.

'Spank me,' she whispered. 'Spank me again, Mark, and don't stop.'

Mark withdrew his hand and picked up the hairbrush. Again, he rested it against her bottom, then raised it and began to spank her. Strong, regular smacks. Amanda writhed around. Ten … twenty … Mark soon lost count as Amanda's bottom took on a rosy glow. Each smack of the brush brought a sharp intake of breath, gradually becoming more tearful, occasionally punctuated with a yelp. As Mark picked up the pace, her breathing came faster and heavier, and her writhing more frantic. He brought the brush up to shoulder height and delivered five extra-hard smacks. Amanda squealed with pleasure and scrambled off his knee, leaping to her feet and clutching her bottom.

Mark stood up and threw the brush onto the couch. He and Amanda wrapped their arms around each other and hugged tightly. Amanda could feel his manhood pushing against her, hot and hard, and her hardened nipples pressing against his chest. Mark slipped his hands down Amanda's back to cup her hot, still naked bottom and pulled her hips tight against him. They kissed again, long and passionate. He reached behind her neck for the zip of her dress, and unfastened it. Amanda backed away slightly, allowing him to ease her dress off her shoulders. He kissed her neck, shoulders and breasts.

Amanda's panties had already fluttered to the floor and with a little shuffling, her dress and bra followed. Mark started to unbutton his shirt but gave up in favour of dragging the garment off over his head to reveal a muscular, well-toned torso.

Amanda reached for his belt buckle and in seconds his remaining clothes joined hers on the floor, freeing his rampant penis. Her eyes opened wide with pleasure and she stroked his erection, slowly and teasingly. Mark picked up the hairbrush and then, taking her by the hand, led her to the bedroom.

He rolled onto the king size bed and pulled her towards him. She pressed her cool hands against his chest and pushed him down into his pillow. With Mark on his back, she knelt astride him and stretched out, catlike, resting her hands on his broad pectorals. Slowly, she started to straighten up, gently scratching the scarlet nails of her slender fingers down his body. Mark sighed deeply. Amanda took hold of his erect shaft with both hands. She parted her deep red lips slightly, tantalisingly licked them, then lowered her mouth over it, plunging Mark into ecstasy as her tongue danced magically.

Before he exploded with pleasure, Amanda knelt upright and positioned herself over his hips. Slowly, sensuously she lowered herself onto his penis, allowing it to penetrate deep into her. Mark reached up and cupped her breasts, pinching and squeezing. Amanda ground her hips, gently rising and falling, her eyes closed, lost in a world of pleasure and driving Mark wild.

With Mark still inside her she slowly lowered her face towards his and kissed him, pressing her breasts to his chest and straightening her legs until she lay on top of him. Mark wrapped an arm around her waist and thrust his hips upwards. With each thrust Amanda's bottom was lifted and Mark knew exactly what she wanted. He reached to his side and found the hairbrush. As he touched the cold wood against her upturned bottom she almost purred. The next thrust was met with a loud smack! Amanda yelped and pressed her lips hard to Mark's. Another thrust – another smack; faster and harder, their passion was wild. Amanda's bottom blazed and in another moment she was drowning in wave after wave of orgasmic ecstasy; an instant later Mark followed.

The couple clung to each other until the moment was spent, both breathless and exhausted. Amanda rolled to the side and flinched as her sore bottom met the mattress. In the throes of passion, she hadn't realised just how soundly she had been spanked. She lay in the crook of Mark's arm and gently caressed his chest.

Christmas, she thought, it's just magical. Who would have imagined when she wrote that letter to Santa that her wish would really come true? Her handsome Knight, sweeping her off her feet and bringing her naughtiest dreams to life. She laughed to herself. Maybe tomorrow, she and Bobby should go and see if there really are fairies at the bottom of the garden.

Melting the Snowman
by Josie Jordan

I *love* my job. But I don't know what else I can try. My client, JJ Green, has both the talent and the balls to go all the way, yet he simply doesn't seem to want to any more. His results have been going downhill all season.

There he is, sitting on the snow with his back to a fir tree. 'Ten days to go,' I say pointedly.

I'm not counting down to Christmas – which is in fact tomorrow – I'm counting down to the Snowly Grail Cup. Because the way things are going, this is the day I'm going to find myself out of a job.

I glare at him. 'Have you even warmed up yet?'

JJ yawns. 'Not yet, no.'

'Well, get on with it, then.'

With a hiss of exasperation, he hauls himself up, all six foot of him. He's tall for a snowboarder. I watch him go through the stretches. Hamstrings, quads, calf muscles. The seat of his baggy snowboard pants pulls tight across his arse as he leans forward to touch the snow and I can't help staring at it. Which is most unprofessional, I know.

Training a guy as gorgeous as JJ is a major test of self-control. I have to sit next to him in the sauna every afternoon, with only a tiny white towel covering his cock. As for rubbing down his body at the end of a hard training session … One touch in the wrong place and I'm pretty sure I'd start ripping his clothes off.

Up until this year, I've only had female clients. A degree of sexism still exists in the snowboard world. People seem to believe a female coach is only good enough to train female athletes. I was all set to prove them wrong, but I'm beginning to think they have a point. I certainly have no idea what's going on in JJ's head at the moment.

'Stiff?' I ask, seeing him wince.

'A little.'

'Come here.' I perch on a nearby tree stump and hoist his snowboard boot into my lap, so I can work my fingers into his calf.

I like to get hands-on with my clients. This way I get to know every muscle in their body. Sadly, there's one muscle of JJ's that I haven't seen yet.

'God, your feet are massive!' I say before I think better of it.

He gives a stunned laugh. 'Are you thinking what I think you are? Go on then, Carrie. Ask me if it's true.'

It's the first time I've heard him laugh for days, but I push his boot away and stand up, dusting the snow from my gloves. 'No thanks. I don't want to know.'

Although of course I *do* want to know. It's something I've been wondering all season.

Despite the sub-zero temperature, I can feel my cheeks burning. To hide my embarrassment, I pick up my snowboard. 'Let's go.'

The conditions today are perfect: clear blue sky and a foot of fresh snow. The cable car is full of skiers in red and white Santa hats. Everyone's in holiday mode and the noise is deafening.

JJ sits beside me, staring at the steep peaks above. His eyes are hidden by his goggles but I can see the tension in his jaw. He's 22 years old and he should be living the dream. So why is he so damn miserable?

This is the guy voted "The One to Watch" in *Whiteout* magazine three years back. A year later, he landed a major sponsorship deal. He picked up three more sponsors last year, thanks to a top ten world ranking. But see him ride lately and you wouldn't know any of that. Passion: there's no passion in his riding any more.

He's doing this tapping thing with his knee. I press my gloved hand over his thigh. 'Stop it!'

He lifts his goggles to his forehead and gives me a belligerent look. His eyes are the same clear blue as the ice up on the glacier. He really is in a filthy mood and I ponder this for a moment.

For a while last year, he dated one of the female pros – a stuck-up little bitch called Annabelle – but they split up last summer. Could that be the problem? That he's a hot-blooded young male and he's not getting any?

Anyway, ten more days and it'll all be over for both of us, unless I can somehow get him out of this rut.

'What's up with you?' I ask quietly.

He avoids my eyes. 'You don't want to know.'

'I'm your coach. I need to know.'

'I guess I'm just not in the mood.'

I struggle to hide my frustration. 'So you'd better damn well get in the mood, because everyone else is training like mad.'

His expression hardens and we sit there in silence. Crap. What can I do apart from give up? Because *he* clearly has.

A wicked idea forms. I take off my glove, slip my hand under his jacket and into his snowboard pants, closing my fingers around his cock. 'My hand's cold.'

JJ sits bolt upright.

'What?' I ask innocently.

He shoots an alarmed look around the cabin, but we're swinging above snow-frosted treetops and thankfully everyone else is admiring the view. JJ's gaze returns to mine. I tug gently at his cock and his blue eyes register his disbelief.

'Bloody hell!' I say softly. 'You *are* a bit stiff, aren't you?'

When I tug harder, his lips part and he slumps back in his seat. Then the cable car pulls into the mid-station and I snatch my hand away.

I feel slightly light-headed as we exit and I know the altitude is only partly to blame. 'Shall we go on up to the top?' I ask.

'OK,' JJ says in a strained voice.

The next lift is a small cabin that fits up to four people. JJ and I scramble for an empty one and the door clunks shut before anyone else can get in. We lean our snowboards against the window.

'I'm going to ask again,' I say. 'What's up with you?'

He throws me a nervous glance. 'You really don't want to know.'

'You said you weren't in the mood, but you're in the mood now, aren't you?' I reach for his cock again. Through the thick nylon of his pants I can feel he's still semi-erect.

I give him a little squeeze. 'Here's how it's going to work. You need to perform and if you perform well, you'll be rewarded.'

He looks incredulous. 'What?'

'I want a nice 720 over the big kicker on your first run. After that, we'll try some flips.'

He struggles to make sense of this. 'And what do I get if I do?'

I give his cock a few hard tugs and he groans.

Our cabin sails over the Snow Park. The jumps have been freshly groomed and most of the other pros are down there training already. They've probably been up here since the lifts opened. Never mind. JJ will have to make up for lost time.

By the time we reach the top, he's so hard I'm scared he won't be able to walk. But he marches across the glacier and fastens his snowboard on with a determination I haven't seen in all the time I've been training him.

Encouraged by this, I give him a quick once over. 'Shoulders down,' I say, pressing into them with my thumbs. 'Relax.'

When he sees that I'm serious, he drops his shoulders obediently.

Soon he's streaking down the slope into the Snow Park. He does back-to-back 360s over the first couple of jumps and hits the big kicker with enough speed to make me catch my breath. He blasts into the air, completing three full rotations, rather than just the two I'd asked for. A smooth 1080, nicely landed. It's good to see he still has it.

He waits for me at the bottom of the park, unable to hide his smug expression. I shoot past him and continue to the lift, keeping him in suspense until the door has shut behind us.

Once again, we have the small cabin to ourselves.

'That wasn't bad,' I say. 'Although you were trailing your back arm a bit. Keep it loose.'

I unzip my snowboard jacket and lift my sweater and thermal top. It takes me a few awkward seconds to wrestle my tits out from the bottom of my sports bra.

JJ's jaw drops. My tits are kind of big and I've seen him checking them out before when he thinks I'm not looking. I glance down. It's bloody freezing up here, so it isn't unsurprising that my nipples are standing to attention.

I unzip the fly of his snowboard pants and pull them down around his arse, his thermal pants along with them. 'Well don't just stand there,' I say. 'We haven't got long.'

But he remains glued to the spot.

I seize him by the cock and tug him towards me. My fingers are icy and he yelps. His cock, however, instantly springs to life, swelling in my fist to an impressive size. I shove it between my tits. They're squashed down by my bra and his dick only just fits between them.

I check my watch. 'You've got four more minutes.'

He finally catches on and begins to fuck my tits, clutching my shoulders for balance. The heat of his shaft burns into my cleavage. I scrape a handful of snow from my snowboard and stick it over his bell-end. Chunks of ice rain onto my nipples as he shoves back into place.

I lower my head so I can lick the tip of his cock with every thrust. *Careful,* I remind myself. I must stay in control. I have a job to do, after all.

'Next,' I murmur, once his breaths are coming thick and fast, 'how about a flip?'

He thrusts hard upwards, giving me a mouthful.

From the corner of my eye, I see the top of the lift approaching. I just hope to God the attendant can't see us.

I push JJ away and tuck my clothes into place. With an anguished expression, he stuffs his cock back in his pants.

The door slides open and we walk across the plateau.

'You're all tense,' I say, trying to keep a straight face. 'Loose, remember?'

He sighs. 'What kind of flip do you want? Rodeo? Misty flip? Wildcat?'

Might as well aim high. 'Double Wildcat,' I say.

I see him weighing this up. Danny Barnes won the Snowly Grail last year with a huge one. For a while, JJ had them dialled too but he fell on his head at the start of the season and he hasn't done any since.

He shrugs. 'OK. Why not?'

I can hardly keep up with him as he speeds off through the Snow Park. I cross my fingers as he flies into the air. He flips head over heels twice in a perfectly executed double Wildcat. A slight wobble on landing, but he quickly corrects it.

'Sick!' a small boy shouts from behind me.

JJ waits for me at the lift, breathing hard. 'How was I?'

'Very nice,' I say as we climb in. I unzip his fly and open my mouth. He wastes no time inserting his cock between my lips and shoving in deep.

I hold him there for a second, nearly gagging at his size but enjoying his low moan of pleasure. His musky male smell fills my nose. Holding him by the hips to keep some semblance of control, I shift my head back and forth along his length. He grips the railing as though his legs are about to collapse beneath him.

I pull back. 'Are you going to talk yet?'

'Hey?'

'Tell me what's up with you.'

He shifts his hips, straining to get his cock back in my mouth, but I grip him by the balls.

'Talk to me,' I say.

'Oh, if you must know, you do my head in.'

'What?'

'Training me.'

We stare at each other.

'Those rub-downs you give me. Have you any idea how hard it is to control myself?' His tanned cheeks have flushed scarlet and he looks like he longs to bury his head in the snow.

I reward him with a quick sucking before pulling back

so I can look at him again. 'What do you mean?' I ask.

'Shit, Carrie, do I have to spell it out? I want to do you, OK? There, I've said it.'

'You want to do me?' I'm laughing now. All along, it was so simple. I open my mouth and allow him back in.

His thrusts rock the whole cabin. 'You're going to make me come,' he blurts.

'Not yet.' I push him away. 'You have to earn it.'

The look on his face is something else, but we've arrived already. I zip him back up. 'I want to see you do that trick again. Bigger this time.'

He nods in resignation. I just hope he doesn't fall, because if he does, he'll break a bone that really doesn't want to get broken.

He lowers his goggles and stands above the jump, biting his lip. Willing his erection to go down, I guess. A couple of snowboarders nearby nudge each other when they see him and one of them pulls a camera from his pocket.

JJ straight-lines down to the jump and flies upwards. Confident as anything; you'd think he'd been doing the trick for years. If I'd known it would be this easy, I would have sucked his cock months ago!

He lowers his pants the minute he steps into the lift. I smile when I see he's still hard. Maybe the extra limb added to his stability.

Gripping his cock in his fist, he advances towards me. I can see I'll have a job holding him back this time.

He stuffs himself into my mouth and shoves in deep enough to make me gag properly.

I give his bare bottom a smack. 'Steady on!'

'Sorry, coach.'

I give him a good hard sucking and pull back when I sense he's about to spurt. 'How about you try that trick again?' I say. 'This time with passion.'

'You want passion?'

I look up into his enlarged pupils but he grips the back of my head with his gloved hands and directs my mouth back down on his cock.

'I'll show you passion,' he says gruffly.

He makes a series of increasingly sharp thrusts that make my eyes water. I close my eyes and imagine him thrusting like that inside me.

'Carrie, Carrie …' he mutters as he fucks my mouth.

Then a muffled curse, his legs buckle, and a hot jet of come splatters the back of my throat.

Our eyes meet as I swallow.

'Fucking hell,' he breathes as he pulls out. He eases himself shakily to the bench beside me.

'This is some training session,' he says when he has regained the power of speech.

'And it's not over yet.' My voice sounds funny. I'm dangerously turned on. 'Now get yourself together. We're nearly there.'

'Do you do this with all your clients?' he asks as we exit.

'Cheeky bastard! No I don't. Anyway, you know my other clients have all been female.'

He chuckles. 'Watch out. You'll get me hard again.'

Typical male. I force myself to get back to business. 'You show me that passion,' I say.

Am I pushing him too hard? I hold my breath as he rides down to the kicker, but his jump is easily as big as Danny's winning one last year and it's technically perfect too.

JJ waits at the bottom, looking pleased with himself.

'I knew you could do it,' I tell him.

When he sits down in the cabin, I climb astride his strong thighs, facing him. 'So you wanted to do me?' I say. 'You only had to ask.'

He lifts off his goggles and there's a sparkle in his eyes that wasn't there before. I realise I'm seeing a whole new side of him. He pulls off his glove and trails his fingertip across my bottom lip. 'You're well sexy, you are,' he says.

When I part my lips, his finger ventures inside to tease my tongue. I abandon all remaining professionalism, lean forwards and kiss him like I've wanted to for months. In the frozen air, his mouth is like a furnace.

'And you give bloody amazing head,' he adds when he pulls back for air.

I laugh to myself at that, secretly flattered. My ex loved me going down on him too. Shame he never returned the favour.

JJ unzips my snowboard pants, watching me carefully, as though he isn't sure if this is allowed. When I don't move to stop him, he delves into my knickers. His eyes open wide. 'Christ, you're wet. Enjoyed sucking me off, did you?'

I laugh again, embarrassed. My laughter changes into a moan as he eases a finger inside me. I buck my hips to urge him on. He presses his finger in all the way to his knuckle.

'More,' I whisper and he pushes in a second finger too.

'Stand up,' he says.

My snowboard pants fall to my ankles. On the slopes below, skiers snake slowly downwards. I worry someone will look up and see my bare bottom. Then JJ starts to pump his fingers in and out and I realise I don't care if they do.

He lowers his face and takes a long lick of my clit. Speared between his fingers and his tongue, the last of my control slips away. Moisture seeps down my thighs and I'm on the brink of an orgasm in no time.

'I want you,' I say.

JJ glances over his shoulder. 'Sorry, coach.'

Damn! We're at the top again already. Cursing, I pull my pants up.

My knickers are soaked. When I sit on the snow to fasten into my bindings, my clit throbs.

'Race you to the bottom!' JJ shouts.

We give the Snow Park a miss this time and instead hurtle down the piste. The nose of my snowboard judders over the ice. My heart pounds and not just because of my speed. I'm relieved to reach the lift in one piece.

JJ and I exchange looks as we wait for an empty cabin. I push through the door, unzipping my snowboard pants as I do so.

When I turn round, he has his cock out already. 'So what do you want, Carrie?'

My desperation to have him outweighs all my inhibitions. I pull a condom from my pocket. 'I want you to do me.'

A surprised laugh from JJ. 'You planned this?'

Actually I've had it there for weeks on the off-chance that something like this might happen. But I ignore the question and rip the packet open. 'We've got exactly five minutes, so get it on, quick!'

I turn to face the window and stick my bottom out towards him.

He thrusts into me and in one smooth motion his cock is all the way inside. The contrast between the heat of his shaft and the freezing mountain air is delicious.

'You want passion?' he asks, drawing slowly out.

'Yes,' I hiss, and he thrusts in again.

'You sure about that?'

I shift my hips back onto him. 'JJ – please!'

'OK, Coach. I'll give you passion.' His strong arms grip my waist and hold me in place while he fucks me forcefully. I arch my back and brace myself against the railing. Just as I'm getting really into it, he pulls out.

A sudden icy sensation makes me squeal. He has stuffed a handful of snow inside me.

'You're burning up,' he says through his laughter.

It's revenge, I suppose, for what I put him through earlier. I try to wriggle away, but he shoves his cock back in and grinds his body against mine. The pain reverts to pleasure as the snow melts.

His fingers find my clit. They're ice cold and they feel amazing. I cling to the railing, giving myself up to him. With his other hand, JJ grips the rail too, using it for leverage to drive his cock deeper.

I'm feeling the full force of my client's muscles and I've never been fucked this hard before. 'That's it,' I tell him. 'Don't stop!'

His breaths are hot and fast in my ear. 'I won't.'

There's an elderly male skier on the piste below, wearing a Santa hat. He does a double take as he catches sight of our cabin and his mouth swings wide in shock. He has a red jacket and a bushy white beard, so it looks for all the world as though Santa Claus himself is watching us.

I shove my bottom back onto JJ's cock. As he impales me, an orgasm rips through my body and my legs crumple. JJ releases the rail to hold me upright. He continues to ram his cock mercilessly into my writhing form until he too crumples.

We collapse to the seat, me on his lap, with his wilting cock still inside me. He holds me like that for a moment. 'How did I do, coach?'

'I'd give you the gold,' I tell him weakly. 'And after another few training sessions like this one, I reckon the judges will too.'

Head to Mistletoe
by Giselle Renarde

Last year, Lars gave me the silliest Christmas gift: crotchless panties with a silky sprig of mistletoe hanging right over the clit.

Actually, he got himself a pair too. His were a little different, obviously. Instead of a strip of crotchlessness, Lars's mistletoe undies had a hole cut out in the front for his dick to poke through. He'd walked into the living room wearing just that ridiculous thong with his hard cock sticking out, and I had no choice but give him the world's best blowjob right there beside the Christmas tree. When I put on my pair, he took me upstairs and kissed my pussy until I couldn't breathe.

After that, the his-and-hers undies sank to the bottom of the laundry hamper with the rest of the "hand-wash only" stuff. I'd totally forgotten about them until I came home from work to find the silly things hanging over the towel bar.

'I washed them in the sink,' Lars told me. 'I thought we could wear them tonight.'

My jaw clenched because I figured he'd forgotten about Ravinia and Stone's Christmas party. It bugged the hell out of me when I told him something 40 times and he was still like, 'Duh ... what?'

But Lars hadn't forgotten. Not at all. He wanted us to

wear the mistletoe undies to the party.

'But your dick!' I cried, which made me giggle even though I was trying to be serious. 'Your dick hangs right out of those things. There's no support. People will stare at you! They'll point at your crotch and say, '"Look at that! Lars isn't wearing any underwear."'

'Nobody's going to stare at my crotch,' he said. 'And even if they do, so what? They can look, but they can't touch.'

That made me laugh out loud, and I picked up my crotchless panties from the towel bar. They were made of that silky-stretchy material that dries really fast, so they were just about ready to slip on.

'I was going to wear that short red dress, the clingy jersey one.' I held the panties up against me. 'What if I open my legs a little too wide and somebody gets a peek at my pink?'

Lars came close. He wrapped his arms around me and kissed my forehead. 'They can look, but they can't touch.'

I craned my head up and kissed Lars's lips, and that kiss drew itself out and dragged us into the bedroom. Lars leaned against the headboard and I leaned against his hard body, running my hands up and down his back. It didn't seem to matter how long we were together. He always turned me on. Always.

But when I reached down to cup his package, Lars grabbed my wrist and held my hand away. 'Not yet,' he said. 'I want you good and horny at this party.'

I gulped. 'Why?'

'Because,' he said. 'I want you willing to do things you wouldn't normally do.'

My heart pounded against my ribcage. It was all I could hear. I didn't know what my man had in store for me, but I couldn't wait to find out.

Ravinia's place was hopping when we got there. Just a house party, but those were the best at Christmas time. You could get good and drunk and know there was always a couch to crash on. The stereo was blasting out a collection of funky Christmas tunes recorded by Mr Tall, Dark and Handsome himself, Ravinia's super-hot boyfriend, Stone. 'As in Stone Cold Fox,' I'd said to Lars when we'd first met him.

Lars had said, 'I think it's more like a tribute to Sly and the Family Stone.' And, judging by his music, Lars was probably right.

But so was I, because Stone was foxy with a capital F.

I giggled when he brought me my fifth glass of eggnog.

'What's so funny?' Stone asked, taking the seat across from mine. I was clinging dizzily to the couch. Even though I was sitting down, I still felt like I could either fall over or float away. I wasn't sure which.

'I don't even know why I'm laughing,' I said. 'Must be the rum.'

'Ahh …' Stone nodded, smiley and joyful as ever. And then suddenly, something changed. His grin fell and his eyes glowed with a darkness I'd never seen in him before. I thought maybe I'd done or said something to offend him, and all at once I felt too sober for my own good.

Then I followed his gaze down, and I realized what he was seeing. I'd forgotten myself and spread my legs. My short dress parted at my thighs. There wasn't enough fabric to hang between them and block his view of my pussy. He was looking at it right now, staring at my hot pink middle. Could he see how wet I was from drinking and flirting with other men while Lars looked on, grinning wolfishly, enjoying my lust? I bet Stone could even see how hard my fat little clit ached to be sucked, teased, toyed with. Lars had gotten his wish. I was horny and

64

ready for anything.

A slapping sound whipped through the air, drawing my attention away from Stone. I snapped my legs together as I looked around the room, thinking something had fallen or ... well, I didn't know what. And there was Lars in an antique rocking chair. He'd taken Ravinia across his lap and pulled up the skirt on her sexy Santa outfit – one of those fuzzy red numbers lined with white fluff.

He'd smacked her ass, and he did it again. My man brought his big palm down across our friend's tight little bum. She had on red panties that probably came with the outfit, and she shrieked when Lars pulled them down. Everybody who hadn't already been looking turned then to see my Lars spanking Ravinia's pink bottom. Slap, slap, slap. The sound was almost as loud as her squeals of, 'No, Lars, stop!' But it was hard to take her seriously when she giggled after every word.

'I hope somebody's taking pictures,' Lars said.

Stone already had his phone out. 'Don't worry, mate. I'm getting it all on film.'

'This could be your big break!' somebody shouted from across the room.

'You're going to be a star of the internet porn sites, Ravinia!'

Everybody teased and taunted her while my man smacked her ass. She writhed in his lap, not enough to escape, but enough that her ample cleavage threatened to fall from her Santa Girl top, which was little more than a bra with red sleeves. She'd styled her dark hair into pigtails which bobbed in the air every time Lars smacked her. I kept staring at her tits, hoping they'd fall loose from that top and I'd get to see her nipples. I don't know why I wanted to, but I did.

'Show her what's under the mistletoe, Lars!'

It wasn't until half the room had turned to look at me that I realised I'd spoken. In a way, I couldn't believe it. I felt outside myself, like someone else had taken over my body. I was possessed by the Ghost of Christmas Sexy.

'What's under the mistletoe?' asked a woman in a sheer gold dress.

Lars had stopped smacking Ravinia's ass. He looked around the room at the audience he'd drawn.

'Yeah, Lars,' Ravinia said. 'I want to see what's under the mistletoe.'

She could probably feel it pressing into her side, the way she was slumped over his lap like that.

'Jess?' Lars looked to me and I bit my lip to contain my excitement. 'You insist?'

I could feel a few pairs of eyes burning into the back of my neck, but they belonged to people who didn't know I was a share bear extraordinaire. If they were waiting for an explosion of jealousy from yours truly, they'd do better to sit back and watch the show.

'I insist,' I said with a resolute nod. I winked, just to show I was extra-OK with this.

'How about I show Ravinia my mistletoe if you show Stone yours?'

A blush came over me because, of course, Stone had already seen it. *And* because I'd never lifted my skirt before a live studio audience. But I said, 'OK. It's a deal.'

Ravinia shuffled off Lars's lap and he stood while she knelt before him. The whole room watched him take off his festive red, white and green check shirt. His clothes looked so normal, with only his 80s Flock of Seagulls hair betraying his rampant freakishness. I remembered how opposed I'd been to us wearing our mistletoe out tonight, and felt silly about that strange bout of prudishness.

When Lars pushed down his grey trousers, the crowd

issued a collective gasp, which made me laugh. The party people laughed too, though I could still feel a few eyes burning into the back of my head.

'My God, what is that?' Ravinia asked.

Everybody laughed and Lars said, 'Well, it's not a fruitcake, but have a little taste. You just might like it.'

His cock was hard as steel. Nothing unusual there, but it did look pretty funny sticking out of the hole in that ridiculous thong.

'Are you one of Santa's elves?' Ravinia asked Lars's cock as it bounced joyfully in front of her face.

'Are you?' Lars shot back at Ravinia.

'You're certainly dressed the part,' someone said from across the room. Her silly red top was tumbling off one shoulder.

The tension in the air was fierce, so thick and hot it was steaming up the windows. Outside, big balls of snow fluttered from the sky. Indoors, the heat was almost unbearable. There were so many people in this room, all focused on Ravinia's mouth as it wrapped itself around Lars's thick cock. They both moaned when she sucked it, but the rest of the room went dead silent. People collectively held their breath. You could feel it. Even I didn't want to breathe for fear of making some noise that might bring this debauchery to a close.

Ravinia wrapped her fingers around my man's shaft and made a fist. She pumped it against her closed lips, pressed right up against his cockhead like she was giving it a Christmas kiss.

'That's what mistletoe's for!' said a drunk man, someone I think I slept with at one of these parties. But that was a long time ago. And we'd done it under a pile of coats, not right out in the open.

'Lars,' I said, and he gazed right at me. 'Look at her

lips. They're almost as red as your cock.'

He looked down. His smile grew as Ravinia planted sharp red kisses up and down his shaft. I wanted to do that too. I wanted to kiss Lars's cock with her, and before I knew it, I was stumbling off the couch and crawling across the carpet, lusting after my man's hard dick.

Ravinia was already kneeling between his legs, so I hugged his thigh and wrapped my mouth around the base of his cock. I bit his dick and he groaned, running a hand through my hair, encouraging more. I knew what Lars liked, and Ravinia knew what everyone liked. She sucked the tip of his cock, just the tip between those cherry-red lips, while I planted slobbery kisses all over his shaft.

I could never believe how hot his cock got when he was turned on. It was a missile, live ammunition ready to launch. I knew what would put him over the top. While Ravinia devoured my man, taking his dick deep in her throat, I plucked his balls out through the tight elastic hole in his thong.

'Fuck,' Lars moaned, and I could hear other partygoers breathing heavily, almost panting behind me. I wondered if they could see my ass, or perhaps my crotchless panties. If not, they would soon enough.

Bowing between Lars's legs, I sucked his balls, carefully at first, building up pressure as I went. Ravinia made kittenish mewling sounds, and I made them too because my man's salty, sweaty balls tasted even better than Ravinia's goat cheese and fig pastries. Even better than her lipstick, which was all over my man's dick.

'I'm gonna come,' Lars warned us, and I could feel it in his body. His balls got so tight I could fit them in my mouth, both at once. I sucked them hard and Lars yelped my name. At first I thought I'd hurt him, but then when Ravinia started sputtering I realized he'd just filled her throat with cream. It was always a never-ending flow with Lars. He just kept coming and coming, and all you could do was open your throat and make room for it.

'Fuck,' he said, stumbling across the room and taking the seat I'd abandoned on the couch. His cock was still half-hard, coming to a rest on the pillow of his balls. The silky green and white mistletoe sat atop his dick like the star on a Christmas tree, greeting the room with the possibilities it had opened up.

'Your turn, Jess.' Lars looked at me and winked. 'Give the people what they want. Show them your mistletoe.'

The air in the room filled with sexual tension so thick I could barely breathe. All at once, it broke into a chant of, 'Show us, show us, show us!'

So I closed my eyes and lifted my skirt. There was a collective silence in the room, and I knew everybody was looking at me. Everyone could see the place where my panties split in the middle, but they couldn't see enough.

Feeling my way down, I sat in the rocking chair and opened my legs. The silence deepened as everyone got a look at the glistening pink of me.

Crotchless panties sure were a crowd-pleaser. The room started chanting 'Eat her! Eat her!' and I felt Stone's mass between my legs. He was all heat, that man, like a furnace. When I opened my eyes, there he was, grinning like a demon. He asked me if I was ready and I said, 'Isn't it obvious?'

He asked again and I simply said yes.

I closed my eyes, feeling dizzy and sleepy, but at the same time very alert. I heard the rustle of his clothes as he drew in close. In my mind, I kept seeing his dark eyes, his lust. And then, for some reason, I knew I had to find Lars. My eyes shot open and I spotted him on the couch, watching, seeming worn out and amorous and amused all at once.

'Lucky you,' he said with just his lips, no sound. Or maybe that was, 'Love you.'

I smiled, so distracted that I really wasn't ready when Stone's lips met my clit. I started to jump, but he caught my bare thighs with both hands and pressed them into the rocking chair. His lips were unbelievably hot.

Stone held me in that chair, which creaked with every pitch forward and back. He followed my body with his, moving with my pussy as the rocker swayed. His lips remained closed and pressed against my clit, but my flesh was so swollen and ready that the mere pressure worked me quickly toward orgasm. I could feel it sitting in my belly like a ball of fire, waiting for something to set it off.

'Suck her clit,' Lars said, which sure enough started a new chant.

The whole room joined in, like a Christmas carol: 'Suck her clit! Suck her clit!'

'But it's mistletoe on her panties,' Stone argued, grinning wickedly. 'You don't suck a woman under the mistletoe, you kiss her!'

The room was adamant: 'Suck it! Suck it! Suck it!'

I'd never had an entire Christmas party cheering for my clit to get sucked. I felt like I should be embarrassed, but I guess I was drunk enough to find everything hilarious. Even the sensation of Stone's sizzling lips against my bare pussy made me snicker.

Stone gazed up at me like a pouting puppy. 'You want me to suck your clit, Jessie?'

I giggled, and when I tried to stop I just giggled louder.

'Is that a yes?' he asked. God, his voice was sexy – velvet gravel, liquid sex.

I nodded jubilantly, laughing until he wrapped his mouth around my fat little clit and started to suck.

70

Arching in the rocker, I grabbed the armrests with both hands. If my nails had been longer, I'd have dug them into the wood, leaving permanent scars. I couldn't believe how immediate the wave came over me, shrouding my body in the tingling warmth of orgasm. It was centred in my clit, but the heat of his mouth radiated out from there, filling my belly with fire, making my nipples hard under my bra.

My climax took over as Stone sucked my clit. I could feel it in my scalp, in my fingertips, needles and heat. Frenzy surged through me, like I had to shake the sensation out. I started fitting and writhing in the rocking chair, hoping to God I wouldn't break the spindled wood.

I wrapped my legs around Stone's head, bucking my wet pussy against his face. I could feel how soaked my panties had become, absorbing the juice of my arousal as it slipped down my crack. Stone's lips splayed mine, and I came even harder watching him savour my cunt.

Then, out of nowhere, Lars and Ravinia opened my red dress and heaved my breasts from my bra. When their mouths found my nipples, my body exploded. It was fireworks everywhere, exploding in the three mouths latched firmly to my flesh.

They held me down as I writhed. Over my screams, I could just hear the room cheering me on, telling me to come harder, scream louder. Everyone was so close, peering over Lars and Ravinia's heads, trying to get a better look at my tits.

Their eyes were everywhere. I could feel them like fingers dancing across my skin, leaving traces of communal lust. Everybody wanted me. Everybody had me, vicariously, through Stone's mouth, and Lars's and Ravinia's.

When I couldn't stand any more, they had mercy. I slid

from the rocking chair like liquid and slumped into a puddle on the floor. My legs were open. In my soaked crotchless panties, I could feel the warm air from the heater right against my naked pussy. My dress was open too, and my boobs spilled out over the cups of my bra, my nipples pointing up at the ceiling.

I could feel Stone sitting beside me. I could hear Lars and Ravinia talking, but I only listened to the tenor of their voices, not to the words they were saying. Closing my eyes, I made myself into art – something to be looked at, and maybe even touched if you were sneaky. Everyone could see me now, see my naked breasts, see the gape of my pussy and my exhausted clit under the mistletoe.

And to think I didn't want us wearing our crotchless undies to the Christmas party. We'd have missed out on all this. Instead, we'd shared ourselves with everyone, and the memory made me smile so wide my cheeks hurt.

All I Want for Christmas Is …
by Kay Jaybee

Holly hesitated, the folded piece of paper in her hand becoming warm and creased. Glancing about her, listening hard to make sure she was alone, Holly stole another look at what she'd written. *Am I brave enough to do this?* She had to be. This had been going on in her head long enough.

Taking a deep breath, she slid the re-folded letter under the oak-panelled door, before running down the short corridor to her own room. Squeezing her eyes shut, Holly tried to calm her pulse as she sat on the edge of her huge bed, her ears straining for the sound of footsteps outside the window, for the thud of the front door being closed as her friends returned from the pub. Nervous anticipation at what might result from her late-night action was joined by the tell-tale frisson of lust that fluttered in her chest each time she thought about the subject of her deepest dreams, her erotic fantasies – and now, her Christmas wish.

Resting against the bed's headboard, his bare legs stretched out across the duvet, Owen's eyes widened as he read the note he'd just spotted on the floor. He hadn't believed Holly's claims that she'd been too tired to join in their traditional Christmas Eve pubfest of mulled wine and too many mince pies. He knew she adored the tradition of it all; it was one of the reasons the three of them always met in this crumbling manor house hotel every Christmas.

Owen re-read the letter, a disbelieving yet curious smile on his lips. So, this was why Holly hadn't gone to the pub ...

Dear Santa,
All I want for Christmas is to have a damn good fuck with the incredible creature that haunts my dreams.

Please, Santa, keep the handkerchiefs I never use and the perfume I never wear, the novelty socks, and the oversized T-shirts, and let me have what I most want for Christmas – Ivy. After all, aren't the Holly and the Ivy supposed to be together at this time of year?

I am a good girl, Santa – although if you'd prefer me to be bad, I could probably manage that as well ...
With hope,
Holly x

The irony of the situation was not lost on Owen as a naked Ivy came out of the en suite bathroom, towel-drying her damp hair, the lingering aroma of her soap floating towards him as he held out the note, 'This is for you. It had been pushed under the door. We must have missed it in our hurry to get to bed.'

Ivy's brow crinkled questioningly as she sat across his legs, her lusciously large nipples only inches from his bare chest. 'You've already read this?'

'Sorry, I shouldn't have, I know it's your room, but well ...'

'Never mind that –' she cut through his unconvincing apology '– what shall I do?'

Owen's shaft stirred, his mind still full of pictures of

her and Holly, naked, their breasts rubbing together …
'Did you have any idea that she liked you?' he asked.

'No! Well –' Ivy's eyes dropped smilingly to his crotch '– I wondered now and again, but as she's never mentioned any girlfriends, I assumed I was imagining things and dismissed the idea.'

His fingers came to her chest, tweaking her nipples gently. 'I thought you had some sort of gaydar?'

Ivy laughed. 'Sometimes that works, sometimes it doesn't!'

'Anyway,' Owen said, 'What do you think? Will you give her what she wants for Christmas?'

Ivy flicked her shiny black hair from her eyes. 'Perhaps we should have told Holly we're together now.'

Owen's eyes sparkled. 'This could be the perfect opportunity to let her in on our secret.'

'And you fancy playing Santa?'

He pushed his palms harder against her chest, 'Well, you always did promise me a threesome one day.'

'And I meant it, but I assumed we'd find someone on the web, someone anonymous, not Holly! She's our friend!'

'Our hot friend with big tits and a beautiful arse.'

'Good point.' Ivy bought her mouth to his, the contents of the Christmas note swirling around her brain. Holly was hot, and if she was honest, she'd had some serious fantasies about her chest – but if they did this and it all went wrong, it could destroy their friendship forever. As Owen's hands crept towards her crotch however, Ivy couldn't help but think how good it would feel. It had been ages since she'd been with another girl, and suddenly Ivy really wanted to caress a woman's breasts again, and if Owen was OK with it, then why not?

'How will we do it? She hasn't asked for a threesome,

just for me.'

Wrapping his arms around Ivy, Owen grinned wickedly. 'Well, it is Christmas Day, why shouldn't she have an extra-special gift? Actually, I have a plan.'

Tilting her head at him suspiciously, Ivy smiled back and said, 'Why doesn't that surprise me! Had a bit of a fantasy in this direction anyway, did you?'

'Let's just say, you could kill two Christmas wishes with one stone!'

Holly tossed and turned in her bed. What the hell had she been thinking? Ivy had probably thrown the note away in disgust. It was only four o'clock in the morning, but she knew it was pointless trying to sleep now. Her eyes ranged over the mini-Christmas tree that stood in the corner of the room. Decked in tinsel, baubles, and traditional gingerbread shapes iced with angels and trumpets, she'd admired it before – now it seemed to be mocking her for being such a fool.

Sighing heavily, she sat up in bed, only to freeze as a piece of paper shot under the door. She didn't move. Was Ivy still outside the door, or had she already returned to her room?

Slowly, with her blood hammering in her veins, Holly slid off the bed and picked up the note. Holding it as if it was an unexploded bomb, her arms shaking, she stared at the creamy paper. Then, taking a deep breath, she read it.

Dear Holly,
As you have been a very good girl this year, I think your Christmas wish should come true.
However, a reliable authority has informed me that Ivy prefers naughty girls – and with this in mind, she would like you to follow these instructions:

1. *At 4.30 a.m. strip off and unlock your door.*
2. *Place the desk chair at the foot of the bed.*
3. *Sit on the chair and fasten your black scarf around your eyes.*
4. *Should you feel uncomfortable with anything that is happening, say the safeword "freeze" and it will stop immediately. Otherwise…*
5. *Obey Ivy at all times.*

With seasons greetings,
Father Christmas x

A faint prickle of nerves ran down Holly's spine. Could this be a joke? Holly examined the loopy, joined-up handwriting. Definitely Ivy's.

Her black scarf? It was hanging over the chair, as if it was already waiting for her. She'd never been blindfolded before, and caught in the grip of uncertainty at what Ivy might have planned, Holly wasn't sure she'd be able to tie it around her face properly, her hands were shaking so much.

It was 4.25. She had five minutes. Exhaling slowly, madly trying to control her heart rate, reminding herself that this was what she wanted, that she'd started this, Holly took off her nightshirt and unbolted the door.

Pulling the heavy oak chair from the desk to the foot of her bed, Holly folded her favourite scarf into a slim rectangle. Then, telling herself she would simply pack her things and leave if this all went wrong, Christmas Day or not, Holly sat down and placed the scarf over her eyes, fumbling with the knot that trapped her chestnut hair behind her neck.

She was adjusting to the unfamiliar disorientation caused by the makeshift blindfold when her bedroom door was opened and gently closed. Her body tensed with erotic anticipation as soft footsteps crossed the room, each step echoing to the thump of Holly's pulse. She could feel her nipples hardening under the imagined gaze of the woman she'd craved for so long. All the fantasises she'd ever had about Ivy, submissive, dominant, and downright kinky, dissolved in the heady excitement of the moment.

Holly didn't dare speak as two perfectly smooth palms came to her knees, her hypersensitive skin jumping in quick response.

'An interesting request to Father Christmas.' Ivy whispered the words, her hands leaving the safety of Holly's kneecaps and gliding down her legs, making every inch of her flesh an erogenous zone.

An elongated sigh of pleasure left Holly as she listened, the temporary loss of her sight making every touch more intense than ever. Swallowing to moisten her dry throat, Holly managed to find her voice, 'Well, you're certainly granting my wish, I …'

'Don't talk.' Interrupting, Ivy placed a cool finger to Holly's mouth. 'That's my first rule, OK? No talking except for the safeword.' Holly nodded obediently.

'Good girl.' Ivy flicked her eyes to the silent figure by the door. A naked and obviously turned-on Owen winked his approval as he held two neckties out to his partner.

Turning her attention back to Holly, Ivy said, 'I'd like you to sit so your delicious arse is perched on the very edge of the seat.'

Shuffling carefully forwards, afraid of going too far and falling, Holly moved as instructed, her brain bursting with the questions she wasn't allowed to ask.

'Open your legs as wide as you can. Let me see that gorgeous pussy.'

Obeying, Holly noticed how Ivy's voice had begun to change from its usual gentle purr, developing an unfamiliar harsh edge as she issued another order. 'You will not move unless I tell you to.'

A single finger traced its way up her inner thigh, and Holly's breath snagged as Ivy's digit wavered around the fringes of her mound, not quite near enough to fondle the light sprinkle of hair that protected her channel, but close enough for her to mentally will it nearer. Finding it incredibly difficult not to beg Ivy to move her hand an inch north, Holly clamped her jaws together and gripped the sides of her chair with both hands.

Signalling to Owen to come to her, Ivy took hold of his rigid length, and used it to steer him to Holly's right side. Taking Owen's ties, Ivy stepped away from Holly, privately pleased at the girl's groan of loss as she was abruptly deprived of contact.

'I thought I told you to be quiet.'

Opening her mouth to protest, Holly immediately shut it again.

'You will not be warned about remaining quiet again.' Picking up Holly's arms, Ivy wrenched them behind the chair, deftly binding one of Owen's ties around her wrists.

Surging with pictures of what she must look like, her imagination at what was going to happen next in overdrive, Holly's pussy twitched and gushed as some silky fabric was tapped against the very tip of her nipples.

'I had no idea you liked me, you know,' Ivy murmured into Holly's ear as she repeatedly dragged the end of the second tie over the girl's tits, observing how they swelled further beneath its touch. 'As it turns out, I've been dying to do this to you for some time. I especially wanted to toy with these amazing globes of yours.'

Holly couldn't help herself. She arched her back, pushing her chest towards the source of the heavenly attention. Ivy's response was instant, her tone acidic, 'I believe I told you to keep still.'

Understanding what Holly's transgression meant, Owen unfurled a piece of silver tinsel from the tree, and passed it to Ivy, wondering how much longer he'd have to wait until his part of their Christmas wish plan came true.

As the scratchy tinsel met her skin, Holly flinched, but Ivy ignored the minor infraction of her rules, as she focused on the chest before her. Threading the garland in a taut figure of eight, Ivy secured it behind Holly's back, well aware of how uncomfortable it would feel. Her mouth watered at the sight of the bound breasts. She'd successfully managed to ignore her personal needs until then, but now, with Holly's breasts all decorated and ready to play with, Ivy couldn't hold back any longer. Bending, she engulfed her willing prisoner's left teat, knocking the exquisitely rough yet smooth nipple around with her tongue.

Despite her efforts to stay quiet, a low hiss of desire shot from Holly, as her whole being reacted to the feel of her dream fuck's lips on her flesh.

Thrilled at having an excuse to punish her friend, Ivy spoke with exaggerated displeasure, 'I told you, you are *not* permitted to make a noise.'

Holly snapped her jaws together, the tinsel around her chest irritating her as a hand slapped her breasts, sending a hot burn rushing through her bound frame.

Smacking Holly again, delighting in the way her tits wobbled and jumped as they were disciplined, Ivy nodded to Owen, who yanked a moon-shaped gingerbread decoration from the tree.

'I can't trust you to be quiet, so I'll have to gag you.'

Holly gulped. Her chest stung, her arms and back ached, and now a bittersweet ginger biscuit was being shoved between her jaws, trapping her tongue beneath it.

She could spit it out if she needed to say the safeword but, as far as she was concerned, that was not going to happen. Saliva gathered at the corners of Holly's lips as the aroma of Christmas filled her nostrils.

'I must say, you're looking more scrumptious by the moment.' Ivy crouched between the girl's legs, feeling the heat of Owen's impatience as his eyes bored into her. Circling a finger around Holly's clit, making the other woman's limbs stiffen and stomach flip, the last of Ivy's self-control broke, 'I'm not sure I can hang on much longer before I taste you.'

Smearing Holly's pussy juice around her snatch, and waving for Owen to come closer, Ivy let her fingernail tickle the top of Holly's clitoris, watching with admiration as her friend fought to obey her and remain still. Then, in one calculated movement, Ivy gave a lingering lick to a half-delirious Holly's clit, before pushing a digit inside her. 'The Holly is definitely in full bud this Christmas.'

Intoxicated by the kinky vision before him, Owen placed his hands on Ivy's shoulders to steady himself, and attacked Holly's right teat.

Sucking for all she was worth on the ginger biscuit, Holly revelled in the combination of sensations her Christmas wish was producing as precise teeth nipped and pinched her with ever increasing pressure, and a rhythmical finger eased itself in and out of her cunt.

Physically unable to keep his hands to Ivy's shoulders, Owen dropped them to her chest, briefly manhandling each globe, before trailing his left hand southwards, urgently seeking out Ivy's pussy.

It was too much for Ivy, the last vestiges of her self-control evaporated as she grasped Owen's dick with her free hand, while attaching her own lips to Holly's neglected breast.

Holly sat bolt upright. A second mouth was lapping at her heated flesh!

Quickly glancing at Ivy for approval, Owen ripped the scarf away.

Blinking, confusion flooding through her, Holly stared in disbelief at both of her friends as they continued to suckle her chest.

Peering up at her through his fringe, the expression of pure and total lust on Owen's face told Holly how much he was enjoying himself.

'It turned out that you weren't the only one with a Christmas wish,' Ivy twinkled mischievously as she pushed another finger inside Holly.

For the first time, Holly was glad she couldn't speak. She had no idea what she'd say, but as Owen licked each of her nipples in turn, and Ivy thrust her fingers faster, Holly knew she was too far down the road of desire to care about the adaptation of her letter to Father Christmas.

'I badly want to kiss you,' Ivy's bright eyes shone with a need Holly had never seen before. 'If I take the gag away, will you let me?'

Holly's nod was so emphatic that Ivy couldn't help but laugh as she tugged out the biscuit, before soldering her face to her friend's, taking pleasure in her taste mingled with a hint of ginger.

With Ivy's fingers deeply wedged within her, her mouth receiving a through workout, and Owen's obsessive domination of her bust, Holly's climax surged up within her. Her chest flushing, her hips raised, she jacked between the two bodies and the chair, the tinsel harness digging into her flesh as she came, her cries of joy muffled by Ivy.

Holly was still quivering with the aftershock of her orgasm when Ivy undid her bindings, and Owen picked her up and threw her to the bed.

In seconds Ivy was on her hands and knees astride Holly, while Owen knelt behind his lover, impaling her with his solid cock.

Ivy's chest swayed invitingly as she was fucked, and Holly wasted no time before she lifted her head and caught a teat between her teeth. Alternately licking and sucking at the succulent nipple, her free hand snaked downwards, cupping Owen's balls as they slapped Ivy's skin.

Through their combined moans of intense satisfaction, Holly beamed up her friends. 'Father Christmas must have thought me a very good girl to grant my wish, *and* give me an extra toy to play with as well. Now it's my turn to give you both a gift,' she said.

Without waiting for either of them to reply, Holly wriggled down the bed and carefully tongued the words "Merry Christmas" over Ivy's clit, while repeatedly squeezing Owen's shaft, sending her two companions into a breathtaking, muscle clenching, Christmas morning climax.

Cinderella Gets her Prince
by Adam G Wright

Fiona heard the "five minutes to curtain up" call and gave her make-up one last retouch before making her way to the stage. She and her fellow actors swapped smiles and friendly encouragements to "break a leg", and as they took their places for the opening scene of the Christmas pantomime, she heard the buzz from the audience gradually quieten down. For Fiona, if her plan worked out, this was going to be one of the best Christmases ever.

As usual, her tummy was doing small flip-flops as she tried to compose herself. She was playing the title role in *Cinderella* this year and this was the last performance of the production's five-day run. It was the first time she'd been cast as leading lady but she loved the theatre regardless of which role she was given.

Everything about it appealed to her, from the chaotic clutter backstage to the friendly banter in the crowded dressing rooms and, of course, the audience's applause at the end of a show. She drank it all in and found it to be a heady mixture.

By nature she was an intellectual who spent her days delving into medieval history and trying to enthuse her students at the college where she lectured. But she was able to indulge her less reserved side when she was, in her mind, transformed into whichever part she was playing in her local amateur dramatic society's productions. In her three years with the company, she'd had great fun portraying a saucy secretary in short skirts that showed off her legs, a mad murderess, and a lady's maid, as well as being in the chorus for musical shows.

Fiona had thrown herself unstintingly into her debut leading role and so far, the audiences had appreciated her efforts. She always got a standing ovation when she and Prince Charming came on to the stage to receive their applause at the end. The added bonus, of course, was that the director hadn't opted for the now rather old-fashioned casting of a female "principal boy" to play the prince. This time around, the role had been taken by Gareth.

Years ago, Fiona had longed for Gareth to notice her at the school they'd both attended but her hopes had all been in vain. He'd been four years older, the Head Boy and much fancied by almost every girl around. He was an all-round athlete, pretty good at academic subjects too, and had a cheerful, attractive personality.

Even then, she'd known it to be nothing more than an innocent schoolgirl crush – the age difference alone, no barrier now that they were both adults, would have precluded them from dating at the time. Also, her parents had been very strict about how she dressed and where she went out, so there was no way she'd have been allowed to go to the places where the likes of Gareth congregated at weekends. She also suspected, deep down, that even if none of this had been the case, he would probably have been oblivious to her anyway. She wasn't the kind of pretty, popular girl he seemed to like.

Eventually, Fiona's intellect gave her the freedom she needed to spread her wings. At 18, she'd begun her first year at Surrey University where she'd matured into an elegant young woman. While away from home, she'd experimented with what she wore, where she socialised – and who she slept with. She was naturally curious and although she was not promiscuous, she did make sure that she got her fair share of attention from the boys who admired both her brains and her long, slim body.

Having attained her degree, she saw no reason to take herself off to foreign parts like so many of her friends had done and was more than happy to return to her home city of Bristol to work. But her time at university had given her a taste for acting and this had led her to join theatre groups and put herself forward for any part she could get. The quiet schoolgirl had definitely reinvented herself as a confident young woman.

Very soon after joining this particular dramatic society, she'd been pleasantly surprised to find out that Gareth was also keen on acting and had been a member for several years. She'd recognised him straight away. After some prompting, he had claimed that he remembered her too, from school, although she wasn't sure how good his memory really was as she couldn't recall ever having been in his company for more than two minutes. In any case, she soon discovered that Gareth was married. And even worse than that, he was married to Marcy.

Marcy had been in Fiona's year but they hadn't been friends. In fact, Marcy and the rest of her gang of cool and sporty girls had gone out of their way to humiliate and exclude Fiona, bullying her for being a "swot" and taking a cruel pleasure in how bad she was at games by leaving her on the sidelines when they, as captains, picked teams.

It appeared that Gareth and Marcy had paired up and then got engaged and married while Fiona had been at uni. And with Gareth being such a catch – he came from quite a wealthy family and his business was thriving too – she didn't doubt that Marcy had dug her claws in deep.

Somehow, she'd managed to avoid any encounters with Marcy until one night, after rehearsals for the pantomime, when Marcy turned up to give Gareth a lift home. Fiona saw them talking and, for a moment, both looked over to where she was standing and she guessed that he'd said something to Marcy about her. But Marcy didn't wave or come over to say hello, she simply turned away and ignored Fiona. This had made Fiona feel uncomfortable – much as she had felt back at school – and was probably the point at which she started to develop her little strategy.

Fiona had almost been breathless when she was told Gareth was to be her leading man. During the days when they were rehearsing she fantasised about him and found it hard to concentrate on her role. Her thoughts of him were invariably followed by a warm, wet feeling in her knickers, especially if she was anticipating the scene in which Prince Charming first kisses Cinderella.

She knew her own body well enough and was by now no stranger to sex, but she was choosy. Although she mingled with a wide circle of friends most weekends, there was still no special man in her life. She knew she wanted more of Gareth even if it couldn't be on a permanent basis – his being married was bound to make things difficult. But now she had a plan.

It was not difficult to mildly flirt with Gareth during rehearsals as she fancied him anyway, and she also noticed that, as well as responding to her in character, he'd often catch and hold her gaze for longer than their roles demanded. They also shared plenty of quiet moments together while the others were going over their scenes. But for Fiona, of course, the best part of any rehearsal was that kissing scene.

At first it was a little unnerving, knowing she had to

lock lips with him in front of the rest of the cast, but she soon forgot that the others were even there. She and Gareth hadn't really talked about what kind of kiss it should be, although both were aware that it had to linger long enough to seem meaningful but not so long that the pace of the play was slowed down. In the end, they just decided to do what they thought felt right – and luckily, the director was happy with their timing.

For Fiona, this was just the starting point – she was determined to allow herself a little pleasure. She also felt she deserved at least some revenge for all the nastiness she'd suffered during her schooldays so she waited until the final performance, when she knew Marcy would be in the audience.

When the time came for the kiss, Fiona made sure her tongue went right into Gareth's mouth – and she held on to him with her hand round the back of his head so he couldn't pull away. He was startled, of course, but reciprocated at the last second with his own tongue over hers. It was a delicious moment for her and she added to it by turning and looking straight at Marcy who was fuming in her seat, unable to do anything about it. And later, Fiona intended to take matters even further.

The climactic scene of the pantomime came almost too soon, as she was relishing every moment on stage – but it marked the point at which phase two of her little plan was about to be set in motion. Prince Charming had just insisted that the Ugly Sisters allow Cinders to try on the glass slipper that had been left behind at the ball. As Gareth knelt before her, Fiona was meant to offer her outstretched foot, as demurely as possible, for to him to hold as he placed the slipper on it. Instead, she reached down, lifted up the hem of her skirt and raised her leg to put her foot up onto his bent knee. This meant Gareth got an eyeful of her thighs, inches from his face. And, rather than wear the costume tights she'd had on all week, Fiona had substituted a pair of sheer black hold-up stockings with lacy tops that flattered her long, slender legs.

Poor Gareth – he nearly dropped the slipper and stumbled slightly over his lines. Somehow he recovered and the scene continued, leading to another kiss as the Prince and Cinderella were reunited. Again she slipped her tongue into his mouth but this time he was ready and rolled his own fully around hers. Then, as they broke away, she whispered to him, 'I've got no knickers on.'

Gareth looked at her, again startled, but luckily it was the turn of the Ugly Sisters to speak so it didn't matter that he was momentarily lost for words.

Following the curtain calls and accolades, including several standing ovations, the final curtain fell. Gareth was handsomely attired in Prince Charming's finery and Fiona, who'd changed back into her ball gown, looked and felt more like a princess than ever before. As they'd taken their final bows, they'd smiled broadly at each other, then, with the show well and truly over, the cast had at last relaxed, hugging and offering mutual praise and thanks.

As it was the closing night of the play, an after-party was held on the stage for the cast and crew, and a round of toasts, laughter and silliness quickly followed the successful production. Various notables came and went, each offering their congratulations on the performance as they too enjoyed the hospitality on offer.

Fiona was happy with how her scheme had progressed so far, but where it went from here would still depend on Gareth. She already knew he was staying for the party and that he intended to have a few drinks – she'd overheard him making arrangements for a late-night taxi to take him home at the end of the festivities.

She played it cool, hoping that her teasing had left him wanting more and eventually, he came over carrying two drinks and offered one to her. She had already consumed two full glasses of champagne but was feeling ready for anything at this point. They chatted for a while about the show, making small talk with some of the other actors as they mingled. Then, finally, they found themselves alone and Gareth turned to her.

'That was very naughty of Cinderella to flash her thighs and put her tongue down Prince Charming's throat!' he scolded her.

Fiona grinned widely. 'The Prince didn't seem to mind though, did he?'

'A bit of warning would have helped!'

'I thought you'd appreciate the surprise.'

'I did. But you also went off-script.'

'Did I?' She pretended to be puzzled, then asked teasingly, 'What did I say?'

'That you had no knickers on!'

'Oh, *that*. Well, it was true – and it still is, as a matter of fact.' She was looking slightly up at him now and directly into his eyes, challenging him to respond – and hoping to get the response she wanted.

Gareth looked around the stage. The party was still in full swing. 'Hmm, I'd like to find out if Cinderella is telling the truth or just winding up her prince.'

'Well, it just so happens I have the key to one of the rooms backstage. If you like, we could …' She left the sentence unfinished.

Under the stage make-up he was still wearing, Gareth looked a little flustered but definitely interested. 'OK, where is it?' He looked around again. No one was taking any particular notice of them now. After a short discussion, they agreed to meet up in five minutes, close to the rear-stage fire exit, and, to make their disappearance less obvious, each made their way there separately.

Fiona wanted her fun and, as a single woman, had no one to answer to. Nevertheless, she valued her privacy and didn't want to be the subject of gossip. Gareth, meanwhile, being married, had even more cause to be careful.

They met at the exit without incident, then she led him to the room and they locked themselves inside it. It was dark outside so the three skylights in the high ceiling didn't offer much if any illumination, and the single light bulb hanging from the ceiling was dim, but once their eyes adjusted to the gloom, it was bright enough for them to find their way around – and see what they were doing.

Immediately, they fell into a clinch that took Fiona's breath away. Gareth's lips were on hers and this was no stage kiss. He took the initiative this time and thrust his hot tongue deep into her mouth. She welcomed the intrusion and rolled her own tongue around his. He was still wearing Prince Charming's tight breeches and as they pressed their bodies together, she felt his hard cock against her belly, despite the many petticoat layers she had on under her ball gown. She reached down and put her hand directly onto the bulge. The material was quite thin and she could feel the heat of his erection. Gareth was caressing her arse as they kissed, cupping her buttocks and drawing her close to him.

Fiona could feel her body responding to the kissing and touching – a hot glow was starting to build between her legs. She knew too that her throat would be flushed, something that always happened when she was aroused.

'Turn around,' Gareth gasped as he broke away from the kiss.

She obeyed but reached behind her to keep her hand

stroking the wonderful hard shaft that she was determined to sample. The gown may have looked authentically old-fashioned but, as a modern copy, it had a zip at the back, which he quickly unfastened to her waist before easing the straps from her shoulders. Her bra too came undone in a flash and his hands claimed their prize, both sliding around to the front of her body to hold her breasts.

Fiona had always worried that men would not find her B-cups large enough, but no one had ever complained and Gareth seemed to like playing with them. She did know that her nipples were wonderfully sensitive and seemed to have a direct link to her crotch, transferring waves of pleasure that radiated around her body. She allowed him some time to hold and caress her breasts while her hand stroked and massaged him through his breeches.

Now he was kissing her throat and she twisted, trying to meet his lips with her own. Finally, she decided the time was right and she squirmed out of his grasp, stepped back and knelt down in front of him. She was now at eye level with the front of the breeches which had an offset button fly. She made sure to concentrate on this unusual arrangement and quickly had the front of them open and then eased them down to his thighs. Gareth wore boxer shorts underneath and she stretched the waistband away while reaching in with her other hand to grip his cock.

Fiona had thought about this moment all day and she was glad that there was enough light for each of them to see the other. She pulled Gareth's cock free of his shorts and spent a few moments with the erect column in her hands, caressing and stroking it. She could hear his deep breathing and she gave a small laugh of pleasure. He was looking down at her and she made sure to look up into his eyes as best she could as she bent forward to take his engorged shaft into her mouth. As she sucked him in fully, he moaned deep in the back of his throat, and then again when she let him slide out far enough to allow her to run her tongue and lips around the head of his cock. Actually, forget all day, this moment had been her dream for weeks – kneeling before Gareth and taking him in her mouth. Right now his cock was hard and it was hers alone, and no thought could have got her pussy wetter.

Fiona stayed on her knees, paying homage to Gareth's cock, alternately licking its length then sucking his balls. She wanted to remember this moment but equally she didn't know how long Gareth would last and she wanted to do more than just suck him.

He couldn't get harder than he was now and she felt the time was right. She leaned sideways and deftly retrieved one of the condoms she'd hidden in a stage-prop cabinet earlier, carefully ripped the foil open with her teeth and handed it to him.

Gareth grinned at her and expertly rolled it on to his shaft before taking matters into his own hands. He reached down and pulled her up by her shoulders and kissed her deeply again. Then he guided her left and backwards, slightly awkwardly, till her buttocks were against a large refectory table that had been left in the centre of the room. After one more kiss, he pushed her back down and further on to the table, raising and parting her legs at the same time. Gareth was firmly in charge at this point.

Fiona's dress was a tangle, with its petticoats and bodice crumpled around her hips. Gareth took the simple expedient of running his hands up her legs from ankles to thighs and pushing back any material that got in his way. Very quickly Fiona's stocking tops, white spread thighs and hairless pussy were exposed to his view.

She lay back on the table with her dress bunched up around her middle and looked at him as he enjoyed this erotic sight of her. 'You're right,' he said. 'Cinderella has no knickers on. She's a very naughty girl!'

With that, he lowered his head and plunged his mouth against her wet and swollen pleasure centre, quickly pushing his tongue as far as it would go into her then withdrawing to concentrate on her clitoris. Now it was her turn to moan aloud as the sensations started to build and spread throughout her body. She held her own nipples and squeezed them, first gently and then harder, to increase the delicious feelings she was already experiencing. Fiona was in heaven but all too quickly she saw Gareth stand up, his cheeks and chin glistening with her juices in the dim light. He raised her right leg high and brought it over his head, effectively rolling her over onto her stomach before pulling her gently towards the edge so she was bent over the table with her feet braced on the floor.

Fiona felt her dress being raised up over her back, the air cool against her skin as Gareth's probing cock began to nuzzle between her thighs. With expert ease he angled her bum up slightly and bent his knees to align the tip of his cock with her pussy. Then, slowly and gently, he pressed forward, sinking deep inside her. There was no resistance at all from her well-lubricated lips and this time her moan was longer and deeper as she felt herself being filled.

Gareth had a good-sized weapon and he was making sure every inch of it was entering fully into her. He paused for a few seconds before starting to circle it in her warm, wet passage. His hands held on to her hips firmly and he moved them counter to his own rotations – and for Fiona, the effect was strong and immediate. She loved the feeling of him being in control and abandoned herself to his ministrations.

Soon, her climax was well on its way, which surprised her – it would often take her ages to even get close to coming and she'd usually end up disappointed when her lover finished first. But the long build-up to this moment, the careful planning she'd done and the excitement she'd got from being on stage had added to her heightened feelings, making things happen so much quicker for her.

Gareth's thrusts were becoming deeper, harder and faster now, creating the unmistakable slap of flesh on flesh, which echoed loudly around the room. Fiona stretched out her arms across the large, heavy table, gripping the far side of it to steady herself and to control the pressure of the near edge that was digging into the front of her thighs. She had no intention of holding back on her climax once the pleasure level had risen to its highest, and very quickly her low moans built up into squeals. She silenced them, suddenly afraid they might be heard, then arched her back, raising her head and shoulders high off the table. Her body shuddered of its own accord then she collapsed.

Whether Gareth took this as his cue or simply lost control at this point she didn't know – she just felt his hands pulling her hips back to meet his piston-like thrusts. He came long and hard, deep inside her body, his strength so great that her feet were raised from the ground by his final lunge. Condom or not, Fiona was sure she could feel his hot ejaculation inside her and then she felt slightly faint as her own pleasure-waves washed over.

It was probably no more than a few moments before Fiona felt able to open her eyes but it seemed like a very long time. As he sensed her movements, Gareth bent his knees slightly to withdraw his still-engorged cock from her and she sighed at the sensation of her own warm juices running down the inside of her right thigh.

Gareth exhaled deeply then stepped back – a little

awkwardly given that his breeches were wrapped round his ankles. He'd kept his ornate dress-uniform jacket on, but as Fiona turned to face him, her gown finally fell off, the fabric puddling at her feet. Gareth wrapped his arms around her and held her tight. She was grateful for the intimacy and hugged him back. Then, after a few moments, she took the initiative.

'We ought to sort ourselves out and get back to the others,' she said.

'I know,' he replied. 'I just need to make sure my knees don't buckle as I walk out. Though I could always pretend to be drunk.' He smiled to let her know he wasn't serious.

Fiona wasn't sure how to play the next few moments. She'd carefully plotted Gareth's seduction but hadn't thought much beyond that. He was married and she knew that well enough. Also, while she'd just received ample proof that the lust between them was mutually felt, whether it was strong enough to warrant anything more than an after-party tryst was a different matter.

They got dressed and did their best to make sure their clothing was properly arranged. Fiona wasn't worried about the marks she found on the ball gown – inevitably, all the actors' costumes got dirty, particularly from the heavy stage make-up everyone wore, so they would all be cleaned before being returned to wardrobe. Once they were decent, Gareth kissed her for the last time before they both, somewhat guiltily, crept out of the backstage room. Fiona headed straight for the ladies' toilet next to the dressing rooms and Gareth, looking slightly less rumpled, decided to pick up a discarded glass and let himself be seen at the party that sounded like it was still going strong.

Fiona spent a few minutes cleaning herself up as best she could before slipping into the communal dressing area.

Thankfully, nobody else was around but, just in case, she crept into a corner and used the cover of hanging costumes and ordinary clothes to effect a discreet but swift change.

Once back in her jeans and top, she made her way through to the party, exchanging pleasantries with a small group of people who had arrived just as she'd been sneaking out to meet Gareth. No one made any comment about her absence, and as other members of the cast were now in their street clothes too, everyone had probably just assumed – if she had even been missed at all – that she'd been in the dressing room getting changed.

The general discussion had already moved on to the next play, with the dramatic society's director giving an outline. They wouldn't need quite so many actors for the production but they would need a leading man to star as a playboy and leading lady to play the heiress he was intent on seducing. Fiona felt she knew just the right two people for the roles …

Naughty … and Nice!
by Tony Haynes

The best career move Sandra ever made was to set up her own company, Sandra's Sinful Sex Toys. From a tiny little office with three people in it when it first opened, the company soon grew beyond recognition. She was happy to acknowledge that that her success was due, in no small measure, to her hard-working employees. Her motto was "Look after your staff and your staff will look after you".

Her policy had definitely paid off because the team she had built up around her was both loyal and dedicated, and each Christmas, she liked to show everyone exactly how much she appreciated them. Along with an extremely generous festive bonus in their pay packets, every Christmas Eve Sandra turned her office into Santa's Grotto for the day, dressed up in a Santa suit and allowed the staff to select any of the products which the company produced as a little extra Christmas gift. Naturally, the outfits that Sandra wore weren't exactly your traditional Father Christmas red and white jacket and trousers – they tended to be rather more risqué.

As Sandra strode into the office that Christmas Eve, she was pleased to find that the Christmas revels had already started. Instead of the usual busy hustle and bustle, the atmosphere was far more relaxed. The punch was flowing readily and the mince pies had already been broken out.

Sandra put down the sports holdall she was carrying and greeted everyone jovially. She was just about to enter her little annexe when Callum called out, 'What's in the bag, boss?'

Callum was a fairly new recruit to the team. Sandra often fondly recalled the morning of his interview, when he had marched into her office with his charming smile and big, broad shoulders. Callum had a confident, slightly cheeky manner about him that she'd instantly liked. As his CV was no less impressive than his physique, Sandra had hired him on the spot. She'd tried her best to square it with her conscience that her decision had been made purely on the basis of the qualifications that Callum had to offer and that it was nothing to do with the fact she quite enjoyed having a bit of decent eye candy around the place. Thankfully, her decision proved correct, for Callum was excellent at his job. Although their relationship had always remained purely professional, this didn't stop the pair from indulging in the odd flirtatious bit of banter.

'You'll see soon enough,' she replied, in answer to his question.

'Any chance of a sneak preview?' he asked.

'You're incorrigible.'

'Thanks.'

Sandra did her best to suppress a grin, then opened the door to her office. After closing it behind her, she set to work immediately. Although she had already put the tree up the week beforehand, it still took her the best part of three hours to hang up all the mistletoe, streamers, tinsel and balloons, then spray the place with glitter. Once she'd finished, Sandra drew the blinds, locked her door and began to change into her outfit. Even though she had done this for the past four Christmas Eves, she still found it felt quite strange to be getting undressed at work.

Unzipping her sports bag, she delved inside and pulled out a cut-off red top and skimpy short skirt, both complete with furry white trimming. She slipped into the skirt no problem, however she couldn't help wondering if she had selected the wrong size top because she couldn't get it to fit properly. Going over to check herself in the mirror, she was rather concerned that she was showing a bit too much cleavage. She tugged at the top once again, but no matter how much she wiggled and jiggled around, her shapely breasts threatened to spill out at any minute. Ah well, she thought, it was too late to select a different one now. The only thing for it was to keep the lights dimmed and hope that no one would make any sarcastic remarks.

Sandra slid her black boots on, donned her little Santa hat, then laid out the fabulous selection of sex toys she had chosen on her desk. There were vibrators, cock rings, anal beads, blindfolds, handcuffs, dildos, leads, masks and collars. Rather disappointingly, Sandra couldn't help musing that she hadn't tried all of the products herself. Making a mental note to rectify this, she crossed over to the door, opened it and called out, 'Merry Christmas!'

The staff in the office all stopped what they were doing, raised their glasses and toasted her. 'Merry Christmas, boss.'

'So, who's first?' Sandra asked.

Jenny, a petite, feisty brunette, didn't hesitate and made her way straight into the grotto. For the next three quarters of an hour, one by one, all of the staff paraded into Sandra's office, selected a gift, exchanged a final season's greeting and then headed off home. Sandra was just wondering where Callum had got to when she heard a knock at her door.

'Come in,' she called out.

Callum entered.

'You don't have to knock,' she said, then added, 'I was beginning to think you'd already headed off home.'

'Are you kidding?' he said. 'This is going to be the highlight of my Christmas.'

'What, are you trying to tell me that there isn't a Mrs Callum waiting at home aching for a Christmas kiss?'

'I wish!' he said, laughing.

Sandra felt her pulse rate quicken. Was Callum trying to tell her something? As she had been out of the dating game for a while, she was wary of misinterpreting the signs. Taking a deep breath, she plucked up her courage and was just about to gamble with a flirty response when Callum strode over to her desk and said, 'So, this is the selection, then?'

'Yes,' Sandra replied, mentally cursing herself that she seemed to have missed an opportunity.

Callum half-turned his back to her as he looked over the array of sex toys. When his hand closed around one of the dildos, Sandra pictured him wrapping his fingers around his own cock. Was it her imagination or was he pretending to masturbate the dildo? As he ran his fingers around the tip playfully, she gulped. In an effort to calm herself down, she went and sat upon the edge of the desk. Callum glanced across at her.

'I appreciate the gesture, but I think I'm a bit too heavy for you,' he said.

'Pardon?'

'Well, I know it's traditional for whoever is receiving a gift to sit on Santa's knee, but I'm quite a big lad.'

'Really?' Sandra slightly surprised herself by responding so suggestively and she blushed slightly.

Thankfully, Callum let it pass, concentrating on the display of toys in front of him instead. After a few minutes had elapsed, he said, 'I don't seem to be able to make up my mind – can you give me a hand?'

Sandra jumped up and scanned the remaining items. Callum gave her a little space by sitting down on the corner of the desk.

Unsure as to his proclivities, Sandra said, 'Any chance of a hint?'

'What do you mean?' he replied.

'Well, what kind of thing do you like?'

Callum shot her one of his award-winning smiles. 'Surprise me.'

Sandra's hand hovered over the table. She was half-tempted to select the dildo that he had been playing with just to see what his response would be – however, deciding to play it safe, she chose a pair of furry handcuffs instead. As she went to hand them to him, Callum patted his lap. 'We could switch roles, if you like. You could come over here and sit on my knee, Santa.'

Sandra suspected that Callum was up to something, but she wasn't sure what. Perhaps he was trying to lure her into a Christmas kiss. Yes, that was it. Deciding to take him up on his offer, she crossed over to him, turned around and then lowered herself onto his knees.

'Comfortable?' he asked.

Sandra nodded. 'Yes.'

'Are you sure? You seem a bit precarious perched on the end of my knees, why don't you edge back a touch.'

Sandra bit her lip. Here it comes, she thought. The cheeky devil is going to take the opportunity to kiss the nape of my neck. Because the prospect appealed to her, she edged backwards. The next moment she got the shock of her life. Through the flimsy fabric of the skimpy Santa skirt that she was wearing, she could clearly feel Callum's raging hard-on – and was so surprised that she practically leaped out of his lap.

It was difficult to tell who was more embarrassed. Callum tried his best to apologise, but, misinterpreting Sandra's silence as stemming from anger, he blushed, then stumbled out of the office. Fatally, Sandra hesitated, so that by the time she went after him, to her immense disappointment, he had disappeared.

Sandra sighed and scolded herself. Why on earth had she acted so foolishly? It was so silly. She'd fancied Callum for ages, he'd presented her with a golden opportunity and she'd gone and blown it. She shook her head. Maybe she'd be able to make it up to him at the office New Year's Eve party the following week.

With the building now empty, Sandra didn't bother shutting her office door as she began to change out of her Santa outfit. Discarding her boots, she then slipped out of her top and lowered her skirt. As she did so her eyes lit upon the dildo that Callum had toyed with so provocatively. It had seemed so alive in his hands. Reaching across the desk, she picked it up. The dildo in question was one of the company's best-sellers. Sandra suspected it was due to the fact that it looked so lifelike. The fake cock was thick and curvy and had an amazing, almost fleshy texture.

As her right hand closed around the dildo, Sandra shut her eyes and imagined that it was Callum's cock. He had felt so big when she'd sat in his lap. As she ran her fingers up and down the shaft of the toy, a wicked thought crossed her mind. Reaching down with her left hand, Sandra eased her knickers to one side. Then, with her right hand, she lowered the dildo until it brushed against her well-trimmed pubes. Teasing the tip of it against her clit she imagined what would have happened if, instead of jumping up as she had done, she had reached around, lowered the zip on Callum's trousers, taken out his cock and allowed him to sink it deep into her pussy.

Picturing the scene, Sandra slipped the tip of the mock-cock between her moist pink lips and began to pleasure herself with it. Resting back against the desk she spread her legs wide apart and worked up a steady rhythm. With her left hand she caressed her breasts, pretending it was Callum's and not her own. She could easily imagine him taking her bra off and massaging her nipples so she reached around her back and unclipped it. As it fell loose, she took hold of her left nipple and tweaked it. A shiver ran down the length of her spine.

'Oooh, you bad boy,' Sandra thought.

'Yes, but you love it, don't you?' her imaginary Callum replied.

She certainly did. The way she could tell was the ease with which the dildo was now sliding in and out of her sopping-wet pussy. Still, she wasn't quite taking the whole length of her toy. She couldn't help thinking that Callum wouldn't be impressed by this, so she sank the dildo in right up to the hilt. As the full length of the fake cock glided inside her, Sandra stifled a gasp. Her thighs felt on fire. She could tell she was on the verge of coming.

'Come on, Callum,' she thought, 'Fuck me, fuck he hard.' Her fingers were only too happy to obey and she increased the tempo.

The orgasm seemed to hit Sandra from her toes up. A tremendous tingling trilled the whole length of her legs. She grasped her left breast tightly, then bit her bottom lip so as to stop herself from crying out aloud. It was a wonderfully satisfying feeling. She luxuriated in it for several minutes as little aftershocks pulsed through her thighs. Only when her orgasm was finally spent did she open her eyes. To her immense embarrassment, she saw Callum standing in the doorway of the grotto, his gaze firmly transfixed between her thighs. Though it was too late to be modest now, Sandra removed the dildo with a wet, sucking sound, pulled her panties back into place and covered her breasts with her arms.

'I thought you'd left,' was all she could mumble.

Profusely apologetic, Callum stammered something about forgetting his present. Only then did he finally tear his eyes away from the incredible scene in front of him.

Just as he was about to leave, Sandra said, 'Oh no you don't!' Then, forcing herself to act with a coolness which belied her true feelings, she crossed over to the door and nudged it closed. 'I don't think that's very fair, do you?'

Callum was puzzled. 'What do you mean?'

'Well,' she explained, 'you've had the pleasure of watching me, I think it's only fair that you reciprocate.'

His face lit up as he realised what she was suggesting. 'You mean..?'

Sandra nodded.

Callum grinned. 'OK, you're on.'

With that, he reached for his flies.

'Hang on,' she interrupted. 'You need to lose a bit of clothing first.'

Happy to obey, Callum stripped out of his jacket, shirt and tie. Flicking off his shoes, he tore off his socks, then paused as he reached for his trousers. 'Ready?'

Sandra nodded. Callum undid his belt, unbuttoned himself, lowered his zipper and slid his trousers and boxer shorts down. No sooner had he done so than his impressive cock sprang to attention.

Immediately, Sandra decided to give it a closer inspection. Stepping forward, she took hold of his shaft in her right hand and stroked his foreskin back and forth. Good though the dildo had been, it was no substitute for the real thing. Sandra loved the way that his cock twitched around. She teased her thumb around the tip until it glistened with moisture. Now that it was fully erect it looked like it was at least eight inches long. It seemed huge. Sandra then took a step back from him.

'Go ahead, then,' she said.

'You want me to play with myself?'

She nodded.

Callum shook his head. 'You're even naughtier than I'd dared to dream.'

'Thanks,' she replied.

With a twinkle in his eye, Callum leaned back against the edge of his boss's desk, took his cock firmly in his right hand and started to masturbate.

Thinking back, Sandra couldn't remember ever having watched any of her ex-boyfriends pleasure themselves. She was absolutely fascinated. Callum alternated long slow strokes with short, sharp ones. He then changed his grip completely. Taking the very end in between his right thumb and forefinger, he toyed with it until his fingertips were covered with precome. Sandra noticed that his breathing was becoming shallower. Callum stopped.

'What are you doing?' she asked.

'If I don't stop, I'll come,' he explained.

'That's the general idea, isn't it?' she mused.

'I was hoping you might help me out.'

Sandra smiled, then shook her head.

Callum shrugged. 'Whatever you say, Santa. You're the boss.'

Taking a firm grip of his cock once more, Callum stroked his foreskin back and forth, faster and faster and faster. Sandra found the sight so arousing she lowered her frilly red knickers and slipped her right middle finger into her pussy. The sight of his boss pleasuring herself was too much for Callum. His cock gave a massive twitch and then shot out a tremendous stream of spunk. Some of it splashed against Sandra's thighs, which she found so ridiculously arousing she slipped a second finger inside herself.

'Don't just stand there,' Sandra said.

Needing no second bidding, Callum took her in his arms and kissed her passionately. She broke off from touching herself in order to receive the kiss. Her arms curled around his muscular back, then she ran her hands down to his bottom. The next instant, Sandra felt something between her thighs. Glancing down she saw that Callum had taken hold of the dildo which she had used to pleasure herself and was rubbing it between her legs. She had never felt so aroused. She broke away from the embrace and turned around. She then leaned forwards, grasped the edge of the desk in both hands, wiggled her bottom high in the air and begged him to continue.

Callum was more than happy to oblige. He rubbed the dildo playfully around the crack of her arse. Sandra closed her eyes – it felt *sooo* good. He then parted her buttocks and slipped the end of the dildo inside her pussy. She grasped the desk tightly, feeling as if she was going to come immediately, she was so turned on. As he worked the dildo in and out of her, she bit her bottom lip, determined to prolong the pleasure for as long as possible. It wasn't easy, though, for Callum proved an expert with the dildo. His tempo was perfect – gentle, but firm.

Just as she felt her climax building he stopped for some reason. Desperate for him to keep going, Sandra glanced over her left shoulder and was about to ask him why he had stopped when she spotted the reason. Unbelievably, his impressive cock was already rock hard again and, with a quick glance to check it was what she wanted, he sank all eight inches of it into her pussy.

Sandra could contain herself no longer. She squealed excitedly and came all over his rigid length.

After allowing her a few seconds to luxuriate in the moment, Callum then took hold of her hips and started to fuck her in earnest. Sandra felt like she was on fire. Her pussy tingled excitedly. No, surely she wasn't on the verge of yet another orgasm? She was, though. With perfect timing, Callum groaned and plunged deep inside her. Sandra cried out once again as a third orgasm crashed over her. As his cock twitched away, she felt as if the pleasure was never going to cease.

It took several minutes for Sandra's climax to subside. Eventually, Callum withdrew from her.

'Wow!' he said.

'Wow indeed,' she replied, then turned around and flopped down on the desk, exhausted.

'Now that's what I call a Christmas bonus,' he said.

Sandra slapped him playfully. 'Cheeky.'

Happening to glance up, Sandra spotted that they were directly under a sprig of mistletoe, which she had hung earlier. Following her gaze, Callum laughed. 'You're insatiable!'

Sandra reached out with her legs, ensnared her new lover's waist between them and drew him towards her. She had the distinct feeling that it was going to be a very Merry Christmas indeed ...

Elf Yourself
by Landon Dixon

There was a new Santa in town.

That's the word I got when I dropped off a load of seal meat at the elf mess hall. It was hard times at the North Pole, economic conditions down south meaning parents were giving fewer toys to their tots – fewer toys, less work for the elves. Coupled with the gloomy global fiscal reality was the fact that the elves had been reproducing like they had long, furry ears, instead of short, pointy ones. Less work, more elves meant lay-offs, discontent, malcontents, full-fledged elf insurrection according to Elvin at the mess hall.

'Emery led a group of other unemployed Elftown elves on an assault on Santa's workshop, captured it and took Santa and Mrs Claus as prisoners!' The guy's face lit up like the Northern Lights, revolutionary fervour burning bright in his acne.

I rolled a barrel of whale oil into the hall. Elftown was where the laid-off and lazy elves had set up digs over the past couple of years, on the outskirts of the Claus compound. 'Yeah?' I grunted noncommittally.

I had my own gripe against the red-suited fat man – I hadn't "fitted into" his plans three years ago, when overexposure to the midnight sun had shot me up on a growth spurt and right out of my green duds. I'd been working in the meat and blubber business ever since, operating a hydroponic oathouse for the reindeer on the side, as well; been living in an igloo a mile south of 90 degrees latitude and zero longitude. Still, I admired Santa and his work, didn't have much good to say about blowhard bully Emery Elf; didn't say it right then, either.

'Yeah!' Elvin beamed on like he'd been sold the moon. 'Emery and his Committee for the Elfin People are going to turn this place into a regular Snowtopia! Better hours during busy season, four-legged stools, free velvet tunics and felt hats, free range for the reindeer! Everybody's going to benefit!'

He kept on lipping like a true believer, lapping the propaganda onto me. I just nodded and grinned right along, reminding myself to sharpen the harpoons and spears when I got back home. Green revolution wasn't my game.

It only took two months for the whole thing to go as sour as Mrs Claus's eggnog come April. There was a knock on my igloo hatch, and Evelyn filled my frosty abode with her awesome physique, and filled me in.

'Emery and his "committee" are working the rest of the elves and the reindeer harder than ever,' she bleated, her sea-green eyes shining like flame-heated ice. 'He's signed contracts with Chinese wholesalers to supply them with North Pole toy products 24/7. And he's using the reindeer for airborne surveillance of US, Canadian and Danish territory, flying them around the clock on the payroll of the Russians.' She bit her plush red lower lip, which went well with her plush red upper lip. 'And – and he's got a team of toy-development elves building a mini-submarine to be used for oil exploration under the polar ice cap – paid for by Iran and North Korea!'

Her pout would've turned most elves to putty – along

with her long, white-blonde hair, long, white-blonde lashes, and larger-than-normal curvy body capped by a pair of tunic-stretching breasts. There was a rumour that one of Evelyn's parents might be a Claus.

But her charms met a chill in my ice shack.

'Won't you help us overthrow Emery and his committee of thugs, free Santa and Mrs Claus?! You were Santa's right-hand man once, after all!'

Yes, I'd been the Belt Buckle's trusted "troubleshooter" once, breaking in bucking reindeer and busting AFL-CIO infiltrations. Once. A long time ago. Now, I was getting by on my own, being left alone. Emery and his committee hadn't butted into my operations, so why should I butt my head against theirs? I didn't owe Santa Claus so much as a cookie.

'Count me out, pretty ptarmigan,' I responded. 'I'm …'

Evelyn unbuckled her black belt and unbuttoned her green tunic. Her more-than-Elfin breasts bobbed out into the open like twin baby beluga heads, complete with jutting pink snouts. She skinned off her green tights, showing me shapely legs of pure sculpted ivory, a white-blonde bush gracing the apex.

She meant business. She suddenly had my full and rigid attention.

Evelyn strolled forward on her pointy-slippered tiptoes, breasts bouncing like weather balloons, lips and eyes and pussy glistening. She bumped up against what had once been an iceberg, melting me to the core with her wicked body heat, running her fingers through my tingling hair. 'I've always admired you, Earnest.' She breathed hot, perfumed air in my face. 'Your long black hair and ice-crystal blue eyes, your rugged physique and manner.'

Her fingers bit into my electrified scalp, her breasts heaving against my thumping thorax, her pussy undulating against the throbbing lump in my slickers; really rubbing it in – her advantage. She put out a good display, had an enticing product.

But I wasn't sold, just yet. Lately, I'd come to desire green as in cash, as well as pink as in gash. I was more reactionary than revolutionary; more doer than do-gooder.

'I want my elf suit back,' I rasped. 'And I want to live in Santa's house, get my old job again.'

She nodded her head, wiped my drooling lips with her wet smile. 'I'm sure I can get Da– I mean, *Santa* to agree to that. So you'll free him and Mrs Claus, overthrow Emery and his committee?'

It was a tall order for short people. It was my turn to grin. 'Give me a little more of your … oral persuasion. I'm not fully convinced yet.'

Evelyn slid down my quivering body like a sealskin, down onto her knees in the snow. She deftly opened the blowhole on my slickers and pulled my pulsating cock out into her soft, warm palm. I groaned. She stroked me with her strong little hand, basting me with her hot breath, turning me hard and long as a narwhal tusk.

Then she scooped up some snow with her left hand and ladled it onto my burning-hot cock. I swear ice crystals had never melted so fast. But before the drip totally overflowed, Evelyn opened her pretty little mouth up wide and immersed my erection in the steambath of her maw.

I jerked, grabbing on to her cotton-floss hair as she gave me a snowjob, bobbing her head back and forth, sucking quick and tight, slow and sensual on my pressurised pipe. The contrast between heat and cold was dick-stunning, shocking to the rest of my system. Water streamed down my balls and into Evelyn's cupping hand.

She'd convinced me. I took immediate action, lifting her up and carrying her over to my musk ox hide-covered bed, draping her down on top of it. She arched her back and bum, seductively curled her limbs, letting me and my one-eyed Arctic snake get a good look at all she had to offer – and then a good lay.

I dropped onto her like a blizzard, plugging into her pussy, mashing my mouth against hers, filling my hands with her tits. I swallowed her moan and she mine, as I pumped my hips, putting it to the erotic elf-woman in hard, unrelenting, sexual terms. She clawed at my back and buttocks, then wrapped her arms and legs right around me, bouncing to the thrusting beat of my lust. Bricks shook loose in the igloo walls, the pair of us melting the permafrost.

'Yes, Earnest! Yes!' Evelyn screamed.

'You've got a deal!' I hollered back.

We surged into one another like the sea into the land, shook together like tectonic plates under the ocean, shattered the Arctic silence with our Elfin cries of passion blissfully consummated.

Evelyn wanted Santa and Mrs Claus freed first of all. But I was running this sideshow. I wanted to keep the Jolly One stewing in his own juices for as long as possible, so he'd be ever more grateful when I finally hauled his fur-trimmed butt out of the fire.

So, first of all, I rounded myself up a posse of fellow elves and friendly reindeer. No inspirational speeches or banners were required – the only ones now benefiting from the new polar regime were Emery and his committee and the axis nations of the world. The revolution had been pre-empted for personal gain, like so many before, hot and cold. The loathing was as palpable in the air as chocolate chip come chimney time.

'Let's string 'em up by their bells!' Elvin exhorted, a

born-again Santaist now.

'No! Let's tie them up to four reindeers and tear them four new ones!' Randolph bellowed, his antlers flaring St. Elmo's fire and his nose blazing code red.

I let them blow off steam. I knew how that felt, I thought, with a smile at Evelyn.

Then I put forward my plan, put the plan into action.

Me and 20 other elves gathered moblike outside Claus House at midnight. We were armed with frozen snowballs and icicle spears, more grievances than even little people had a right to bear against the world. We tripped the security wire that ran around the perimeter of the compound and strolled resolutely forward.

Huskies and wolfhounds started barking and snapping at us, charging. We pelted them with the snowballs, sending them yelping and whimpering and scampering away into the darkness. Emery's brutish form and face quarter-filled the front door of the house.

'We're taking our pole back!' I challenged the goon, Evelyn alongside me.

Emery sneered, and snarled, 'Back to your seals and oats, Earnest! Or be crushed by the revolution!'

The guy was self-indoctrinated to the point of delusion. He turned and shouted instructions, and six husky, black-uniformed elves armed with driftwood fungo bats boiled out of the front of the house.

Icicles flew through the air like a frozen string hailstorm. The thugs retreated back into the building under the onslaught, battened down the red and green gift-wrapped metal door.

I raced around to the rear of the house, where I'd already hitched up a team of 20 reindeer to the floor of the structure. They were impatiently waiting in their traces for me to give them the signal, lined up out onto the summer ice two by two, Reginald the blue-nosed reindeer in the lead. He was a prude, yes, but he was powerful, had taken to the revolution like a walrus to a razor.

Santa House was set up on cinder blocks because of the permanently frozen soil. So when I gave the signal, and Reginald and the other reindeer leaped forward, the house lurched right off its blocks and smashed the ground running, dragged forward over the snowy earth. The snowballs and icicles pelting the front of the house kept any of Emery and his committee from escaping.

Faces began to pop up in the lit windows in the back of the building – scared faces – as the reindeer strained at their traces and pulled the houseful of elfvolutionaries grindingly out onto the ocean sea ice. This was thick at the shore, thinner further out. The reindeer picked up speed, the house skidding along at a good clip, and the elf faces turned terrified.

I raced alongside. And just as the house crashed through the ice, I pulled the pins that held the traces onto it, and the reindeer flew up into the air right before they reached ice-chunked open water.

The house wallowed, started to sink. Emery and his panicked committee busted out of the windows and bolted out the door, right into the freezing waters. Their thrashing forms quickly hardened into blocks of ice, elfcubes to be fished out and thawed for future rehabilitation and release, as required.

Thank you climate change.

We freed Santa and Mrs Claus from their cramped gingerbread house imprisonment. And then a celebration ensued of Boxing Day proportions, with all the trimmings.

'Santa says you can have your old job back, just like you wanted,' Evelyn murmured into my kisser, lying on top of me, as we partook of our own private celebration at my soon-to-be-abandoned igloo.

'Better red than dead, I say,' I muttered back, kissing the gorgeous elf-woman and pulling the musk ox bedspread more fully over our naked bodies. I was already inside of her, rocking her gently with my cock.

She rocked me, by adding, 'And he even threw in a couple of things you didn't ask for, just to make sure you're totally satisfied.'

Evelyn called out, and two more female elves squirmed into my snow shack, Evangelina and Esther, two of Santa's own "personal assistants". They were smaller than Evelyn, but just as curvaceous. They quickly shed their green duds, and showed off their treats.

Evangelina was a redhead, Esther a brunette. Their lovely little features glowed and bobbed and stiffened and glistened in the dim light shed by the whale oil lantern. The musk ox came off and they came on.

Esther straddled my face, splatting her hot, moist, furry mound down onto my open mouth. I gripped her bubble buttocks and licked her dripping slit. She quivered and squealed. Evelyn kept on riding my cock, tall in the saddle now, cowelf-style, as Evangelina heaped snow onto my nipples and nuts, and then licked it off with her melting wet tongue.

The ceiling started dripping, too, the heat rising in waves from our roiling bodies. I thrust up into Evelyn, pumping my hips, lapping Esther's pussy like a horny reindeer at the trough, stretching a hand up to clutch and squeeze her full breasts. Evangelina twisted my balls with one hand, pulled my cock right out of Evelyn's slit with her other hand and briefly sucked on the slickened candy cane before stuffing it back into Evelyn's satin pink sleeve.

They switched positions, elf-quick in their movements. I stayed supine, sublime, eating out Evangelina's cute little ginger muff, fucking Esther's tight velvet cunt, getting my torso and sack fondled and licked and sucked and snowed by sweet, nasty Evelyn. They all got a ride on my north pole. Until they piled off and piled up, and I drove them hard and fast like Santa's sleigh on Christmas Eve.

Evelyn was on the bottom, on her hands and knees, Esther and Evangelina stacked on top of her in that awesome order. I was in behind them all, gripping my dick and staring at the three sets of buoyant butt cheeks and three gleaming slits, then sticking them.

I fucked Evelyn, plunging deep and pumping hard; then Esther, then Evangelina. Up and down the stacked-up snatches I went, delving and drilling. Then I snatched up a pair of foot-long icicles lying on the snowy floor of my melting hutch, rubbed the points smooth and round then slid them into the heated holes I wasn't torching with my own cock.

It was a frenzy, a fuck-for-all. The three girls moaned and screamed and shuddered, rubbing together as one. I grunted and growled, pistoning pussies, the icicles melting, my cock gone molten.

The roof almost caved in on us. Ecstasy did. I slammed one cunt after another with my cock, the icicles liquefying in my hands and their pussies. Then I bucked, belted by orgasm.

I jerked my spurting hose out of Esther and plugged into Evelyn, doused her tunnel, then jumped up into Evangelina, blasting her pussy with my sizzling ball-nog. They quivered and shrieked with their own orgasms, all four of us sharing the joy. *Viva l'end of the revolution!*

Good cheer had been restored to Santaland. And I was back in the green – tights, tunic, cap and slippers, that is. We run a non-profit up here, after all.

Christmas Keeps Coming
by John McKeown

There's probably a medical term for a woman obsessed with having sex with a guy dressed up as Santa Claus. Clausomania, Santaitis. I should look it up sometime. Though I'm trying to forget my entanglement just last Christmas with one of the worst sufferers of the disease. Maybe this confession will help. I certainly couldn't take it to my local priest.

Anita had just divorced me and not only had I lost the wife I still loved, along with three wonderful kids, I'd lost my business in the recession, and it was only the goods unloading at the warehouse, the cold calling for a car insurance company and – I still wince when I think of it – being Santa in a mall in Queens that were keeping me out of the soup kitchens. It wasn't just my neck on the line. I had alimony payments to make, and I wanted to make them. I wanted to keep on putting food in my kids' mouths.

So there I was, sitting in that sparkling, twinkling, snow-speckled grotto wearing a red fat suit and a big fluffy white beard, dandling kids on my knee and listening to them reel off lists of toys they'd been working on since the summer. At least, I told myself, way out in Queens I was safe from anyone finding out how low I'd sunk. But then, ten days before Christmas Day, Nuala McCarthy walks into the grotto. Boy, total disaster has never looked more mouth-wateringly gorgeous.

Nuala had more curves on her than a bagful of bowling balls, and whenever she appeared the men went down like tenpins. I was no exception and the moment I recognised her I had a woody as big as a California redwood straining against the fabric of my Santa pants. It didn't matter that this Irish broad had a personality meaner than any of the snakes banished by St Pat from the Ould Sod, her looks overrode everything.

I hunkered down deeper within my flowing beard and put extra bass notes into my greeting of the little boy – her nephew – who climbed fearlessly onto my knee and peered cynically into my eyes.

I went through my spiel on automatic, with not just the kid's eyes but Nuala's burning into me. It was as though she could feel that hard-on throbbing with months of frustrated desire just a few feet away from all her lovely weight slouched on one long, sharp high heel. But I got through it, losing half a pound in sweat, and then they left.

And then, a minute later, she came back in, with her fur coat over one arm and stood, hand on hip in front of me.

'Hi, Jerry.'

'Huhhuhhummm!'

'I know it's you, Jerry. And you've never looked more fetching.' She brought her tight, silk-clad ass down onto my thigh.

'I can understand your reluctance, but your secret's safe with me, as long as –' she plucked my lips free of the coils of beard and kissed me, her tongue slipping in '– you do exactly as I say.'

I had no choice. She knew Anita. She'd tell Anita. Anita'd be happy to tell the kids. My daughter especially would die of embarrassment. Also, Nuala was a Mob wife. And not just any Mob wife. She was the wife of

Michele Angeli, the head of a big outfit sanctioned by the Gambino Family. If I didn't do exactly what she wanted I was as good as dead.

I spent the afternoon with one ear cocked to the endless stream of kids and the rest of my head considering what to do. And how crazy was I? My pride got the upper hand. I'd rather risk death than have Anita and the kids know I was a Santa Claus in a shopping mall!

Nuala came back just as I was closing up the Santa shack.

'Room for one more, Santa? There's so much I have to ask you.'

'Relax, Nuala, you'll have me fired – the supervisor's a total bastard.' But that woody was back, and Nuala could smell its resin.

'Don't worry about him, I locked the door.'

'You *what?*'

She had.

'Gimme the key, Nuala!'

She dropped the ornate gold key down the front of her red silk blouse and wriggled it down.

'Now, you sit down and play Santa for me. The works. You have no idea what Santa does to me. Maybe it's those big boots –' she patted my fur-lined waders '– maybe it's the big buckled belt –' her fingers tugged at it and moved down to press against my woody '– or maybe it's that last secret toy Santa always has tucked away for really good girls.'

'You haven't been good, Nuala. Ever.'

'No, I confess I've been a bad girl, Santa. Maybe you can spank me a little –' she had a firm grip on my cock through the red velveteen '– in fact, I insist.'

What the hell, I thought. If I'm a dead man, then let's die happy. I pulled the curtains over the munchkin windows and sat down. Nuala dropped her jacket, shimmied out of her split silk skirt and bent herself over my parted legs. She was wearing the briefest sliver of black panties beneath the garter belt that held up her fishnet stockings. I pulled them down and gave her piled-high cheeks a good hard slap, and then a few more. She was a flood of wet already. I parted her thighs and slid a finger in. A tight quim, for all the action it must've seen, and so soft. I pushed in deeper, letting her pull my other hand down to the breasts she'd popped out of her half-cups. I gave them a good squeezing massage as I worked her with my fingers. Suddenly, a footstep outside. The door rattled. The supervisor's voice. I put my hand over Nuala's mouth but couldn't stop my fingers doing the frontstroke and backstroke in her wetness. Then he was gone.

'We have to be quick, Nuala.'

'Anything you say, Santa.' She raised herself up, pulled, then tore away the restraint of her panties and bent to free my cock from its red-hot prison. The suit had a long zip that often got caught in stray bits of fabric. It was halfway down when it happened and she had to do quite a bit of tugging that, awkward though it was, got both of us breathlessly excited. The zip wasn't fully down before the head of my cock poked itself free and was met by her super-heated quim. The teeth of the zip bit into the shaft as I pushed it up into her, but Christ, I felt as wild as a 19-year-old losing his cherry.

I got all, or most of it in and, gripping her hips, forcibly matched our motions into one fast seesaw of sliding, grinding penetration. It was quick. But we were so perfectly in sync, in such harmony, that the time element didn't matter for once. Biting her backthrust neck, sucking at her stiff nipples, and digging my nails into the thick, rippling outflow of her ass, I shot months of backed-up come into her lovely, nasty insides.

In my stupidity I thought that might be the end of it. That Nuala might move on to redder Yuletide pastures. After all, there must be a couple of hundred thousand Santas in New York over Christmas, she could've had her pick. But no. It was this big, hairy Italian Santa she wanted. She'd had the hots for me ever since we'd known each other as teens back in Brooklyn. She'd just been waiting for her chance. And now she was making the most of it. She hired a suite in a plush Manhattan hotel and, after a gruelling day in Santaland, I'd go over there, change back into my Santa suit in the janitor's closet and find her waiting.

I hadn't forgotten that, sooner or later, when Michele Angeli found out, I was a dead man, but I was so damn exhausted from my three shitty jobs, plus servicing the insatiable Nuala, that I hardly gave it a thought. At least I was still earning for my kids, and going out with a bang – several bangs – per festive night.

One night, three days before Christmas Day I think it was, I staggered into the suite to see Nuala trussed up tight in Christmas ribbon in front of the decorative gas flames of the fire.

'Come right in, Santa, I'm primed and ready.'

And she really was. Her thick black hair was tied into pigtails with red ribbons. A red choker, a short red basque, thin red straps holding up crimson stockings, shiny red patent leather heels. She was on all fours, legs together, pantie-less, her pussy moistly gleaming. I dropped my sack and fell down behind her. There was woody again, thicker than a Christmas log and eager to burst into flame. Instead of tugging at the zip I pulled my pants straight down, released him from his red jockstrap and pressed him against Nuala's fine, wet labia. I felt like teasing her. There

122

were moments when I enjoyed my power over her – she was really hot for me. If Anita had been this hot I wouldn't be … Well, I was, and if I was to get out of the situation I had to get deeper into it. I painted her lips with it a little longer until she was whimpering, pleading for me to push in. A little more painting … and a little more, the head nosing in a half-inch and then nosing out.

'Fuck me, you bastard!'

'Santa won't give you anything if you talk like that.'

'Fuck me, Jerry, for Christ's sake, before I get on the phone to Anita.'

'Naughty Nuala!' I rammed the whole length in and hammered her into the rug, tearing off the rest of my suit as I nailed each of her backthrusts with a savage forward lunge. I hadn't been this brutal with her as yet, and maybe I shouldn't have been, because she was even more insatiable after this episode.

She'd managed to get back on her knees and was now ramming her ass back into me like a rabbit on amphetamines. Still feeling brutal I pulled out, pressed a thumb against her asshole, just to signal what she could expect next, and then replaced thumb with cockhead. The eternal question – would it fit? She was certainly eager to accommodate and after some stretching and angling I got enough of it in to produce loud gasps of pleasure. I worked her pussy with my fingers and gave her a tight screwing in the ass, squeezing her swinging boobs at the same time. I was getting close to coming. But it was always better if I waited for her. I scooped her pussy out with three fingers and got my cock into her ass up to the balls. What a pretty picture it made, my tanned, muscled navel with its black hair pounding into those pale, flawless, flushed-pink Hibernian ass cheeks.

She was on the point of coming now, thanks to the

fingers. I pulled out quick and drove it into her pussy. She was flat on the rug again, her fingers gripping the marble floor-lip of the fireplace when I let all my frustrations rip, forgetting everything in the violence of release. I collapsed on her back, our sweated bodies embracing in one giant kiss.

'By the way –' I was rolled on my back now, fingering those busted gift ribbons '– who tied you up?'

'My elfin friend.'

'Come on, *really*. You couldn't do that yourself.'

'Really, I have an elf helps me out.'

'You've been at the eggnog again. Tell me.'

'Elfinea! Come in here.'

Jesus, I thought, I've literally gone and fucked her brains right out.

Then the bedroom door opened and in walks a short but very shapely chick in a bare green whisker of an elf costume: a saw-toothed green bra, each point ending in a little brass bell, and the same below, the belled points knocking against inches of firm, bare, creamy-white thighs above tight, pale-green stockings.

'Elfinea, this is Jerry. He needs a shot of bourbon.'

'Ice, Jerry?'

'Yeah, Elfinea, please.' As she walked to the kitchenette I leaned up to see the tiny back bells of her slip-skirt knocking merrily against the naked cheeks of a cute, ultra-tight little ass.

I don't know how it is with other guys, but with me, the more exhausted I'm feeling, the hornier I get. It's a kind of automatic horniness. My body just takes over. What happens is all my remaining energy drains into my cock and balls, and stays there. It happened now. 'Timber!' in reverse.

'Darling, I think Elfinea's made an impression.' Nuala

tapped a finger against the head of my new stiffy. 'Let's retire to the bedroom, she'll bring the drinks there.'

I lay on the bed, totally exhausted in body, but frisky as hell in cock. The ladies were giggling as I sipped my bourbon. I let them play. I didn't care any more. Hell, I was already sleeping with the fishes in the East River.

Nuala, naked but for her red silk kimono, put my Santa hat on my head and kissed me. Elfinea gave me a foot massage that gradually worked its way up to be a cock massage. She seemed genuinely amazed by its dimensions, as I was myself. Sometimes, ladies, a man and his hard-on really are two-different beings. I watched, as if I was watching someone else, as Elfinea's lovely white fingers stroked and kneaded that big monstrous thing, like they were ten naked maidens bathing some naked god.

What was Nuala doing? Nuala was sitting at her dressing table, sipping, looking on, a couple of fingers at her puss. Was this some new kind of trap? Would she start videoing me to show to Anita? I couldn't care. I was nothing but a dead prop for a cock that kept getting bigger and bigger as it slipped through Elfinea's fingers like a shuffled card-deck.

Then little Elfinea had climbed up my legs and was bending over me, teasing me with the bells on her bra like they were grapes. She was certainly a pretty little thing. And then my big boner was being lifted up and I closed my eyes as I felt it being guided into a tight, juicy pussy. I had no energy for aggression now. In my exhausted, dreamlike state, I let those elfin fingers take me into that hot miniature grotto under the fringe of bells at their own pace. I closed my eyes and felt its suckering mouth slide up and down, eating, regurgitating my cock's hard length. The swallowing and slippage speeded up, the little bells jangled. I looked. Elfinea was riding me, ecstatically, caressing her little breasts under the green bra. I raised myself up, and started sucking them. Nuala was moaning, legs pulled up onto the chair, fingers deep in her quim.

Elfinea's breasts were so small, but so prettily compact, that I could get almost a whole one in my mouth. She loved it. I sucked hard and started driving up deeply into her. A sudden surge of new bodily energy. I pushed her back slowly onto the bed and gave her some good old missionary.

Nuala got jealous and got onto the bed. She lay down next to me and got two fingers round my cock as it drove in and out of her friend. She also got a finger in my ass which gave me an extra surge of stiff. Elfinea was moaning pretty loud for such a little woman, one of her green stockings down by her knee, the other still firmly in place. I like to feel material – stocking, panties, a long shoe heel – when I'm fucking. I gripped that green-nyloned thigh and let myself snap, shooting my load into little Elfinea's twisting, sucking, contorting body.

I never found out who Elfinea was, or saw her again. Nuala confessed she got incredibly turned on by watching me fuck other women, but though we tried it a couple of times, it never worked out to anyone's satisfaction. Nuala got so crazy-jealous she ended up slinging her woman friend – usually another Mob wife – out on her diamond-ringed ear. In fact, as Christmas got closer, Nuala got more and more possessive.

She was, of course, blackmailing me and (I know this isn't a very masculine thing to say) treating me like a sex object, something to slake her lust with, but the weird thing was, I started to feel a kind of tenderness toward her. I couldn't let this show, though. I tried it once, but it made her even more crazily possessive. I was trapped. I just couldn't see a way out. Maybe, just maybe, her obsession with me would tail off after Christmas? But that year it felt like Christmas just kept on coming without ever arriving. And even when it did, I could count on Nuala wanting to celebrate each of its Twelve Days to the full.

And then, finally, it was Christmas Eve, my last day in that fucking Santa shack with an endless line of overweight spoiled brats breaking every bone in my legs. There was also relief in the fact that Nuala had to be at home for Christmas Eve and the big day itself, playing the happy housewife with Michele and their five young kids. My balls could have a well-earned breather. They were getting seriously sore.

I was in the queue in the mall's staff canteen, on my generous 45-minute lunch break, when there was a commotion behind me. I think you can guess who it was. Spot on. There's Nuala fighting her way toward me. Stepping on toes and winding hungry people. She grabs me just as I'm within touching distance of the meatloaf, gravy and fries, and pulls me back through all those irate people and – back to the Santa shack. What the hell's going on, I'm wondering. Has Michele found out? I push her in the shack and lock it.

'What's up? Tell me, quick.'

'I have to have you, Jerry. I can't face two days without you inside me, I can't! Fuck me, now!'

She's finally flipped, I think. She's tearing at my pants. I'm starved, I've had nothing to eat since 8 a.m., and the kids'll be clambering back on my knee in 20 minutes. If they don't find a festive bundle of fatherly joy waiting for them, it's goodbye paycheque.

'Goddamn it, Nuala, this is the last time! You can't treat me like this! I'm not a fucking machine!'

'Oh yes you are!' she snapped. 'Now hurry. I'm

already wet as Niagara Falls so you go straight in.'

'I'm not even fucking hard yet, Nuala!'

'You will be. Get it out!'

There's no time to argue. I tear the zip down, her fingers go in, she pushes me, and I land with a crash in my big Santa armchair, all of me except my cock which she has firmly in hand, and then firmly in her red-lipsticked, greedy, sucking mouth. With her oral skills, Nuala could get a dying man's dick stiffer than rigor mortis in no time. That mouth, that vacuum-pump of a mouth of hers didn't stop, and though we had no time, her sucking and blowing motions paid attention to every detail. Every minor and major ridge, bump, swelling of my cock was lathered, basted in her oven-hot mouth. I just rose like a pudding in its perfectly timed rhythms of concentrated heat.

'OK, stuff me like a turkey, baby.'

Instead of climbing onto me, she pulled me up.

'Where?'

'Under the tree. I want you to fuck me under the tree.'

'You're a romantic broad, Nuala I'll give you that.'

She lay down under the thick spruce clogged with balls and drapes of beads and lights in the corner, and pulled up her skirt. I pulled her soaked panties to one side with a finger, which alone always sent a visible shudder through her, and got in between her thighs. That pussy of hers always looked so … pristine, virginal, those fresh, pink, gleaming lips like the flesh of a just-cracked oyster, and always so soft. And as my cock slipped in easily as an oyster slipping down a well-oiled throat, she gave out a gasp that you could surely hear outside.

'We have to be quiet, Nuala, please!'

'I'm sorry – stuff something in my mouth. Let me bite on something or I'll start screaming.'

I pulled out my silk handkerchief, balled it and put it in

her mouth.

'Don't worry, I don't have a cold.'

'Amfks!'

She slid her head way under the tree, leaving me in danger of poking my eyes out on the branches as I boned her, fluid as a dog in rut. But no mastiff had a cock like this. She'd really given me a whopper with the blowjob. It was like she'd inflated it with a whole extra layer of ultra-sensitive skin. There was more of me to feel with, and so much more of her to feel too, each push opening out fresh, moist quivering layers of … the only word to describe it is *bliss*. Hot bliss matting cock and pussy together into one thing, a liquefied cocoon. The deeper cock drove, the closer pussy clung …

Dimly, somewhere, I knew the tree was shaking, balls dancing, some crashing on the floor, but cock and pussy kept on weaving, winding, poking, pulling, rolling themselves together in the stuff of shared sensation. Then there was a snap, like something had finally fused somewhere deep between us. It was like matter and anti-matter coming together. A violent, blinding loss of control. Nuala's thighs were way up. I was gripping her ass-cheeks tight, trying to keep her bucking steady as I released a careening truckload of jism into her. Her stillettos were kicking in the branches when the tree toppled over and the supervisor burst through the door.

I was fired on the spot but Nuala terrified the bastard into handing over my paycheque, with a nice bonus. We had a drink in a bar round the corner then she went back home to Long Island. I stayed on in the bar, brooding. It was all kind of sad in a way. Our bodies were obviously made for each other, I'd never had a better fuck than the one I'd just had, in my life, with anyone. But our minds … well. I was a guy who wanted a quiet life. Corny stuff: happy kids, going to the ball game. Nuala was wild. She needed a constant diet of danger and excitement. But who could blame her? Being married to the Mob couldn't be much fun. There was no way Nuala could do the dutiful domestic Italian wife thing. I'd forgotten about Michele. The guy who was doubtless soon sending me to the bottom of the East River in a pair of cement shoes, or worse. Would I get the barrel of acid treatment? Again, I had to do something, but what?

Meanwhile, Christmas just kept on coming. Two days after Christmas Day and with Michele away on business, Nuala and I were in a snowbound cabin in the Catskill Mountains and she had no plans to let me go. Telling Anita about my Santa job was forgotten, the promise now was that she'd tell Michele if I didn't stay with her.

Where was my self-respect, where was my Italian honour? Why couldn't I just call her bluff? Why couldn't I just go to Michele, confess – word was he was a man of reason, not a crazy hothead – explain my predicament? Hope for mercy? But no. That would be too much like pleading. I was at least man enough not to plead.

Man enough! What a laugh! There I was, lying on the bed in the cabin, wearing the tight red leather pants from the new Santa suit Nuala had bought me, sipping a flute of Bollinger, waiting to be massaged with fragrant oil.

I dozed off and was woken by the feel of something tight around my cock. My pants were off and I was naked. Nuala had given me the massage while I slept, I was gleaming with oil. I was also gleaming with fairy lights she'd wrapped all round me. The ones wound round my balls were shooting their red and green glow up the thick shaft of my cock, which Nuala sat gripping, a boozy smile on her face. The tight feeling was getting painful.

'What the hell's this, Nuala?'

She released her fist and there, gleaming round the end of my glowing woody, was a silver key on a chain.

'Merry Christmas again, baby.'

'What's a key doing on the end of my cock, Nuala?'

'That's the key to your new apartment. It's in our old Brooklyn neighbourhood, which is, admittedly, a bit gentrified now. But it's quiet. And we won't be disturbed. And don't worry, you won't be lonely. I'll be visiting you there a few times a week.'

'I can't afford that kind of place, Nool, not on my paycheques.'

'I'm paying for everything from now on, baby – no more shitty jobs for you. Now, enough talk.'

She pulled the little chain-ring off my cock and soothed the pain with her mouth.

This is the last time, I swore to myself – Jerry Sacchetti is no one's male mistress! I pulled her onto the bed, yanked up her kimono and spanked her ass hard until the cheeks were redder than the fairy lights. I smacked her with my woody too, rubbing a little of the leaked-out semen into her hot, mottled flesh before driving it through the sticky lips of her pussy.

A week later, I was putting the key into the door of "my" apartment. I was about to tell her it was over, she could tell Michele, or my ex-wife, anything she liked. I'd go and kiss my kids goodbye and take the consequences. She was there already, in the living room – and another woman, sobbing. I closed the door quietly and crept along the hall.

'What are we gonna do, Nuala? Boccanegra is gonna kill my husband. I hate that dumb *bischero* of mine but he takes good care of me.' I recognized her voice – Gaia

Ventresco, another Mob wife.

'And Michele, they're gonna blow him up in his car. What are we gonna do?' More sobbing. Nuala patting her back. I could imagine how Nuala was greeting this news. But could I believe it? It made sense. Carlo "The Bull" Boccanegra was always on the make. And Michele had made a lot of enemies. But then Boccanegra's ambition could be my ticket out of the mess. I crept back out the apartment, back to my car and headed to Michele's office in the Bronx.

Getting an audience with the Pope was easier than getting in to see Michele Angeli. It was late that night before I was finally ushered in. I won't say I wasn't scared. I was shitting in my pants.

I told him about Boccanegra's plot to kill him. There was only a flicker of surprise. Then he asked me how I knew. I told him how. I told him where. I told him about Nuala. Barely a flicker of surprise. Then he gets up, walks round the table. I mentally tell my kids goodbye. Michele bends to my ear.

'Did you fuck my wife, you son of a bitch?'

'Yeah, Michele – I did, I have, I …'

The warm muzzle of a Glock .357 presses against the side of my head. I piss myself. An eternity later I hear him put it back in his pocket.

'Yeah, well, you got her off my back for a while. I can't satisfy that girl. Crazy Irish, I should've married Italian like everyone else. But if I was like everyone else you'd be in black bags this instant, understand, Jerry?'

I did. The gamble had paid off. I'd saved his life, I'd saved his kids from being fatherless, I'd saved the Gambinos from a long and costly war. He lectured me a little on not being ashamed of anything I felt I had to do to help my family. But he'd see to it that there'd be no more stints as Santa Claus for me.

And there won't be. Michele got me a job with one of his legitimate businesses out here in sunny Pasadena. It's secure, easy, well-paid. I can pay off my alimony quick. But Christ, I miss New York! I miss the snow at Christmas. And, I still wake up in a sweat at night, thinking of Nuala.

Santa's Knee
by Bethany Goring

Angela Crawford sighed as she piled biscuits onto the plate. The school's Christmas fête was by far one of her most hated times of the year – as the deputy head of the school, she couldn't get out of helping out, but children hyped up on too much sugar and parents who expected you to know every single one of them even if you'd never met them before weren't her cup of tea.

She always volunteered to help police the Santa's Grotto; it was constantly busy and lessened the time she had to spend with others. It also meant she'd be in charge of taking wanders to the staff room every so often to get Santa more water, sandwiches and biscuits. But now it was Santa's lunch break, and she was going to have to take this plate in to him then spend the next half-hour mingling. She'd rather spend the time hiding in the toilet.

She popped a digestive into her mouth before turning towards the door, finding herself all too soon in front of Santa's Grotto, despite the fact she'd walked as slowly as she possibly could.

'Right, kids, Santa needs his lunch – the grotto will be closed for half an hour,' she called as she wound her way through the crowd of children gathered outside it, despite the "Closed" sign hanging on the door. A collective groan came from them but slowly they dispersed and she was able to wriggle through them and knock on the door.

'Santa, it's Miss Crawford – I've brought your lunch,' she called through before opening and entering.

The man in the chair this year was fairly wide-set. He hadn't asked for any extra padding to fill out the suit but he was solid rather than fat. In all honesty, having to call him Santa all morning meant she had entirely forgotten his name, and had no idea which of the children's fathers had been stupid enough to volunteer for it this year.

'I'll lock the door so you can take the beard off,' she said, closing it and snapping on the deadbolt.

The man smiled at her, or at least there was a movement behind his beard that caused his eyes to get smaller – so she presumed he had smiled. He gave off a happy vibe which somehow managed to soothe her on this, her most hated of days, so it made sense to think he'd smiled.

'Where will I sit these?' she asked him, looking around.

"Santa's Grotto" was the school photocopy room, the shelves on each of its walls thinly disguised with tacked-up, sparkly fabric. The photocopier had been stowed elsewhere, leaving a space in the middle just about big enough for the large throne upon which Santa sat. Santa nodded to his left but said nothing. The sack of presents was in front of his feet on that side so she moved to his right and leaned over to place the plate down. She couldn't help but wonder, was this a ploy for him to check out her backside in her jeans? Not that she was entirely against the idea. She hadn't had any in a while.

This thought coincided with the moment she placed the plate down – which was also the same moment she felt a firm hand shove her in the back, so she half-fell, face down, over Santa's red suit trousers. Her mouth dropped open and her eyes widened as she felt him wrap both hands round her and move her so that her backside in her tight jeans was raised over his lap and her upper body was pushed forward and angled further towards the floor.

He seemed to pause. She could have said something at this point, or cried out or struggled. Instead, she stayed stock still. She felt oddly unafraid, sure on some deep level that she could trust this man. And, for the first time in a while, Miss Angela Crawford, Deputy Head of London's finest primary school, was lost for words.

Her silence didn't last for much longer, however, as a series of sharp smacks landed on her upturned rear.

'What the …? What do you think you're – ow! – doing?' she gasped, her questions punctuated by loud, sharp cracks as his palm struck the tightly stretched denim.

'Miss Crawford, I am spanking you, as you deserve,' he answered, seemingly unperturbed by the strangeness of the situation and his own answer, as he continued his methodical smacking.

It was the first time she had heard him speak and his lascivious voice sent a shot through her lower belly and into her groin. Well, either his voice or the word "spanking" – she wasn't entirely sure which.

'Why – ow! – would I – ouch! – deserve this?' she questioned, wriggling from his hand.

'You're not interested in doing your job properly – you're here by obligation,' he answered, wrapping his left arm around her waist and holding her firmly while his right continued to spank her. She blushed at the thought, and more moisture shot downwards. She was being spanked. She couldn't lie and say that she'd never fantasised about it, nor that she was completely averse to what was currently happening.

'So are at least half of the staff at this thing!' she shrieked, as he landed a particularly hard smack that covered both her cheeks at once.

'Yes, but you're the deputy head. You – *smack* – are – *smack* – supposed – *smack, smack* – to – *smack* – set – *smack* – an – *smack* – example!'

His voice was enticing, smooth, but stern. She was wetter than she'd been in … actually, she was wetter than she could ever remember being.

The strong arm encircling her waist hauled her to her feet and she was standing in front of him, in between his legs. He reached for the button on her jeans, but she slapped his hand away. It was more the principle than any real objection. She couldn't allow him to …

He spun her round on the spot and landed a series of quick, sharp, stinging smacks to her rear, 'Get your hand on your head – now.'

There was no arguing with him, not in that voice. It was the voice she'd always imagined telling her what to do … the voice that relieved her of her own responsibilities.

Slowly, she moved her hands to her head, shutting down her brain as it screamed at her not to, and listening instead to her groin, which was indicating that she should just let this man keep doing exactly as he was doing.

His hand went to her navel and undid the button on her jeans before slowly pulling down the zipper. The sound was loud in the silent room, and she had entirely forgotten about the gym hall full of people outside.

Now she was definitely wetter than she ever had been before – there was something about standing helpless as a man undressed her. And he didn't look up at her, but instead kept his eyes fixed firmly on her mound as he pulled down her jeans, and she was aware that he was looking. And that he was seeing her, all of her, due to the fact that the moisture had spilled through her white underwear. Slowly, he inserted a hand between her legs and stroked her over her knickers, cupping her mound and pressing down, before trailing up to the top of her underwear. She shifted her legs slightly apart and saw his face twitch with that same smile again, as his hand went into her virginal-looking pants and one finger trailed slowly up and down her soaked inner folds.

She felt empty, she wanted him to put his fingers in her, but after that one, incessantly slow and tantalising stroke, he pulled his hand out. Then, in one swift movement, she was facing the ground again, and her backside, which must already have been a fairly pink shade by now, she thought, was once again being spanked. The smacks were sore, and concentrated more on her under-curve and the tops of her thighs than they had done before. She tried to kick but she could feel her jeans constricting her movements, which for some reason only turned her on more. The heat from her backside was spreading through her and she started to wriggle around over his knee, rubbing her swollen and sensitive clit as best she could against the velvet of his trousers.

A series of sharp smacks landed, not on her backside, but between her legs, causing her to cry out, loudly.

'Don't you dare,' growled Santa. 'Try it again and I'll get a paddle out of that sack.' He was certainly strong – his voice was strong, his hands were strong and she could feel the muscles in his legs beneath her. He shifted her forwards so that she was entirely over his left knee, clamping her firmly in place by closing his own legs together, his right pinning down both of hers with no room for movement. There was something delicious about being held down over Santa's lap. He raised his left knee and landed a series and quick smacks on her bottom, with no rest. She was really crying out now, welcoming this mixture of sweetness and pain.

His hard strokes stopped, giving way to his hand

rubbing, tweaking and pinching her backside, while she groaned and pushed out towards him, craving more, spreading her legs subconsciously as the leg that had been pinning her in place loosened off.

'Angela, reach into the sack. Take out the first present you find,' he ordered, his voice slow, sexy, deep. She wriggled a little and put a hand into Santa's sack, though her impulses were telling her to wriggle off his lap altogether and reach for the sack inside his red trousers. But she figured she'd best continue on his terms, pulling out the first thing that her hand came into contact with.

'Open it,' he ordered.

Her hands were trembling from sheer arousal and excitement, which she hadn't felt at all in far too long. And she had never felt them like this. She was soaking, to the point that her knickers really needed to come off as she was verging on uncomfortably wet. And she felt empty. She wanted her legs spread and her cunt full. But she knew she wasn't in the position to ask or to tell. She had to wait, to accept, to take.

The paper came off and she was nose to nose with a bottle of baby oil and a blue cone. A butt plug. She shivered. She'd seen them, thought about them, but she'd never had the guts to actually try one.

'Pass me them up,' he said, and she took them in her shaking hands, gasping as he reached down and took the items from her with his left hand while landing one of those hard smacks that crossed her entire arse in one stroke with his right.

His short nails scraped across her lower back, just at the top of her knickers, and she shivered, goosebumps appearing on her arms. Slowly, excruciatingly slowly, he grasped at the elastic waistband and pulled down her underwear, tugging first at the centre part and then hooking that onto the under-curve, then pulling down each side one at a time, until he had worked her sodden knickers down to her knees.

His hand rested there for a moment before ghosting back up, brushing against her inner thighs, then eventually rubbing her moist slit. She moaned and pushed against him, silently begging, desperate to feel filled.

He chuckled and slid two fingers into her hole and she sighed, feeling sated for a moment before his thumb slid up between her arse cheeks and started to massage her back hole in circular motions. It drove her wild. She felt her face get hotter, knowing that he could feel how much wetter this simple action was making her. She hadn't thought she could get any wetter but her warm backside and the thumb probing where nothing had probed her before were certainly managing to make her so. She had fantasised about being touched there, too. But nice girls weren't meant to like it. Nor were they meant to like being spanked. But she did. Angela certainly did. And Santa seemed to know exactly what to do.

She was at the point of orgasm when the fingers withdrew and she heard him open the bottle. The next sensation was of her cheeks being pulled apart and the oil being poured in between them, against her anus and trickling down into her front. She gave into the sensation and came, hard.

'Tut-tut,' he murmured. 'I didn't give you permission, you've still not been punished enough, Angela.'

Angela. The way he said it. It made her – supposedly a grown woman, in a position of authority – feel like a naughty schoolgirl being told off by a strict schoolmaster. Not that any schoolmaster she'd ever known had been this sick and sexy, she mused.

Again, his hand began to collide with her backside,

and since she had already come she was able to feel the full force of it. He wasn't being gentle, but she wasn't sore, not sore enough, not yet. She wanted him to punish her, she wanted him to fill her.

As his hand smacked against her and she wriggled, the oil that had dripped down to her cunt moved, obvious and cool against her hotness, thicker and less sticky than the come that was mixed with the moisture of her arousal.

He stopped the spanking for a minute and she heard him pick up and uncap the oil again, and she squirmed, pushing her arse out, expecting more. But she didn't feel anything. And then his hands were on her backside again, massaging, oiled and slippery. One slid down between her lower folds for a moment before working its way up and one, then two fingers were slipped into her anus. She sighed and lay there, enjoying the sensation of being stretched. She felt the hardness of his fingernail against the inside of her back passage and she bucked wildly, completely out of her own control. He chuckled quietly and then, quick as a flash, he was back to spanking her.

Each smack stung more now that he had oiled his hands. But she craved the soreness, pushed her arse out for every blow, each one being a sweet mix of pleasure and pain. She knew that as soon as the heat from each smack rippled out from her cheeks it would travel through her groin. Her backside was glowing, but her cunt was glowing too. She may have been lying heavy as a sack of coal over Santa's knee, but she felt light as air.

It was only when she stopped struggling and just lay there, lapping it up, that he stopped spanking her, and his hands circled her cheeks, the heel of each digging in to the bones in her arse, manipulating the flesh, grabbing big handfuls of it, twisting, tweaking, kneading.

She was enjoying the sensation when his hands pulled

apart her arse cheeks, to the point she could feel the skin stretch and the air kiss her arsehole. With her legs lewdly spread, her cunt and arse pushed up over his knee and her buttocks splayed, she was exposed. Really exposed. But she didn't care. In fact, this only served to make her cunt even wetter.

He switched the way he was spreading her arse to holding it with one hand – his strong left thumb on one cheek, and his fingers on the other. Then, with his right hand, he probed round her front, scooping some of the juices that they found there, and then smearing them round, over and just inside her arsehole. She gasped as, a second later, the butt plug was slowly pushed into her in its entirety. Now she was full. Stretched, full and probably looking ridiculous with a blue circle highly visible between her now exceptionally red arse cheeks. But she didn't care. She was humiliated and tears ran down her face, but they were tears of relief and joy, for she was more aroused that she ever had been before. This was what she had fantasised about her whole life.

He wrapped an arm round her waist and stood up, lifting her easily, then he sat her down in the chair where he had just been. She felt this push the butt plug totally into her, as though she were sitting on a spike, making her aware of how full her arse was.

He kissed her, hard, sucking so strongly on her tongue that she cried out into his mouth. He moved to her neck, sucking and biting, his teeth leaving light, bruising impressions where she knew anyone who looked would be able to see them. But she didn't care. He was marking her, and she wanted him to. He pulled her top over her head then moved to his knees, cast her bra to the side and cupped one breast with his hand and let his tongue flick over the other, before biting down on that too. She cried out but felt even more wetness between her legs. His hands went to her thighs and, roughly, pushed them wide open. She didn't fight. His tongue then delved into the dark passageway her lower sex offered him, before sliding up to play with her engorged and sensitive clit. She closed her eyes and threw her head back, about to come again – but he stopped.

This time he reached into the sack that was on the floor where he was kneeling, and pulled out a dildo.

It was bigger than any cock she'd ever encountered, but she was so turned on that nothing she'd experienced before would have been enough to fill her – to truly fill her – now.

He pulled her forwards to the edge of the seat and instructed her to put her legs in the air, grab the backs of her knees with her hands and hug them into her. She was thrust out, exposed, open. She could feel air on places air had never touched before, she could feel the butt plug stuffed into her at the back, she could feel the wetness inside her trickle out onto the edge of the seat.

Slowly, he pushed the dildo into her, pumping it in and out, and she screamed. She had never felt so full. Now she knew how good sex could be, she could never go back.

She came hard but, rather than feeling like she had reached a satisfied place after her orgasm, she felt instead like a pot on a hob that was boiling over and wasn't ready to stop. And he didn't stop; he shifted his hands so that his left one continued to move the dildo in and out of her as the right began scratching her exposed and red lower arse cheeks, reigniting the flame from before.

When she came again it was with such a scream that she wasn't sure how the walls were still standing.

He removed the now hot and sticky dildo as Angela, finally spent, let her legs go and just lay sprawled in the chair. That was how to have sex. Proper, earth-shattering sex. And yet they hadn't even had sex.

She pushed herself up in the chair, trying to gather back the breath that she had lost and get a look at the man who was already on his feet, and turned towards the door.

'Where are you … who …?' she managed, her breath still gone from the effort, her throat and mouth dry from her screaming.

'I'm going away now, Angela, I have other Christmas presents to give. Also, the man dressed up in the imitation of my suit, he's almost finished his lunch,' the man replied, before tapping his nose and unlocking the door of the photocopy room, slipping through it and disappearing before Angela could say another word.

Mistletoed
by DK Jernigan

Marcus blew into the hotel lobby on a wave of icy air, and the dry heat of the building hit him like a slap. He considered skipping the holiday party for the hundredth time that night, but yet again he continued toward the inevitable, giving up his final hope of escape along with his coat at the coat check station, and accepting a numbered slip in return.

He braced himself one last time, and stepped into the combined Christmas party of his own firm, Sweet Charity Marketing, and two other businesses that shared their building downtown. The banquet hall had been decked out for drinking and dining, and he admired the decorations, even as he scorned them. They were tasteful, classy, and elegant, and a complete waste of time and energy.

'Bah, humbug,' he muttered.

'Pardon?' Marcus turned to see another man standing next to him, likewise surveying the scene.

'Looks lovely,' he said, trying on his first polite smile of the evening.

'I suppose,' said the other man. 'Seems like a bit of a waste, to me. I'm a bit of a Grinch, I guess.' The man shrugged and smiled apologetically before moving away, and Marcus couldn't help but watch him go. His trousers clung to his ass in all the right ways, making the tight curves look completely irresistible. He shook his head and moved to greet a group of colleagues, trying to put the bad mood out of his mind.

It was hard to remain neutral, however, with co-workers, acquaintances, and strangers alike all chatting about their holiday plans and the lovely holiday decorations and holiday foods and the holiday presents they were planning to buy. If he took a sip of champagne every time he heard the words "holiday", "Christmas", or "Chanukah", he would probably have stopped caring about any of it by now.

It wasn't that he was against people being happy, but there was something about the forced, frenetic cheer of the season that made him want to hibernate, especially when he had no one to spend the time with. He sighed and took another flute of champagne, nodding politely to the waiter.

'Aren't you going to dance?' a male voice asked from his elbow. Marcus turned to see the same man he'd been admiring earlier.

'Ah, no,' he replied, and with his tongue loosened by the bubbly, he added, 'I'm not a fan of the ladies, and most gents don't react well when I ask.'

The man flashed a grin, and Marcus thought he might swoon like a lady. The bastard was adorable. 'I'm Rob,' he said, and stuck his hand out.

Marcus gripped it, surprised. Most men heard he was gay and scrupulously kept their hands to themselves from that point forward, as if homosexuality were contagious. Rob, however, shook firmly, and neither held his hand too long, nor yanked it back nor surreptitiously wiped it on his trousers like Marcus had seen some men do before.

'And you?'

'What, dancing? I wouldn't inflict that on anyone without grave cause,' Rob said, flashing that handsome grin again. Marcus found himself wanting to move toward Rob – wanting to touch him – and he turned and grabbed a small plateful of prosciutto rolls to keep his hands occupied. It didn't occur to him until he turned around again that he didn't have a hand left to eat with.

Rob watched him for a moment, that grin never slipping, and finally gestured toward the small round tables clustered around the edges of the room. 'Perhaps we should take a seat?'

Marcus nodded, and then followed as Rob grabbed a handful of finger foods and a glass of dark wine before leading the way through the crowd – more standing and swaying than dancing – to one of the unoccupied tables. They were far enough from anyone else to converse quietly under the blaring sounds of cheerful Christmas music, and Marcus leaned over his little plate, eager to hear what Rob might have to say.

Rob nodded politely as he sat, then turned his attention to his snacks, popping bite-sized vegetables into his mouth and sucking the meat from a couple of chicken wings with gusto. It was a long moment before Marcus realised that apparently Rob had been hungry, not actually in the mood for conversation, and he blushed and hid it behind his glass.

The prosciutto was actually quite good, rolled up with basil leaves and mozzarella, sliced thin, and laid on bland, stale crackers.

He glanced up from his intense snack-food study to find Rob watching him, a mysterious smile on his face. 'You see intent,' he said.

Marcus straightened, immediately feeling defensive. 'So did you!'

But Rob only laughed. 'No offence! In fact, do you know why I chose this table?' Marcus shrugged, wishing he hadn't had so much to drink, and followed Rob's gesture as the handsome man pointed at a spot up the wall near their heads. 'I've been fantasising all night about getting you alone under the mistletoe,' he said quietly.

Marcus blinked. 'You're gay?'

'Bi, actually. Does that bother you?'

Marcus shook his head. 'No, of course not. But I can't – I mean, I'm out, but – I can't just kiss some strange man in the middle of my own office party.'

'Plenty of other people are doing it,' Rob pointed out, gesturing to the dance floor, where a number of couples, new and old, were indeed draped over one another, many with their lips actively engaged.

'Yes, but most of them probably don't own any of the companies here tonight,' Marcus said.

Rob blinked, and Marcus was pleased to see the other man thrown off for once. 'Which one?'

'Sweet Charity,' he said. 'We got our start doing marketing, promotions, and public relations packaging for non-profits.' He paused, and then felt the need to add, 'And it's my favourite musical.'

Rob laughed. 'My brother and I are co-owners of Blue Star Promotions,' he said, naming one of the other firms represented tonight.

'Robert Chalmers?'

Rob leaned back and spread his arms as if to say "In the flesh!" and Marcus pushed his champagne away and considered him. The two had exchanged the occasional email over the years, including several regarding tonight's party, but Marcus couldn't remember ever meeting the man before, and he was certain he would have remembered a face like that.

'Well,' Marcus said at last, 'as an executive, you surely planned ahead by booking a room for tonight.'

'And I'm sure you had the same foresight,' replied Rob. I've got a room on the 22nd.'

'They gave away my room. My assistant tells me I got bumped to a suite on the 31st,' Marcus said, a grin starting to spread over his face. The warm tingle of tipsiness was slowly being pushed out by the even more intoxicating tingle of desire.

'I've never seen a suite here,' Rob mused, leaning forward. He had a way of idly swirling his wine before sipping it that drew the eye, and Marcus found himself admiring everything about the way he sipped, from the broad palms that cupped the goblet to the way his lips caressed the rim and the way his throat bobbed as he swallowed.

Marcus had to cough before he could speak around the lump forming in his own throat. 'It's, um, quite nice, I'm told. Perhaps you'd like to take a look?'

'Delighted to,' Rob said, his grin more and more wicked with each moment that passed.

They retrieved their coats and went upstairs, the elevator ride blessedly silent except for the sounds of their own breath. Rob shifted until he stood behind Marcus, who had taken a position in the middle of the car, and Marcus closed his eyes and shuddered as the other man's warm breath blew lightly over the back of his neck.

The elevator chimed softly as it passed each floor – 23, 24. He nearly moaned each time Rob exhaled, and his cock, merely interested before, was now straining desperately against his suit pants. Floor 29. *God*, the ride was interminable!

He nearly jumped through the doors the moment they sprang open on the 31st floor, and coughed as he caught his footing and allowed Rob to saunter up to him to keep pace. He glared, but Rob only grinned his infuriating grin, and Marcus found his pace increasing as he searched for his room. Three-one-what? 3114, that sounded right. He fumbled in his pocket for the key card, nearly dropped it, and took a firmer grip on the flimsy plastic.

'Hurry,' Rob murmured behind him, 'I think I'm going to die if I don't get my mouth around you soon.'

'Holy *shit*.' He might have fumbled the card again, but it was already in the lock, and he pulled it out with a twitch of his arm. It fell to the ground just inside the door as it swung open, but they both ignored it, hurrying past the open door and letting it slam shut behind them. Both of their coats joined it a second later.

Marcus found himself slammed against the wall as Rob pressed himself against him, their tongues clashing as they kissed, rough and hard. He moaned and his cock surged with arousal as he felt Rob's hands on his belt, fumbling desperately with the buckle. Then his pants fell away, and he gasped with the suddenness of the end of their kiss as Rob followed Marcus's pants to the floor.

'Oh, *God*, your cock looks delicious,' Rob said, and then his mouth was on him, and Marcus groaned, insane with pleasure. Rob sucked and teased with skill, making the hairs on his arms stand up with the electricity of his arousal, and Marcus gasped and groaned at each technique, thrusting into Rob's mouth as the other man sucked hard, teased with his tongue, or scraped his teeth gently against the underside of his cock.

'If you don't stop that,' Marcus finally gasped, 'I'm not going to be able to fuck you.'

Rob pulled back and grinned up at him, and Marcus groaned at the sight of the gorgeous man between his legs, nuzzling up against his throbbing erection. 'Then I hope you don't mind if I fuck *you* when I'm done here.'

Marcus groaned again, and Rob took it as permission,

sucking Marcus's cock deep into his throat. Marcus felt his eyes roll back in his head and he leaned against the wall, breathless with pleasure. His balls tightened and he dug his nails into his palm, trying to hold onto that elusive sensation, willing himself to wait, wait, *wait* …

But Rob had apparently heard the hitch in his breath or the desperation in his moans, because he increased his pace, licking and sucking with fervour until Marcus thrust his hips forward and buried his cock in Rob's throat. His orgasm pulsed through him as he shot his come into the sexy businessman on his knees before him, and for one electrified moment, he felt like he was floating in the clouds. Then his knees went weak, and he nearly collapsed to the floor. He gasped and leaned heavily on the wall as Rob stood and started stripping his own clothes off.

'Please tell me you have condoms in here.'

He'd never thought he'd actually need them, but … 'Duffel bag, side pocket.' He pointed and Rob hurried to the bag. When he had the strength to stand again, Marcus moved toward the bed, pulling the rest of his clothing off on the way.

He climbed happily onto the bed, bracing himself on his hands and knees as he heard the tear of a condom wrapper and the snap of the tiny lube bottle he'd tossed into his bag 'just in case'. Thank God.

Rob's hands on his thighs made him jump, then groan with anticipation, and behind him Rob chuckled and let his hands wander over Marcus's bare flesh. 'I'll bet you say that to all the CEOs,' he quipped.

'Most of the CEOs I meet are straight, believe it or not,' Marcus teased back, barely able to speak coherently as he waited, with tingling excitement, for the sensation of Rob's cock pressing against his tight asshole. 'But I hope you'll make tonight memorable for more than that.'

'Oh, it hasn't been memorable enough already?' Rob's cock teased at his tight opening, pressing gently against the muscles and sliding away again. Marcus groaned and gritted his teeth, and Rob laughed. 'Be patient, Marcus, we've got all night. And I want to be sure you're ready for me.'

'I'm ready, believe me. Fuck me, Rob. Fuck me, now.'

Rob teased his fingers around Marcus's hole, and Marcus growled in frustration. 'Are you sure?' Another wordless growl, and the fingers moved away. 'We'll see, then …'

He'd barely had a moment to become aware of the head of Rob's cock against his ass once again before Rob plunged forward, letting the bulbous tip penetrate Marcus's straining body. Marcus cried out and his fingers tightened convulsively on the bedspread as he rocked back in pleasure. The fire of sudden penetration only made him burn hotter as he drove himself against Rob, loving the other man's hiss of pleasure as Rob's cock was buried deeper in his ass.

'Shit, baby, you weren't kidding,' Rob said, and moaned as he rocked gently, his cock sinking deeper in Marcus's ass until he was sheathed completely.

Marcus moaned in response, and his cock ached with desire when the tip of Rob's dick bumped against his prostate as he rocked back again. It had been more than long enough since he'd found someone willing to screw him into the bedsheets and make him beg for mercy, and the fact that Rob was game made him want to come right then and there.

Rob thrust faster and faster, establishing a grunting, primitive rhythm, and Marcus pushed back against him, embracing the flaming pleasure of the other man's cock plunging deep into him again and again. His own cock was hard again, and he groaned and the sensation as it bobbed along with their animal thrusts, tapping gently against his belly with each stroke as Rob's balls slapped against his ass.

The pleasure mounted in him as Rob's breaths became ragged and his rhythm broke down into desperate thrusts. Rob roared behind him, and Marcus groaned, tightening his muscles around Rob's cock as it pulsed inside his ass. Rob took a couple of panting breaths, then pulled free and shoved at Marcus. 'Turn over. Come for me.'

Marcus hit the bed with his chest and rolled onto his back, his hand immediately finding his cock. He locked eyes with Rob and stroked hard and fast, encouraging his eager cock to discharge his arousal. His balls tightened and the pleasure built to a knot low in his belly, then he groaned as it broke free and throbbed through him. Molten heat splattered his chest and belly as he came with a long, low groan that resurrected Rob's grin.

He panted, spent in more than one sense, and looked up at the man standing over him, the filled condom still hanging from his near-flaccid cock. 'This was completely insane.'

'Completely,' Rob agreed, tossing the condom. He handed a box of tissues to Marcus and sat down on the bed, running fingers through his mussed hair. 'But as long as we're here, we might as well enjoy ourselves. And Merry Christmas, by the way.'

Marcus took in the man's mischievous grin as he cleaned himself off, and echoed it. 'Merry Christmas.' It was going to be a long, merry night indeed.

A Christmas for Carol
by J Smith

What Carol hated most about Christmas was that she was going to be spending it alone. She had been six months without a boyfriend now and, possibly even worse, six months without sex. She couldn't even remember what the argument had been about but it must have been something important otherwise Jack would be here and she wouldn't be sitting on her sofa in her dressing gown on Christmas Eve with a bottle of eggnog, her vibrator and a copy of *Babes in Sex-Toyland* in the DVD player to keep her company. Well, she didn't need a man to have an orgasm – in fact she was better off without them. She'd make it her New Year's resolution to become celibate.

Carol watched the couple steaming into each other on the telly, the unbelievably flexible woman mewing with every thrust like the cat that got the cream – or, more accurately, was just about to get it. Nobody had orgasms that lasted that long, Carol thought, although there had been that one time when Jack had surprised her in the shower and … but Jack was a thing of the past.

She sighed. She'd thought he was the one, her soulmate, but she had to stop thinking about him. She reached for her vibrator instead. It was cold and hard. Maybe another few eggnogs would loosen her up.

The DVD played on, her supply of eggnog diminished and the flexible woman was now dressed as a Christmas fairy who was making a Christmas elf's wish come true. Carol had never thought that a Christmas fairy would do it cowgirl, but then why not? She felt under her dressing gown and between her legs at the growing moist patch in her trimmed thatch of hair. She was warm and slippery, and her sex-starved clit seemed to be reaching up to her finger in desperation. The Christmas fairy was slowly sliding up and down the elf's cock and as her breasts bounced before him, his hands toyed with her swollen nipples, a look of ecstasy on her face. Again, Carol reached for the vibrator, brought her knees up and slowly began to run it along her scarlet slit. God, it felt good, like food to a starving person. She turned the speed up and let it buzz across her hard little bud. Carol sighed and the fairy sighed with her.

'All the way,' the fairy said to the elf. Carol slid the vibrator inside and let it tingle delectably in her depths.

'That's so good,' the fairy said. 'Further in, all the way.'

Carol pushed her toy in deeper, she spread her knees apart and felt her insides stretch.

'Pump it … faster.' The fairy sounded as though she were about to climax.

Carol pumped it faster, sliding the slippery shaft in and out of her tight little hole, parting the wispy halo of hair in time with the happy little elf's thrusts.

The fairy groaned, her little wings flapping behind her as she bobbed up and down. The elf's fingers dug into her breasts as his eyes started to glaze over.

Carol felt her own orgasm starting to build, her finger slipping on the plastic as she swirled it around her opening.

'Yes, yes …' The fairy's mouth pouted her pleasure. 'Oh yes … harder.'

Carol began to pant and the warm glow began to spread out.

The fairy screamed in pleasure. In the last moments of her orgasm, she looked towards the camera. 'You know, Carol, the real thing is *sooo* much better.'

The elf gave a flushed nod in agreement, as the Fairy lifted herself off his spent penis.

Carol was almost oblivious, fixated on her own orgasm as it began to pulse.

'Anyway,' the fairy continued. 'You will be visited by three ghosts tonight – spirits who will show you the error of your ways.'

Carol shuddered as her finger joined the vibrator.

'The first will arrive at midnight, so be ready.'

With a last jerk of electricity, Carol's climax came to an end. Out of breath, she slumped down on to the sofa and drew the still-buzzing sex toy out of her.

The fairy looked back down at the elf who was holding his re-swollen cock enticingly in the air. She licked her lips and bowed her head down. 'Don't forget, midnight and … mmff…' Her voice trailed off. It was rude to speak with your mouth full anyway.

Carol pulled her dishevelled blonde hair from her eyes and looked at the screen. What had the fairy just said? Midnight? And something about being visited? She rewound the DVD a few minutes and played it again but the fairy said nothing. Must have been too much eggnog.

Carol looked at the time. It was 11 p.m. on Christmas Eve – she bet she was the only person alone in the world. Bloody Christmas, she thought. Bloody Jack and bloody men. She took what remained of the eggnog and her vibrator and headed for her bedroom. As soon as her head hit her pillow, she was asleep.

As her clock chimed midnight, it woke Carol from a fitful dream, which she thought was strange because it was digital and had no chimes. She shook the dancing sugar plums from her head and opened one groggy eye. Her room was bathed in bright light. There beside her bed was the robed, thin figure of a man.

'I am the ghost of ...'

Carol leaped out of bed, grabbed the nearest weapon she could find, which happened to be her vibrator, and hit him as hard as she could and then again just for luck.

'What the hell are you doing?' the man cried, rubbing the side of his face.

'You're in my bedroom, in the middle of the night. What did you expect me to do?'

The man paused for a second. 'Oh, I never thought of that,' he said, then added, 'but it's never happened before.'

'Who are you and what do you want?' asked Carol, holding the vibrator out like a cudgel.

'OK. Calm down. There's no need to be nervous.'

'I'm not nervous. I've accidentally switched it on.' She turned off her vibrator and her hand stopped shaking.

The man picked himself up then cleared his throat. 'I am Abstinence, the Ghost of Christmas Past. And to prove the error of your ways, I shall show you how you once enjoyed sex.'

'Ghost ...? Christmas ...? Sex! Oh my God, the fairy!'

Before she could protest, Abstinence had taken her hand and walked her into a vortex of memories.

Instantly, Carol knew where she was. It was the previous Christmas Eve. She was on the back road in the woods beside the golf course.

'Do you remember this place?'

'Yes.'

'You and Jack had been heading to a party when you suggested a quickie.'

'I know. He pulled off into the woods.'

'And then you pulled his wood off.' He waited for a

157

laugh but none came. 'Anyway, if you look behind you, you will see his car.'

Carol turned and saw it. The estate's windows were steamed up and it was rocking rhythmically.

'You're in there having sex.' Abstinence cupped his ear as a loud groan filled the air. 'Sounds like you were enjoying it,' he said.

'And it looks like you're enjoying it now,' Carol retorted, looking down at the huge bulge that was jutting from his robe.

'Give me a break, I haven't had any in two centuries and what do I do for a job? That's right, I go around watching people have sex. I'm fit to burst. But we're not here to sort me out, more's the pity, we're here to sort you out. Look in the window. They – you two – can't see us.'

Carol looked through the window. The rear seats were folded back, her skirt was round her waist. One foot was strapped up in a seatbelt, the other wedged against the opposite door. Jack had his head firmly placed between her legs, the tip of his tongue running along her slit, his fingers expertly opening her up – then his tongue vanished inside her. Carol watched herself squirm and she felt a longing spark in her stomach. Younger Carol looked lost and content at the same time – had she really felt like that?

'Remember how good it was?' Abstinence asked.

'Well I …'

'Maybe this will jog your memory.'

'What do you …? Oh, ohooohhhooo!' Carol had suddenly taken the place of her younger self and was taking the full onslaught of Jack's probing tongue. All at once her pussy was hot, incredibly wet and tingling as though an electric current was passing through it.

'You OK?' Jack asked.

'Er, yeah. Good.' Carol caught her breath.

'It's getting a bit constricted in my boxers, if you could lend a hand.'

'Erm ... OK.' Carol tentatively reached down to Jack's flies and undid them. She could feel the heat of his cock escape, the hard nub of his manhood press out, tenting his shorts towards her, a small, damp patch spreading out from the peak.

'Take it out. You're not normally this shy.'

Carol reached into the elastic waistband and took a firm hold of him. She sighed at its forgotten touch, her fingers barely able to meet around its girth. It was warm and velvety-firm, not like her vibrator. She ran her hand along its length, feeling every ridge and bump. Her thumb slipped on his silvery precome and slowly she started to wank him, bringing that look of peace to his eyes.

'You're the best at that,' Jack's muffled voice rose from between her legs, sending another shiver through her.

As he slid a finger inside, Carol wiggled down onto it and with his tongue lapping at her clit, she began to lose herself to the sensations starting to take her body.

His finger moved faster and so did her hand, running the full length from root to knob. He groaned and his cock bucked in her grip and it felt good to know she could do that to him.

'You keep that up and I'm going to come. In fact ...' His love-juice smile glistened like frost as he took his head from between her legs. He slipped her sticky hand from his shaft and lined the head of it up for a collision course with her puffy mound.

'Do you know what I'm going to do now?' He had a wicked look on his face.

'What?' Carol panted expectantly.

'I'm going to slowly push my cock as deep into your pussy as I can.'

Carol said nothing but subconsciously her thighs parted a little more. She looked at his manhood, engorged and large, and it was as though she could already feel it dive into her.

'God, you're so incredibly wet.'

'Well, it has been a while,' she replied, still transfixed by his cock.

'I don't think three hours is a while,' he laughed.

She had forgotten about their Christmas shopping quickie in the department store changing room, but said, wistfully, 'It seems longer than you know.'

'So, you ready?'

Carol pouted a nod.

'Guide me in. I like it when you do that.'

'OK,' she said a little nervously. She felt as though she was having an affair with him. Gently, she took hold of him again – he seemed even harder than before, if that were possible. She looked at him as he watched her steer his cock to its target. Carol gave a small gasp as he nudged at her opening. Would he feel like she remembered? She closed her eyes as he parted her lips and eased himself forward, inch by inch, slowly sinking into ...

'There. I bet you remember it now?' Abstinence said.

'What?' Carol opened her eyes to find herself outside the car looking in at a mildly surprised younger Carol.

'I said ...'

'I know what you said,' Carol muttered angrily. 'How could you bring me out? I was just about to ... he had his ...'

'And here was I thinking you didn't want it any more.'

'That's not the point,' Carol sighed. 'If you get a girl worked up, of course she might want it.

'Only might? Well, I guess it's a start.' Abstinence turned to walk away, inadvertently bumping her with his

160

erection as he spun round. 'You did look good in there.'

'Thank you.'

'Any chance you could wank me?'

'No.'

'Didn't think so.' He looked at his watch. 'It's getting late, anyway. Next ghost will be here at two. It's time to get you into bed – I wish.'

Carol woke up with a start. 'That was one weird dream,' she said. But what a dream it had been! She reached between her legs – she couldn't remember the last time she had been this juiced up. Yes she could, it was when she was last with Jack. Well, she didn't need him now. And to prove it, she determinedly slumped back onto her bed, tucked the duvet up to her chin and turned over to go back to sleep.

She hadn't expected to see an attractive blonde lying next to her, and she definitely hadn't been expecting to be kissed by her. As Carol's mouth opened in shock, the blonde's tongue made full use of the ease of access and before Carol came to her senses, she couldn't help but think that it was rather nice.

'Wha do noo dink yer nooing?' Carol said.

The attractive blonde pulled out of her. 'Pardon?' she said in a raspy voice, like hot chocolate being poured over stiletto heels.

'I said, "What do you think you're doing?"'

'Well, I thought that if you've sworn off men maybe you fancied a bit of the flip side.'

'What? No. Who are you anyway?'

The blonde got off the bed and Carol saw that she was dressed in stockings, a basque and high heels – and the tightest thong Carol had ever seen finished the look.

'I am Climax, the Ghost of Christmas Present and I'm here to show you how others enjoy this time of year. You sure you don't want me to hop back into bed with you and show you a woman's touch?'

Carol still ached with longing from her first ghostly encounter but she'd never been with a woman before. Would another female's touch be as soft as her own?

'You think about it, and let me know.' The ghost leaned over the bed and offered Carol a hand, her melon-round breasts almost falling from the basque as she bent forward. 'I saw you looking,' Climax said.

'No I wasn't,' Carol lied. 'Let's just go wherever it is we're going.'

'OK.'

The room spun round in a kaleidoscope of lights and, just seconds later, Carol was standing in front of a door.

'It's a cupboard,' she said.

'Turn around.'

Carol did. 'Oh my!'

There in front of her was her friend Lucy. Lying on top of Lucy was a rather attractive man, in his early twenties, with the body of a stallion and a mane of hair to match. Beside both of them was as sensuous a woman as Carol had ever seen. All were naked.

'That's Lucy. What's she *doing*?' Carol couldn't believe her eyes.

Climax leaned in for a closer look and licked her lips. 'I think she's having sex. It really has been a long time for you, hasn't it?'

'But I didn't even know she was with anybody.'

'She only met them tonight, Tim and Annabel. The universe is trying to balance itself out for the people who don't have sex.' Climax looked accusingly at Carol.

'My God!' Carol gasped. 'He's definitely not Tiny Tim, is he?'

She watched Lucy squeal with delight as Tim rolled

one of her nipples between thumb and forefinger while Annabel descended vampire-like on the other breast. Lucy had a hand between each of their legs.

'That doesn't turn you on?' Climax asked. 'Watching them tangled together in a lovefest.'

It did turn her on. Carol squeezed her thighs together and felt a shiver run up her body. 'Well it's …'

'Look at all those sticky little fingers.' Climax ran her own hand down her lace basque and rubbed it over her silken thong, making herself purr like a kitten. 'God, it makes you hot, makes you want it.' She pouted her ruby lips and moved behind Carol.

The merging bodies on the bed transfixed Carol. It was difficult to see where one started and the other stopped but the more she looked at the scene, the more she enjoyed being a voyeur.

'Just say you want it, I'll even do it for you.' Climax snaked her hands around Carol and cupped her breasts through the flimsy dressing gown. Her nipples hardened at the touch and she gave a small moan despite herself.

'There is more to life than … mmm… ohh… mmm…' Carol found herself naked on the bed. One mouth clamped onto her nipple the other between her legs, and two pairs of hands were massaging her body. Her hand was rubbing something soft and moist – she knew it was a pussy, similar to her own and yet different, and curiosity dared her to explore deeper.

'Finger me,' Annabel whispered in her ear.

Carol's finger ran along her slit, parting the puffy lips then falling inside. Her heart beat faster – she was actually touching up another woman! Then the man opened up her lips with his fingers and she felt the tip of his tongue enter her, his other hand still moulding her breast. Annabel moaned in her ear and Carol could feel the hard buds of those perfect-looking breasts drag her arm as she rubbed against her. She rolled closer and the woman's lips met hers, soft and plump like her pussy. Then another tongue began exploring, this time inside Carol's mouth.

Over her shoulder, she could see Climax watching the proceedings, one hand in her thong furiously rubbing away as she brought herself to a climax.

Tim pulled his face from between her legs and kissed up her body, occasionally nipping at her skin, biting her nipple. Then he began to alternate his kisses between Carol and Annabel, their greedy tongues meeting somewhere in the middle. Carol could taste her love juice in his mouth, or rather Lucy's love juice, and the thought turned her on. She grabbed his cock, and played along its shaft. Annabel knelt over and as Carol held it she slipped the member into her mouth, almost to his trimmed pubes.

As she sucked him, the round globes of her backside wiggled in front of Carol, sticky pink pussy lips poking between them, opening as she rocked back. Well, Carol thought, in for a penny … Like burrowing between pillows, she pushed her face between Annabel's cheeks and let her tongue run up and down the moist furrow. It almost tasted sweet, and the musky smell begged her to go deeper. Annabel pushed back onto her and Carol twisted in further, lapping into the depths of silken pleasure, feeling her chin become sticky as though she were eating melon.

Carol came up for air and watched Annabel sucking Tim off, marvelling at how she made his large cock disappear into her mouth. He looked at her with smouldering, dark eyes. She was being watched by a man as she watched him get a blowjob – and that was making her feel hot. Really hot.

'Your turn,' Tim said, offering his cock to her now.

Both eager and hesitant, Carol leaned forward and

opened her mouth ready to receive his shaft. She guided its length in with her hand, feeling the foreskin pull back as it slid past her tight lips. She ran her tongue over the helmet and felt it spasm.

Annabel slithered her head between her legs and Carol firmly planted her snatch onto the woman's extended tongue, and instantly felt her orgasm start to build. Her saliva dribbled from the cock as she sucked it in and out, keeping to the same rhythm as she bounced on the tongue jabbing into her depths. She heard Climax squeal like a porn star as she fingered herself to orgasm.

Faster she went, swallowing globs of precome, Tim's shaved balls swinging onto her chin. Annabel nuzzled her mouth against her pussy opening and Carol shivered as sparks began to shoot round her body. Tim took hold of her head and began to groan. Carol felt her own pressure building almost to tipping point.

'Oh God, I'm about to come!' The man gritted his teeth as his cock throbbed harder, preparing for release.

So am I, Carol thought. Annabel now rubbed her clit with a finger while her tongue wiggled inside her. The sparks grew bigger, Carol felt her muscles tense.

Tim groaned loudly and Carol prepared for the load …

'So you didn't enjoy that, then?' Climax asked Carol as once again she was in her own body, looking at the threesome on the bed.

Carol was still panting, her knees shaking from expectation. 'I was about to … why must you ghosts do that?' She looked on as Lucy arched in delight, a trickle of come slipping from her lips like melting brandy butter.

'I can't believe she did that,' Carol said.

'Did what? Decided that she didn't want to be alone at Christmas? Decided that she wanted to have earth-shattering sex with two gorgeous people?'

'No. Steal my orgasm.'

Climax seductively moved beside her, her palm stroking the round of Carol's bottom and slipping down between her cheeks. 'We could always do each other – sixty-nine is my lucky number.'

'I think I've had enough of ghosts, thank you very much. Take me home.'

'As you wish.'

Carol took one last, jealous look at the trio then found herself back in bed. The room was bathed in a bluish moonlight as it reflected from the snowy roofs. In a few more hours, Christmas Day would dawn and then it would be over – and it wouldn't matter if she were alone or not. Roll on New Year, she thought. She screwed her eyes shut, wished for morning and fell asleep.

At five o'clock, Carol woke up but she didn't open her eyes. She didn't want to see the figure standing at the end of her bed. At last, she dared a quick peek. There was a man covered in skin-tight black leather. The gimp mask on his head had only slits for eyes and a zipper for a mouth.

'Don't tell me, spirit, let me guess. You are the Ghost of Christmas Yet To Be?'

The ghost nodded.

'And you want to show me my future?'

The ghost nodded.

'Then lead on.'

The ghost was carrying a spanking paddle. He waved it like a wand and suddenly they were in a church yard.

'Oh no, I'm dead! You've come to show me my grave!' she stumbled back into the snow.

The ghost tried to unzip his mask. The zipper was stuck.

'Here, let me.' Carol managed to tug it open.

The ghost took a deep breath. 'Thanks. It was getting a bit stuffy in there.'

'Hold on, you're Abstinence! I recognise your voice.'

'Bugger, you weren't supposed to notice. I'm standing in for Christmas Yet To Be as he has the night off. I think his outfit suits me, don't you?'

'Er, lovely. Why am I in a churchyard?'

'Took a wrong turn, I think. I normally do the past.' He waved his spanking paddle again, there was a rush of wind, and when it abated, they were standing in a bedroom.

The ghost looked into his hand. 'What you are about to see is only a possibility of the future. For your actions tonight can change your fate and …'

'You're reading that off a piece of paper, aren't you?'

'Look, we're understaffed and I'm doing my best. Oh, just have a look.'

Carol stood and waited. It was dark outside and Christmas lights twinkled along a neighbour's drive. There was the smell of cinnamon and pine in the air. A stocking was hung at the end of the bed but this wasn't a child's room. A picture stood on the dressing table. Carol moved over and looked at it. It was of her and Jack – she didn't remember it being taken but this was the future. Suddenly, the door flew open and Jack burst in carrying an armful of wrapped parcels.

'It's manic out there!' he gasped, and dropped the presents onto a chair. Then he turned to face her. 'God, you look beautiful!' he said, with his lopsided smile.

Carol looked around her – the room was empty, not even Abstinence was there. 'You talking to me?' she asked.

'Is that a trick question or a Robert de Niro impression?'

'You can see me?'

'Have you been at the eggnog already? Of course I can see you – in fact I can see rather a lot of you.' His gaze wandered over her body making her feel even more naked than she was.

Carol glanced in the mirror. She was dressed to thrill in hold-ups with a seam, and tanga panties and a half-cup bra in matching red silk, all trimmed with black lace. She couldn't remember ever looking so sexy.

'I take it this is for my benefit?' He moved closer.

'I guess it must be.' She felt her heart skip a beat.

He kissed her softly on the lips. 'Do you know how much I love you?'

'About seven inches, judging by the bulge.'

He pulled her blonde hair aside and kissed her neck. Carol's nipples stiffened as if touched by ice. His arms wrapped round her back, strong yet gentle. Slowly, he peeled away one bra strap and cupped her breast, strumming his thumb over her raspberry bud.

'Oh, Jack,' she gasped. 'Finish it this time.'

'Don't I always?' His lips moved down her neck and on to her breast. Small, damp kisses alighted on her like falling snow

'Oh my God!' Carol made a fist in his hair and pulled him down harder. After the encounters of the night, she was on a hair trigger. His teeth found her nipple and grated against it, then he sucked it inside. His tongue circled her bud.

'Don't climax yet, I haven't finished with you,' he whispered.

He left her saliva-covered breast and got on his knees as he trailed kisses down her stomach. He dipped his tongue in her belly button and continued south, past the elastic of her panties and further down.

'You smell *sooo* good.' His nose nudged at her though the material.

'I smell even better with those off.'

He dragged her silvery-wet panties to the floor and she moved her feet apart. He breathed deeply.

'You're right. In fact, you smell good enough to eat.' His hands grabbed at her arse cheeks and he pulled his mouth hard onto her pussy. As his tongue wedged its way inside, she felt her pubes grate against his face. Carol closed her eyes, threw back her head and gyrated onto him. Gradually, he eased her back against the bed. She lay down with her stockinged legs dangling over the side, his lips still stuck to her like a limpet. She let him part her knees and caught his eye as he probed deeper. She drifted in pleasure for what could have been seconds or minutes – and it didn't matter if this was the past or the future. For this moment at least, it was now and she was with him.

'Shall I finish you like this?' His voice rose from between her thighs. Carol ran her fingers though his hair.

'No. I need you inside me.'

He gave her a few more laps. 'I haven't even got my trousers off yet.'

'We can soon fix that.'

As he stood, she smiled to herself as she saw a small dark patch at the front of his trousers. 'What can I say?' he asked her with a grin. 'You turn me on.'

'Good.' Carol reached out and undid his flies. His trousers slid to the floor, his thick manhood already peering out from his boxers. She took hold of it and slowly masturbated him.

'You seem eager to have sex tonight,' he said. 'Not that I mind.'

Carol thought back through all the encounters of the evening. 'Not sex – I'm eager for you to make love to me.'

He descended on top of her, his strong body against hers. 'I think I can manage that.' They kissed and he tasted of her.

Still holding his cock, she moved it to her entrance, leaving a sticky trail along her leg. For a second she wondered if the ghost would take her away from him, then decided there was only one way to find out. She raised her hips and he started to sink in. He toyed with her pussy, easing it open with his swollen cock head, each teasing push sending it only fractionally deeper. She sighed and looked deep into his eyes, he smiled back and she felt as though they were one.

Then, suddenly, he plunged all the way in, and a breathless moan escaped Carol. Long, rhythmic pushes in as deep as he could go and then back out again. She knotted her legs behind him and pulled him tighter. She could feel the heat building, spreading through her body, her mind floating. He sped up the pace, rising onto his hands, a look of concentration frowned onto his face.

'Come inside me,' she whispered.

His cock jerked and she tightened her muscles around it. He groaned loudly and the sounds set off her own orgasm, the wave of pleasure washing her senses away, their climactic sounds merging into one. Then, spent, he slumped on top of her before rolling off.

'I love you,' he panted.

Carol rolled over to face him. 'And I …' But he wasn't there. She was back alone in her own room. The clock said 8 a.m. It was Christmas Day. Had it all been a dream? She felt lonelier than ever. She wanted Jack back, she had always wanted him. The ghosts had been right, there was no substitute for the real thing.

The phone rang. Carol picked it up – probably Lucy wanting to boast. But no, it was a man's voice.

'Hi, Carol? It's Jack. I know this sounds crazy but I just had the weirdest dream and well … I wondered if I could come over.'

Carol smiled.

A Seasonal Victorian Spanking
by Victoria Blisse

I pulled myself into the constrictive and expensive corset. It was a struggle but when I'd finished, the scarlet silk and bone fitted like a charm. I admired my waist for a moment, hands on hips as I swayed from side to side. My breasts jutted out and were cupped gently, the magnolia white of my flesh standing out in contrast to the fabric.

I had to stand up straight and true – the garment gave me no room to slump – and I felt like I was presenting my breasts proudly for inspection. I hoped Edward would approve, after all it was he who I hoped to impress. I had taken on the job of waitress at the local museum simply to make ends meet as I studied medicine at university. I came to it late, after a few years of farting about deciding on what my career was to be. It seems weird but I am a mature student, though sometimes I don't feel very mature, especially not at work. I am one of the youngest there.

I'd never been much of a history buff until the day I saw Edward conducting a museum tour. His tall, sleek body encased in the smart grey of his work suit first took my eye. I couldn't get close to him when I worked. I was in the café and only glimpsed him through the opened doors. I fantasised about him even then. I imagined him coming in for his dinner, chastising me for not cleaning his table just so and flipping up my skirt and spanking me right there in front of the customers. I was even more convinced of his dominance when I took his tour one day. I hung on every one of his words and by the end of the tour, I knew a lot more about Victorian Britain than I thought I ever would. Edward made it fascinating and not just because of his purring upper-class accent, his rounded vowels or his perfect bubble butt and square-cut jaw.

He made it all ever so interesting because he was so enthused by it.

Especially the corporal punishment.

I joined his tour once a week just to hear him speak lovingly of the cane and in explicit detail about the pain of a wooden ruler chastising naughty buttocks. Soon, we exchanged names and chatted generally about the museum, work and our mutual love for history. Well, *his* love for history which I was catching on top of my feverish lust for his hand on my arse and his severe lips pressed to mine.

So when the Christmas party invite was handed to me, and when Edward confirmed he'd be attending the Victorian-themed event, I decided I had to go. I blew more than a month's salary on my costume, the corset and the dress. I couldn't just hire something or pick up a cheap fancy dress – Edward liked authenticity. So I found a dressmaker who made my gown from a genuine 1890s pattern. She was the one who told me I needed a corset and I couldn't refuse. I knew it would look spectacular. I spent a long time thinking about knickers too – technically, I should have worn long bloomers that covered me to my knees but I just couldn't bring myself to don anything so terribly mundane. I thought about buying a sexy red pair of exotic undies to match the shade of my corset but I knew that would be wrong. It would spoil the whole outfit and I knew Edward would certainly not approve.

So when I walked into the museum that night, I had no

undergarment over my bum. Not that anyone could tell as there were several layers of lace-edged underskirts covered with scarlet satin that stretched out from my waist like an opened umbrella. And the bodice clung to my chest like a second skin. I hid a little of my extensive cleavage behind an intricate network of red, garnet-like jewels that spread out from my neck like fine lace.

If my own mother had walked in she wouldn't have recognised me. My hair was professionally piled up on my head, held in place with more pins than I care to imagine. I had even applied a little make-up, light and fresh, but the length of my lashes and the sparkle of my lips showed that I'd spent some time making myself look pretty.

I was incredibly self-conscious. I certainly felt sexy but I didn't feel comfortable flaunting it around people I worked with every day. And as much as I looked for him, I couldn't see Edward anywhere. So I did as any shy girl would do. I went and stood in the corner by the buffet.

Everyone seemed to be having a good time. There were people swaying and swishing on the dance floor, others in small groups chatting and laughing and all lit by a thousand or so candles, surrounded by springs of holly and mistletoe and overshadowed by the huge Christmas tree in the corner. The vast hall of the museum was alive with vibrancy and mirth.

I was mulling over in my mind whether the candles on the tree were real or fake when a familiar voice broke into my thoughts.

'Well good evening, Miss Jones, I didn't know you were going to be here.'

'Ed– I mean, Mr Butterworth, I'm glad to see you.' I had to act the Victorian lady, it was central to my plan. A very loose plan, admittedly – well, more of a hope than anything else, but I was going to stick to it all the same.

'And I you, miss. I must say I think your evening gown is just splendid.' He raked his gaze up and down my body. He lingered on my curves. I wanted him to linger on them in a more literal sense too. 'It fits you to perfection.'

'Thank you. I had my seamstress make it to my specifications. I think she did a very thorough job of it.'

'I quite agree. It's quite *à la mode*. I do hope you have the undergarments to match it.'

'Sir!' I gasped with fake affront. 'That is a very personal question indeed but if you must know, I have a corset on that matches the dress in colour and style.'

'And your bloomers?' he leaned in as he whispered those words and I licked my lips nervously.

'I am not wearing any.'

His groan vibrated in the base of my stomach and tickled past my ear. 'That is wicked of you, Miss Jones, completely wicked.'

'Yes, sir,' I replied huskily. I was turned on but I had to say everything within little gaspy breaths because of the constriction of my stays.

'I think it is my duty as caretaker of this establishment to take you in hand and punish you for your wanton ways. What do you say to that, miss?'

'I'm sorry, sir,' I stuttered, 'it's just I find them so uncomfortable and …'

'There is no excuse for indecency, Miss Jones. You deserve to be punished.'

'I do, sir,' I replied, my head bowed. My heart thumped with desire as I awaited his next words. They would reveal if he was being serious or not.

'Follow me to the schoolroom. I refuse to spank you in front of the guests, it may disturb them.'

'Yes, sir.'

He grabbed my hand, the first proper physical contact

we'd ever shared and pulled me away from the hubbub and down the corridor towards the Victorian Life exhibit. We have working exhibits depicting many aspects of day-to-day life in that era, including a schoolroom, complete with rows of tables attached to wooden benches, a teacher's desk and a blackboard. Edward pulled me to the centre of the room before a table. He left me standing there as he moved to light candles around us, using the light pouring in from the corridor to guide him.

'Right, Miss Jones. You do know that such morally loose behaviour cannot be tolerated within these walls, don't you?'

'Yes, sir.'

'So why did you choose not to wear bloomers to such a formal affair?'

'They looked frumpy, sir. I didn't want to spoil the effect of my dress and my corset.'

'Vanity!' he exclaimed. 'One of the seven deadly sins.'

'Actually, sir, I'm pretty sure it isn't. I think that's pride–'

'*Hush*!' he shouted as he slammed his hand down on to the desk before him. 'You do not interrupt me, you do not contradict me and you certainly do not mock me, miss. You do realise the more infractions I mark on my list, the more severe your punishment?'

'Sorry, sir.'

'We'd better get to it, then. Step up to the desk, Miss Jones, and bend over it with your arms outstretched.'

I followed his instruction without hesitation. The hard wood dug into my ribs and my breasts souffléd forward as the slope of the authentic desktop left my hands dangling lower than my body. I swear more flesh was out of my outfit than was confined within the elaborate silk.

'I'll add a few extra swats for indecently low cleavage

too,' Edward mumbled as he took off his long, black jacket and rolled up the stiff, white sleeves of his shirt to reveal the strong arms I'd so often fantasied about.

He walked behind me, his shoes clacking on the wooden floor. I felt my skirts being lifted and pulled up over my back. I inhaled sharply as cool air caressed my now exposed buttocks. He could see my naked arse and I wasn't sure how he'd respond to its size and its curve. He stroked gently over my left cheek and I let out a gasp of relief and arousal.

'Lucy, I don't want to hurt you, only arouse you. If at any time this gets too much please shout out "mistletoe" and I swear I will stop.'

"Thank you,' I whispered and he squeezed my arse in response. I was a bundle of nerves and waiting arousal. I was glad that Edward had thought about my well-being. That warmed my heart. His hand on my posterior heated a whole different part of my anatomy to boiling point too.

'I am going to start your punishment with ten hand-slaps. That is for your insolence. I will follow with another ten for answering out of turn. Then we will get to your punishment for going bare-cheeked. Five swift slashes with the cane.'

My eyes widened and I gasped but clamped the words down before they escaped and earned me even more punishment. I'd seen the cane many times and heard Edward talk of its uses for chastisement. When he would swing and flex it, my cunt would contract in pleasure as I imagined its hot sting on my flesh but I wasn't sure I was ready to experience it at first hand. I waited impatiently. The strain in my calves from stretching up over the high desk made me shuffle, the ache in my arms made me want to let go and straighten but I couldn't. I didn't want to. I wanted to feel Edward's hand on my arse. I tensed myself for the first spank.

It came out of nowhere and I felt the warmth of his hand first, then the exploded heat of the impact a moment later. He didn't give me time to react but hit me again on virtually the same spot and that time I cried out, unable to hold in my response.

'Oh, hush, girl. We've only just started.'

He slapped my arse again, hitting the other cheek. The sting was at once painful and arousing. I wanted more but I also wanted him to stop and to just fuck me. My cunt was wet. I wondered if he could see my juices shining on my thighs? As he hit again and again I listened to the rustle of my skirts around my shoulders, felt the wobble of my tits as my whole body shook with the impact. My arse was on fire and I wanted him to soothe me. I wanted him to dip his cruel fingers between my sex lips and to frig me to completion.

'Good girl, that's the first ten down.'

I'd lost count and was startled to realise I was a third of the way through my punishment.

'OK, for the second ten I'm going to treat you according to your childish behaviour. Stand up.'

I straightened my buttocks, which stung as my skirts fell back down to cover them once more. I didn't want to be covered. I wanted more. Edward walked past me and retrieved the simple chair from behind the teacher's desk. He set it on the floor just behind me. He then returned to the teacher's desk and reached up to the wall behind it to remove the cane from where it hung on a peg.

'Right,' he sat down and let the cane fall with a clatter to the floor beside him. 'Over my knee, now.'

'Yes, sir,' I replied. I didn't want to hesitate. I wanted to feel his spanks again. I wondered as I arranged myself over his lap, if he'd seen into my darkest fantasies or whether his own were simply similar? I had fantasised so many times about being spanked in just such a position. I hadn't really thought about the strain in my legs and arms as I fought to keep my balance. It added to the erotic suspense, as did being able to feel the generous rod prodding into my belly from Edward's crotch.

He flicked up my skirts and pulled over my back once more. I was exposed again. My facial cheeks flushed in humiliation. I knew he liked what he saw, though, as his cock jumped and I heard him growl his approval.

'Naughty girls get spankings like this,' he said as he slapped down, 'because they cannot be trusted. They need to be held down.'

He spanked again and my flesh wobbled. I held my breath, waiting for the next explosion of erotic pain.

'And you're a very naughty girl aren't you, Miss Jones?'

'Yes, sir,' I yelped.

'A *very* naughty girl.' He spanked me several times, the heat building, the pain escalating to a point where I wanted him to stop. I whimpered and wiggled in his lap.

'No more,' I gasped. My already sore buttocks throbbed with the heat. I knew I shouldn't have spoken but I couldn't help it.

'Oh, shush, you adore this.' He dipped his hand to cup my arse and his fingers trailed between my thighs and brushed my sticky lips. 'You're so wet.'

I couldn't deny it. I was aroused to a point where pain blossomed into pleasure.

'Tell me you love it.'

'I love it,' I whispered.

'Beg me for more, girl, beg me for it.'

'Spank my naughty arse, sir,' I moaned. 'Spank me, please. I need your punishment.'

'Yes, you do.' Each word was emphasised with a

spank that shook me. I felt so close to complete ecstasy I was honestly convinced I might come from one more spank. 'And that's your ten hand spanks up. I gave you an extra two for the insolent words you uttered.'

'Thank you, sir,' I gasped. My nipples were hard, my breasts ached and the constriction of the corset made me oh, so aware of them dangling free beside Edward's knees.

'And now for the cane. I want you to count each impact and thank me for it.'

'Yes, sir.'

He leaned to the side, holding me in place as he picked up the whippy piece of birch from beside my head.

'Brace yourself.'

Nothing could prepare me for the harsh, focused sting that was the cane whipping my flesh.

'One,' I squeaked through my pain. 'Thank you, sir.'

As two and three followed, I managed to squeal out the number and thanks. The fourth, however, hit in such a way as to cause me exquisite pain and bring tears to my eyes.

'Say it,' Edward whispered, gently rubbing my back. 'You're doing so well. Almost done, darling. Say it.'

His tenderness melted my heart and I managed to groan out.

'Four, thank you, sir.'

The fifth hit was torturous and glorious. It fucking hurt but it was the last beat.

'Five, thank you, sir,' I gasped.

'Good girl.' Edward gently stroked my arse. 'You took that well.'

My buttocks stung but I was so proud of myself. I'd taken it. I had been a good girl for Mr Butterworth.

'Now, good girls deserve a reward. Stand up.'

I got unsteadily back to my feet and Edward wrapped himself around me and crushed his lips to mine in a ferocious kiss.

'I've wanted to do that for so long,' he gasped as his long fingers worked at the buttons on the back of my dress, 'and to have you over my knee in this dress, Fuck, Lucy. It was a dream come true.'

'It's all for you,' I said as he nuzzled kisses on my neck between the criss-cross of deep red gems. 'I dressed like this just for you.'

'I love it,' he moaned. 'But now I want you out of it.'

He undid the buttons with far more dexterity than I had managed when I'd fastened them, and the heavy dress fell to the ground with a satisfying "whomf", leaving me deliciously exposed.

'So beautiful,' he moaned, tracing a finger down over my cleavage and corset, then he added, 'and the stays are pretty too.'

'The corset was specially made too. Do you approve?'

'I love it,' he replied. 'Look at how it accentuates your delicious tits –' he dropped kisses in my cleavage before continuing '– and how it pulls in your waist and showcases your feminine hips.' His fingers gripped my hips and pulled me closer to him. 'And draws my attention to what lies between your thighs.'

He kissed me again and as passion blazed between our lips, he slipped his fingers between my legs and rubbed against my clit. My knees buckled and he grabbed me tightly to stop me from falling.

'Bend over the desk again, love,' he panted. 'I want to fuck you.'

'Yes,' I replied, 'fuck me, please.'

I stumbled out of my dress and over to the desk. I bent over and spread my thighs, eager for him to fill me.

'Happy Christmas to me,' he mumbled before pressing his hard cock against my hot slit. 'Fuck, you're so wet.'

I moaned and pushed back and helped him sink deeper into me as he thrust forward.

'You're a naughty girl, Miss Jones,' he moaned into my ear, 'getting turned on by a spanking.'

'Yes, sir,' I replied. 'I'm a very naughty girl for you.'

He grasped my hips even more tightly, almost painfully, and slammed into my pussy. Sensation exploded through my arse from the impact of his crotch against it – a sharp reminder of the stinging blows he had inflicted earlier, which now melded with the flow of pleasure shooting from my clit to take my breath away. I had never felt so turned on in my life before. I was going to come just from the friction of his thick dick inside me. I screamed out as ecstasy overtook me and I held on to the desk, my legs no longer able to support me.

'Tell me you're my naughty girl,' he gasped. 'Tell me!'

'I'm a naughty girl for you, Mr Butterworth. I'm your naughty girl. I want you to spank me, to fuck me, to keep me in line. I'm yours.'

'Yes!' He exclaimed and held himself deep within me as his orgasm blasted through him. 'Thank you.'

'No, thank you. You gave me just what I wanted for Christmas. The perfect punishment.'

'Hmm, Let me book you in for New Year, Epiphany, Mother's Day – well, you get the picture.' He smirked as we pulled our clothing hurriedly back into place.

I giggled. 'Any day I'm naughty, sir, I'll come to you.'

'And come on me if I have any say in it,' he added, and pulled me into his embrace.

'Yes, sir,' I whispered. Then I kissed him deeply as I wondered what scenes we could come up with to make more good use of my new gown and corset.

Designs on the Boss
by Poppy Summers

The day I left the most boring Christmas party on earth
and walked in on my boss having a wank in his office was
the greatest day of my life. You doubt me? You haven't
seen my boss. He would make angels fall from heaven.
He would stop traffic in the street.

Cool and reserved with more than a touch of
megalomania, he didn't seem to notice he was beautiful.
People joked about him and said he was asexual or frigid
or whatever the male equivalent is. Forty and not married,
they had him down as gay with his sharp suits, expensive
cologne and immaculately coiffured black hair. People
hadn't even seen him out shopping, never mind in a bar.
There was no gossip to be dug up about which way he
swung and when he ever got laid, and most people had
written him off as some weirdo, married to his job and not
even bothering to wank.

Me, I knew better. I wanted my boss with every fibre
of my being and I had waited two years in purgatory for
him to even notice me.

I'd done something really risqué the week before the
office party. Maybe I'd been hoping word would get
around to my boss and shock or excite him or maybe it was
simply for the thrill but either way, I'd agreed to bare my
bum for a calendar of sexy office girls organised by the

firm. OK, it was cheap and degrading but all proceeds were for the RSPCA and the guys were doing one too – hot men in and out of suits. I already had a copy of that stashed away for lonely nights. Why they hadn't asked my boss to participate I can't imagine. They must have been blind.

The office closed up, the party started and people passed around copies of my calendar, leering over me. It was my own fault for doing it but I warned the culprits to put the photo away if Michael ever came out of his office. People were taking bets that he'd stay in there all night like he had done last year, not even tempted out by the copious amounts of alcohol, which he'd paid for anyway. That was his contribution. He gave us money rather than himself. His social skills left a lot to be desired and I wondered how exactly he had progressed to a six-figure salary when nobody ever saw him.

It was Gavin from accounts who egged me on to entice him out and, as I'd already had a couple of glasses of wine, I was up for it. I approached his office in my slinky party dress and tapped lightly. No reply. I listened with my ear at the door and heard nothing. I frowned, glancing back to see my colleagues had gone back to their party and my attempt to lure the boss out was forgotten about. Nonetheless, I'd started so I had to finish. The door creaked like Dracula's coffin as I pushed it open, peering around.

Michael's desk was empty. My gaze tracked across the room to his en suite. I heard a stifled sound come from behind the open door. My ears pricked up. My heart picked up speed. Whatever he was doing in there, unless it was sitting on the toilet, I wanted to see. I crept inside.

The sink was next to the door in the bathroom and I saw his shiny Italian loafers before the dark cloth of his pants and then his hand and … oh God.

My boss was standing at the sink, fisting his straining

cock. He was flushed, a thin gleam of sweat on his upper lip. Never had he looked more stunning. And his cock? Well, it was as lovely as I had expected, big and thick and just made to satisfy. I was mesmerised by the rapid movement of his hand, the slick sound of his palm on his shaft, the guttural groans he tried to stifle. With his other hand, he clung to the edge of the sink as though his knees were buckling.

I stood pressed against the wall, peering in. The flimsy lace between my legs was soaked at the evidence of my boss's sexuality. Never had I spectated on anything more erotic in my life. I brushed a hand over my breast, found the nipple rigid below the silk dress and ached to touch myself in more intimate ways. Reckless in my need to see it all, I leaned closer – too close – and he spotted me.

Michael went rigid. He gave a little cry of horror and snatched the hand-towel from the rail, holding it over his arousal. His cock merely poked it upward like the lewdest of tents. He stood there blushing tomato red.

Trying for nonchalance even though his embarrassment had leached into me and made me nervous, I struck a pose against the wall. 'I came to see if you wanted to join the party but I can see you're having one of your own.'

My boss coughed. He turned away, fumbling furiously with his pants.

'Don't put it away on my account.'

'Genevieve,' he said, looking sternly over his shoulder at my teasing. 'What do you want?'

'I already said. I know you like to work alone, boss, but *really*.'

Michael turned around and gave me a little glare. He swept a hand nervously through his raven hair. It was then that I saw it. A photo balancing on the edge of the sink of a woman wearing a red and white Santa outfit, bottom bared with a cheeky grin over her shoulder.

My jaw fell open. My boss had been wanking over me.

He saw the direction of my gaze and his face burned ever brighter. He dropped the hand towel over the picture. His cock pressed rigidly against his tight, well-tailored pants, showing no signs of flagging.

I recovered myself and smiled although my heart was racing. I just couldn't believe it. 'We shouldn't let that go to waste –' I motioned to his hard-on '– why don't you let me finish you off?'

My boss's dark blue eyes bulged from their sockets. 'Are you serious?' He nearly stammered.

'Deeply,' I replied.

'Is this some sort of … are you going to do me for sexual harassment?' Poor man looked increasingly fraught.

I cocked my head. 'What? You mean if you let me blow you –' his face went purple at the word *blow* '– then you think I might say it was sexual harassment?'

He nodded, looking miserable now.

I stepped into the bathroom. He had nowhere to go. He tried to squeeze into the corner by the sink. 'Michael,' I said, 'if anything, it will be you doing *me* for sexual harassment. Seriously, I'm wet just thinking about sucking your delicious cock.'

I thought his eyes were about to bounce onto the floor at my dirty talk. I don't know where it had come from – well, probably two glasses of wine and finding my boss wanking over me in my Santa outfit. It wasn't my usual approach, though. If he could have got past me without pushing rudely, I'm sure he would have fled. I stepped closer and put out my hand. He gave a little strangled sound and jerked his hips away as my fingers closed around his shaft. But he was up against the wall and I had him.

His cock was velvet steel. He whimpered as I tightened

my hand, slid it up and down, dwarfed by his size.

'Do you like that?' I asked.

By way of reply, his eyes darted wildly to the door. 'Someone might come …'

'The only one who's going to come is you, boss,' I said before I threw the door shut and dropped to my knees. Blowjobs weren't always my cup of tea but never had I wanted to give one more. This beautiful man deserved all the pleasure he was owed.

Eye to eye with his prick, I saw a pearl drop running from the slit. I swiped it up eagerly and smacked my lips. 'You taste good.'

He looked like he was going to stroke out. His pants were undone but his cock was sticking through the slit in his Calvin Kleins. I freed it entirely by yanking down both pants and briefs, exposing his undercarriage to my greedy gaze.

He had a nice little manscaped bush. His rod reared up to his belly proudly, looking even bigger now, while his balls were in a tight little sac with no hair. Well he trimmed for someone, that was for sure, unless he just liked to fondle a nice smooth bag. I certainly did.

I lowered my head and flicked my tongue over his delightfully pink scrotum. He hissed and gripped my shoulder. I sucked each ball into my mouth in turn and then I lifted up his equipment and pressed my tongue to his perineum.

'Holy fuck!'

I glanced up with a smile. I had the craziest thought of tonguing his tight arsehole, but all in good time. There was a certain protocol, after all. It would be like him not touching my tits first. If only …

I went down on him, taking my time and easing every inch of his wonderful cock deep into my throat. It felt good, so good to suck my boss off. His meat throbbed in my mouth, rock hard and making my jaw ache.

Michael moaned. He touched my head tentatively, fingers easing through the waves of my long hair. I squeezed his balls in one hand while the other ran over his belly, up under his shirt to his chest. He writhed under my touch as I pinched one tiny nipple, then the other, rolling them erect.

I drew back, leaving his dick glistening with saliva. I used my hands on his balls and nipples and my tongue on his slit, all the while looking up into his stormy eyes.

Michael gripped the sink as though trying to stay upright. His fingers slid under my hair, stroking my neck, his touch feverish.

'I want to make you come,' I said in a whisper. 'I want to see your beautiful face.'

My boss blushed again, but he held my gaze, his own intent. He touched my face with reverent fingertips and I sensed that this wouldn't be cheap to him, whether I was his employee on my knees or not. Warmth surged in my belly. I smiled up at him. I couldn't have picked a more worthy recipient of my affection. He wouldn't forget this.

I sucked his cock down again, feeling my pussy clench with every inch I took. I was beyond wet and desperate for him but it was OK. I'd said I was going to make him come and that was enough for me.

His hand slid over my shoulders and down my neck. His fingers rested on the zip at the top of my dress. I took it as a hint even if it wasn't meant as one, and unzipped, shrugging out my arms, letting the silk fall to my waist before unhooking my bra, tossing it away.

Michael drew in a deep breath. While I sucked his cock fervently, he eyed my breasts as though afraid to take liberties. I helped him on. I cupped my left breast and rubbed the nipple, pinching the stiff peak. He liked that. His pupils overwhelmed the blue of his eyes. He gave a soft little moan and his thighs trembled, his cock pulsing.

He was ready. Should I swallow or not? I had a better idea. Something nice and visual for him. I let his cock slip from my mouth, grabbed the shaft and wanked him all over my tits.

Michael let loose a cry. He creamed my cleavage in hot pumps, splattering me with jizz. I milked every drop from his cock. Then I let go and pushed my breasts together, lifting them so I could tongue the semen from my hard nipples.

Breathing hard, he slumped against the wall, eyeing me. I rose to my feet and drew my finger through his spunk before sucking it, keeping my gaze fixed on his. Then I turned to the sink and washed my hands, but left the semen on my boobs.

He tucked himself away and fastened up and then he hovered there a moment. As I was drying my hands, he moved behind me. I shivered in excitement as he lightly drew my hair back over my shoulder and kissed my neck. I hadn't expected him to touch me, only zip himself up and go back to his lonely ritual at the desk. Instead, my legs started to tremble as his hands released the rest of my zip and my dress pooled around my feet. I stepped out of it, standing there in my lace thong, hold-up stockings and high heels. Michael looked down, taking in my body. He drew in his breath, cupping the cheeks of my bottom. Our eyes met in the mirror.

'I want you,' I said in a whisper. 'Please, Michael. I want you so much it hurts.'

My boss swallowed. He looked nervous and unsure again. But his prick told a different story. It pressed rampantly against my arse.

I turned around and then I pressed my come-soaked breasts into his chest, against his expensive silver tie and black shirt, my arms around his neck. His eyes sparked flames. His hands smoothed down my hips. I knew he was all man and that sooner or later he would show it.

He lifted me under my backside and I wrapped my legs around him as he carried me out of the bathroom and into the office. Holding me firm he swept everything off his desk with one strong arm, stationery and silly glass paperweights and books clattering to the floor. For a moment I held my breath as he lowered me down on the edge, glancing towards the door. He did too, both of us afraid someone was going to come running at the noise.

But the noise outside consisted of Queen's *Bohemian Rhapsody* and the office denizens screeching about *Figaro, Magnifico* in unison and Michael gave a shy smile as he pushed my thighs apart to stand between them. I grasped his face in my hands and kissed him.

My boss kissed like an angel; that won't surprise you by now. His tongue was hesitant and so sweet when he finally introduced it to duel with mine. He stroked my inner thighs through the silk of my stockings and then I gasped as his forefinger slipped beneath my thong and he circled my clit.

I arched under him, hot and hard and so wet. His fingers caressed my slit, spread my juice over my clit and rubbed it teasingly. I whimpered and grabbed his wrist, urging him on and he speared me with two fingers while using his thumb to stroke my bud.

Oh fuck, he knew what to do. Asexual, my arse. He breathed into my mouth while he frigged me and I felt myself rushing towards climax, shaking with pleasure. He stopped abruptly before I could come. The protest died on my lips as he fell to his knees and hooked one of my legs over his shoulder. I tensed with excitement and then he mouthed the wet lace of my thong before his tongue crept under the edge, licking my slit. I trembled and moaned, gripping his hair, dishevelling it. He pulled the soaked gusset aside and lashed my clit with long licks and I cried out, lifting my backside, pushing into his face. He held me firm with his hands under my arse and God, he ate me until I thought I would pass out.

Of course, once again, he didn't let me come. Instead, he straightened up and I saw his face had changed. He was all masterful, flushed with arousal and I wriggled excitedly on the desk to know that finally, I was going to get it.

He ripped his trousers open and yanked them down, his boxer briefs barely containing his tumescent cock. His prick sprang out heavily and he pulled me up off the desk, spun me around dizzyingly and then shoved me down face first. He pulled my thong aside. I yelled an unladylike curse as he penetrated me, sliding in up to the hilt, filling my pussy so full so quick I could barely breathe. I scrabbled at the desk as he pounded me into it, quick, hard strokes, taking me all the way.

Oh God, it was delicious! Like something from those delectable fantasies I had at night of him with my hand between my legs and gasping into the darkness.

He gripped my hips and pulled me to the edge of the desk. Then he slid his hand under me and fingered my clit. I panted and slithered around on the smooth mahogany. I groaned his name uncontrollably. He leaned over my back, cupped one breast, squeezed the nipple and mouthed my neck.

His cock stretched me so deliciously. His finger didn't stop tormenting my clit as he rammed me. I was going to explode and scream the place down. I shook and writhed as I ascended the peak and fell into the climax.

Everything faded away as I convulsed on that desk. I

was barely aware of Michael any more, of the Christmas party carrying on beyond our ecstasy. Of the fact that I had *fucked my boss.*

I regained my senses, damp and sweaty, face down on Michael's desk with his cock still embedded inside me. He eased free and I felt wetness seep down my thighs. He moved across the room and softly closed the en suite door. I got stiffly to my feet and adjusted my underwear. My dress was still in the bathroom. I perched on the edge of the desk, covering my sticky breasts with my hands and glancing nervously towards the outside door. God, what if someone started to wonder where I had been all this time and came looking for me?

And just as I thought it, a shadow loomed up behind the frosted glass and there came a knock on the door. I dived ignominiously under the desk. The rap came again and I heard the en suite door open cautiously, Michael no doubt peeking out and wondering where the satiated, nearly naked woman from his desk had gone.

He cleared his throat nervously and called to the visitor to enter. Then he sat in his executive chair and pulled it up to the desk, kicking me with both Italian shoes. I grunted, clapped my hand over my mouth and nursed my bruised arms. Michael withdrew his feet instantly, muscular thighs tensing perceptively and … was he still hard in his pants? It looked like it from here. I smiled, forgetting about my pain.

Meanwhile the interloper had entered the office. It was Gavin. 'Boss, I was looking for Genevieve.'

Michael's lie was smooth and surprisingly easy although his voice wasn't quite steady. 'She was here briefly. I think she went out for some air.'

Air? In my party dress when it was snowing?

'Oh, OK.' Gavin seemed unsure. 'I'll go and look. Are

191

you coming out?'

'In a little while,' Michael said. 'Save me a drink.'

'Sure, boss.' The door closed.

Michael pushed his chair back and looked under the desk. 'I'm so sorry,' he said.

I shrugged. 'What's a few teeth?'

Michael looked appalled. He held out his hands and I took them and climbed up. He settled me on his lap, studying my face intently. 'I kicked you in the mouth?'

'No, I'm joking. I'm fine.'

He seemed relieved. He stroked my hair back and nuzzled my neck. 'Thanks for the Christmas present.'

I grinned. 'My pleasure.'

He trailed a hand down my back, making me shiver in renewed arousal. 'I guess you must have lots of plans for Christmas Day?'

'Only a family dinner that I'd love to get out of,' I said with my heart beating hard at the connotations of his words.

'OK.' His fingers traced my thigh, smoothing over my stocking and fondling the lace at its edge. 'Perhaps I could ...' He stopped, then tried again, head bowed, teeth nibbling at his lip. 'I'm a good cook.'

I put my arms around his neck. 'I'd love to.'

'Really?'

I laughed. 'Really. Michael, I thought you'd never notice me.'

He gave a shy smile. 'I noticed you all right.'

He kissed me and I thought about what a perfect Christmas this was going to be and how I would have never hooked my delightful boss if I hadn't shown my bum on that photo.

The Twelve Days of Sexmas
by Rosalía Zizzo

'Are you really a virgin?'

'Well, not any more,' I chuckle as I toss my wheat-coloured hair and throw aside my cranberry-red, velvet Santa outfit. Other than my black, supple, thigh-high boots, I am currently naked and feeling very satisfied. Very. Satisfied. Running my hands over my legs, I've never felt sexier. I like to massage lotion into my newly shaven legs and run my palms over their smoothness, so I'm sure Luis is telling the truth when he comments in his cute Spanish accent on their crazy, wonderful feel when he caresses them. But I get ahead of myself.

Exactly one fortnight ago I went to the local mall to purchase some holiday gifts, but we're not talking about one of those mega malls you'd find in a fairly large, suburban area. Our teeny, tiny town has a population of 8,000. That number of mainly migrant farmworkers in the Sacramento Valley – where the closest thing to a white Christmas is a drop in temperature to 45 degrees and hailstones as big as blueberries – does not justify a building that takes up an entire block with several dozen stores as well as a frozen yoghurt shop, a pretzel shack, and a couple pizza places.

Sure, the small strip of stores housed under the same roof has a drugstore, where I stopped to purchase my mom's favourite cheesy celebrity perfume, but to get something special, I had to order online. I received a package today that contained the thigh-high, soft-vinyl fuck-me boots that retail for a couple hundred dollars. I had been eyeing them for several months, then they went on sale for 50 bucks, so I bought them along with the velvety Santa suit that was just long enough to cover the pantyless space between my thighs.

Of course, our little mall still had a Santa so the kiddies could plop their little behinds on his knee and share their Christmas desires, but not the fancy decor and 20-foot tree decorated with egg-sized lights and ornaments the size of baseball mitts. No, just a brown-skinned young man in costume with a fake white beard seated in a little pagoda next to the pretzel shop. Families huddled nearby, clicking their cameras and hoping to savour the memories within the photographs.

After quickly making my purchases, I made a rapid stop at the pretzel shop beside the holiday pavilion and got a crazy idea – what if I sat on Santa's lap? What if I whispered to him in his ear my naughty intentions? As I sat with my salty piece of warm, twisted dough, taking bite after bite, I strategised my plans. I was a 19-year-old virgin, and I thought I'd discovered a way to have a discreet, first-time experience. I didn't know this guy who was probably making a few bucks for college playing a holiday character, and it seemed a simple way to get the whole thing over with. And besides, it could be fun.

Looking over his form, I tried to get a sense as to what he really looked like under the beard and red suit. His brown skin looked touchable, and he appeared young and fit and like someone I wouldn't mind getting into bed with. His broad chest under the coat was also a turn-on, and he seemed like a sweet guy too – every little visitor brought a genuine smile to his face, lighting it up like a holiday accessory that spurred on an electrical surge in my body. I was convinced my plan was a good one – clandestine, easy, fun, and a way to get past the idea of being a "bad" girl. Until now, I had always been a good girl, but I was truly looking forward to being the bad one, a naughty one, the girl my typical, religious, American parents tried very, very hard to stop me from becoming.

So when I got up the nerve, I trailed behind the last in line to speak with Santa Claus while the crowd dissipated and slowly wandered away. As I approached the bearded fellow, pulse racing, breathless and feeling like I was a million miles from the pretzel shack, he appeared confused. His eyes drifted down to where I should have been holding a child's hand, yet my hands were empty aside from the greasy napkin that belonged in the trash. Starting at my chest, he scanned my body up and down, and his dark eyes met mine as I stepped forward, escorted by one of his elves.

'Can I help you?' He whispered in quasi-English and shifted in his seat. Starting to blush, I smirked and nodded as he questioned me further. 'Do I know you?'

'I sure hope not.' I didn't want it getting around I was fishing for erotic adventures by cruising the shopping mall and taking home the first guy I met. I grinned, feeling the heat spread over my face, which I'm sure looked like a ripe tomato at this point. 'But maybe you can help with my extraordinary problem.' *You can do this Margie. You're strong enough. Get a grip. C'mon.*

He paused, looked me over again, then waved me forward, beckoning me to the green carpet with his white-gloved hand as the rest of the holiday employees started to pack things up, including his cute teenage elf. The anxiety increased a bit as I started to move, my knees weakened as I took a single step, and in my nervousness my throat constricted so it felt like I was gasping for breath.

But I knew it had to happen sooner or later, and I was sick and tired of masturbating to movies like *9½ Weeks* or *Original Sin* or the even kinkier *Blue Velvet*. Walking onto the plush, dark-green runner in my skinny jeans and tight, white V-neck sweater that accentuated the valley between my breasts, I approached him and leaned in close, my heartbeat pounding in my ears.

'I could be wrong, but I sense you're not married, so let me tell you what I was thinking,' I whispered hoarsely as my knees brushed his, almost buckling, and I slowly climbed and settled onto his lap. He smelled so good, so warm, so manly. His thighs felt strong, and I felt the urge to squeeze his muscles, but I suppressed it for the time being and just softly vocalised my wishes. 'I'm not interested in commitment or a boyfriend.' Heart pounding, my voice dropped lower. 'I am a 19-year-old virgin who wants an unknown someone to do the deed. To take my virginity.' When I saw his eyes bug out of his head, I continued, 'It's a weird request, but I'm ready, and I'm eager to learn.' It felt like I was sucking on sand as I waited for his response. *Please, please, please* ...

After a length of time with him silent, somewhat stunned by my proposal, I asked him, 'Are you interested at all?' I bit my lower lip and brushed the dirty-blonde bangs from my eyes. He shifted under my weight, and I felt him nudging the back of my thigh with his rising erection, which proved his obvious regard for my idea.

Oh boy. This is going to be fun, I thought. Breathing a sigh of relief for completing the task I had set for myself, I looked into his bearded face. 'I'm Margaret, by the way.' I brushed away the strands of hair sticking to my oily lips.

'Luis,' he whimpered, after another pause. I could hear

the accent in his voice, so I knew English wasn't the only language spoken at home. Seeming to hold his breath, he stammered, 'Let me sign out first. Then I'll follow you home.' I could feel his hard chest under the coat. He must pump iron regularly. I wondered his age as I stood up from his lap and strolled to a nearby table and chairs.

As I waited, I dug in my purse until I located the spearmint Chapstick and coated my mouth, smacking my lips and rubbing them together. I tucked my hair behind my ear, letting the ends fall to my collarbone, and watched as people passed me on their journey to a chosen store. The smell of cranberry, nutmeg, and pine wafted from the holiday store while I pondered my plan and wiped the corners of my mouth with a finger. As I crossed and uncrossed my legs, I thought about finally releasing myself of the good-girl persona and how my life was about to change forever.

When he returned from the back room, I studied him more intently as he was better-looking than I had at first suspected. He'd taken off the beard, suit, hat, and clunky black boots to reveal a Chippendale's dream body dressed in blue jeans and a snug-fitting T-shirt. I couldn't believe my luck. Obviously, the portly exterior had just been a façade, and what I saw instead was a firm, toned, athletic farmworker's body that called to me like a siren's song. My wish really had come true, and it took some serious willpower to not attack him on the spot.

'Shall we go?' he asked while offering me his arm.

After bursting through my apartment door and telling Luis I'd be right back, I made a beeline for the bathroom, where I used the toilet and stared at myself in the mirror, giving myself a pep talk. I was about to have sex for the first time. Sex. S-E-X. 'You're about to have sex with a guy who looks like he belongs on a magazine cover,' I told the mirror. I stared at the Eva Mendes mole on my upper-right cheek and at my stormy blue eyes staring back at me and ran my fingers through my blonde hair before grabbing my toothbrush and giving my teeth a quick clean.

'Can I offer you something to drink?' I asked when I got back to the kitchen. 'We have water and juice.'

'Just water,' he said.

After pouring from the jug in the refrigerator, I moved to the sofa with his glass and patted the cushion beside me, requesting he join me. When Luis sat close enough, we proceeded to kiss softly and slowly while touching each other's body. He seemed so strong, so beautifully put together. The tight-fitting jeans and snug T-shirt displayed his muscles perfectly, and I couldn't help but touch them through the cloth. His hard chest and strong thighs against my palm made me giddy.

The kisses were getting more intense and our breathing heavier. Threading his fingers through my hair, he cupped the back of my head and pulled me to his mouth, lightly licking and nibbling on my lower lip. His own lips were so soft and warm, and I was easily lost in a romantic embrace. I felt like I was back in high school making out on my parents' couch, kissing his lips and throat hungrily.

When the situation progressed quite rapidly and he wiggled his fingers under my sweater, I stopped suddenly and grabbed his hand, giving it a tug and leading him down the hall to my bedroom where I flipped back the beautiful floral Laura Ashley comforter, revealing the 650 thread-count sheets that had been a gift from my parents last year. Then I reached for the open package sitting on my dresser beside the bed.

'How about a fashion show?' He nodded as I reached

into it. 'I bought some things today, and you can tell me whether or not you like them.' I felt myself getting stronger. Now that he was here, I felt like a superhero, and I was ready to don my costume. Why I hadn't done this before is beyond me. I'm sure plenty of men would have gladly taken Luis's place, but I was extremely glad to have found a hunky man to fill that position by sheer luck instead.

Removing my belt, unbuttoning my jeans, and kicking off my shoes, I blew upwards at the stray hairs that hung in my face, and as I crossed my arms over my front to pull my sweater off over my head, Luis moved to the side of the bed and stared. I started humming Christmas songs to break the silence and to comfort me, and for some reason I cupped and lifted my breasts in their bra before reaching around the back to unclasp and shrug out of it. This gave me more reason to fondle them and caress their smooth, creamy texture prior to stuffing them into another bra – a black push-up number. Unzipping and dropping my jeans, I continued to strip, even removing the satiny bikini panties that were my last proof of modesty.

Luis gazed at me from the edge of the bed while I slipped out of my remaining clothes and slid on the long boots, zipping them up my legs, which only accentuated the white skin above the shiny vinyl tops. Then I put on the suit. No panties. He gasped, leaning toward me closely and whispering, '*Ay, Dios mio!*' as he reached out to stroke an uncovered upper thigh.

'I don't know what to say, Margarita. You look like a Christmas present, and I would love to unwrap you,' he said. His foreign tongue thrilled me, and I was both apprehensive and aroused, both tight with anticipation and dripping with desire.

I tentatively reached out to touch his chest and dragged

my hand down his belly, and silently told myself not to treat this as a movie, not to treat Luis like an actor bent on bringing me to the highest heights. For all I knew he was as inexperienced as me and did not deserve such expectations. While he ran his palm up my booted leg and touched his fingers to my inner thigh, I trembled and even wrestled with the idea of calling the whole thing off, but I had come this far and nothing was going to stop me.

He lifted the hem of my suit and breathed '*Quiero tocarte*' as he fingered his way up to my moist pussy lips. His dark eyes got darker still as he placed his hands around my waist. '*Poca cintura*,' he muttered. It's true. I do have a tiny waist. '*Perfecto para agarrar*.' He circled my waist with his hands then dropped a palm to an ass cheek. After massaging it, he squeezed it firmly and pulled me to him, looking into my eyes. '*Quiero besarte*.' Leaning toward me and closing the distance between us, he barely touched his lips to mine, slowly increasing the pressure until both sets parted and our tongues slowly danced the tango, returning to devouring each other. He kissed along my throat, all the while keeping a hand on my body by running a palm up my leg.

After rapidly stripping, he kissed the swell of each of my breasts in turn, while stroking my thigh. Lightly running his fingers up my leg to that V under my belly and lifting his eyes to meet mine, he spoke more strongly. '*Quiero comerte*.' My Spanish vocabulary consisted of words I'd learned in high school, but I very much understood what he was saying as he pressed me to the bed and proceeded to place a hand on each leg and his lips on my inner thigh, kissing me in a trail up to my intimate area, which made me gasp and tense because it was so foreign to me to have someone's face there.

When I relaxed, he gently licked along the seam,

opening me with his tongue, after which he sucked each of the fleshy lips and very delicately made slow circles and figure-eights around my swelling clit. While holding me down to the bed and spreading my legs, he very lightly stroked with his tongue and continued to do so until I writhed beneath him, my arousal inching its way upwards. His lack of urgency released any pressure I felt about what to expect, and by the time he spread my legs with his knees, clothed his hard cock with a condom, and approached my entrance with the tip, I was ready to beg him to take me.

So that I wouldn't be alarmed at seeing a real, flesh-and-blood cock, I had purchased some magazines featuring nude males a month ago, but those images didn't match up to the real thing. What you see in the magazines is clean-shaven. Reality has much more hair – Luis had much more hair. Both his chest and crotch sprouted a thick, dark forest when all of his garments were removed, making me doubly aware of what we were about to do.

However, that didn't matter. When I saw him unroll the condom onto his firm dick, I was prepared and aroused by his confidence and sexiness. I could smell him. He smelled like a man, and it made it so much easier to desire him. While keeping the boots on, I slowly unbuckled the black belt of my suit, awaiting his approach.

Flipping open my suit, he caressed my body all the way down to the top of my boots, all the time making appreciative noises. He made me feel beautiful. While he gently squeezed my breasts, teasing each nipple with a finger till they were erect peaks, he very slowly climbed on top of me, getting on all fours above me before pushing my legs wider and slowly inserting the tip of his cock and lowering his body. The weight of him was indescribable and made me pant with need. His bare, hairy chest pressing against mine spurred me on so that I wriggled under him as the head of his cock gradually pushed through the entrance. The pleasure took over, and his slow pumping, with a finger constantly teasing my clit drove me crazy.

As he gradually pushed in further, it felt as if my body were swallowing him completely. It was amazing, really. Because his tempo was so slow and gradual, I wanted to pull him to me, imploring him to give me what I deserved. He felt so big inside me, filling me up, and the pressure made it seem like I was stretching widely around him, like I was hugging him tightly. Then, every time I lifted my hips, grinding his groin against my clit, I could feel myself getting closer and closer to climax.

The continual attention to my clit and his easy thrusting brought on a steady climb of arousal, and, eventually, he coaxed an orgasm from my body – the pleasure spread until I tensed my legs and the fireworks burst behind my eyes. It was the first orgasm I had ever experienced aside from by my own hand, and I couldn't believe it. I couldn't have asked for a better first time. I had heard so many horror stories, so I was prepared for the frustration and disappointment that many women experience. Coming with a cock inside me that first time wasn't something I had been expecting, so I knew the experience was a memory to treasure.

That was the first day of Christmas, and although Luis was not my true love, he was quite an amusing and pleasant toy, and because the first day was somewhat awkward, we decided to make the next 11 a lot more exciting by planning a buffet of sexual pleasures once we figured out our schedule a couple days later. I was 19, and now my adventure had begun, I wanted it to continue.

Once we resolved to enjoy our very own Twelve Days of Christmas, the days flowed into each other, one after the other, with Luis returning each time to fulfil a new fantasy. The second day found me on all fours so he could ride me doggie style and the third had us testing different styles of kissing – French kissing in a French maid outfit was definitely new. The fourth day was a fun day of phone sex, me rolling around the bed nude, cell phone on my ear and my hand between my legs; the fifth, experimenting with different toys, including a cock ring; the sixth, skinny-dipping at my apartment pool when no one was looking; seventh, joint masturbation; eighth, dirty dancing and me riding on top; and we tried anal sex on the ninth day with a whole lot of lube. A blowjob, a threesome, and drumming on my ass with a spanking finished off our set with the last day again including my Santa outfit and the boots.

By the time we finished our string of sexual delicacies, I was ready for Luis's broken English to tell me he was done. An evening of regular vanilla sex in the missionary position on my queen-sized bed was a breath of fresh air. Even his request that I wear the suit and boots seemed normal to me, and I was happy to do it. I sighed and chuckled, 'You know, it's really amazing how far I think I've come.'

I could hear him mumble 'And how often …' which only made me smile more.

Freeing my silky pillow from my clutches as I stretch out across my bed, I realise I now feel comfortable in my own skin and at ease sharing my bed with a man. When I think how naïve I was, how nervous about sex, and all of that just a short time ago, I find the whole thing comical and can't help but laugh as I wrap myself up in Luis's warm arms.

'You're so wonderful,' I hum into his shoulder, grazing it with my teeth as he caresses the skin along my thigh.

I roll to the side and prop myself up on my elbow, facing him as he continues to stroke my hip and the dip in my waist.

'What's so funny?' He presses his lips to mine, and I smile underneath the kiss.

'I was laughing because I thought maybe it was time for some virgin margaritas.' I continue to chuckle and meet his eyes with mine.

'Oh, I think we're well past that now, Margarita.'

Willing Spirit, Hungry Flesh
An Erotic Ghost Story for Christmas
by Demelza Hart

An isolated, timeworn house just outside a small moorland village. Christmas Eve. And it was snowing.

As far as Emma Padmore was concerned, she couldn't have asked for more.

Christmas was normally spent at home in London: party after party, one-night stands, an endless hangover. Not this year.

This was how she wanted it. Alone. No parties. And no sex. Now that *would* be different – and taking herself off to a remote Yorkshire village seemed the only way to ensure it. Now a successful editor in her late twenties, she could do without the haze of fast living. It would be tough, but she would go without sex for three days this Christmas. That was the plan, anyway.

But on arriving at the dark and oppressive house she'd rented half a mile outside the nearest village, Emma was suddenly unsure. It seemed lifeless, unnerving, and she almost turned around and left before even stepping foot into the place. But, not one to be defeated, Emma pushed open the heavy door and, once inside, despite her misgivings, was reassured that she'd made the right decision. The house immediately seemed to welcome her.

She'd loaded her MP3 player with carols and had even

brought along a small tree and some fairy lights. After lighting a fire, she put on the carols and happily set about decorating. Emma surveyed the twinkling scene with a satisfied smile. Yes, this was the Christmas she'd been longing for.

Later, she walked the half-mile into the near-deserted village. She approached the pub, not that the ramshackle old inn looked very inviting against the cold, darkening sky. Still, she would give it a try.

'Hi there,' she beamed when inside, but was met by only a glower from the taciturn landlord. The gloom wasn't even relieved by the comfortingly annoying refrain of *Merry Xmas Everybody*. The only other drinkers were a morose pair of elderly men, their faces as wrinkled as the shrivelled sprigs of holly over the bar. They barely registered the attractive, slim brunette ordering a drink. 'Dry white wine, please.'

This was poured without a word by the landlord.

'Ready for Christmas?' she tried again. He grunted. 'I'm in Lane's End House for the next few days. Thought I'd pop in for a quick drink.'

The landlord at last fixed her with his eyes. 'Lane's End, eh? There's a curious thing.'

'Why's that?'

'It's not often that people stay there, especially over Christmas.'

An expectant shiver ran over Emma's skin. 'Oh?'

The landlord leaned towards her, his eyes narrowing malevolently – clearly, he was trying to intimidate her. 'It was derelict for years and years. Then some rich boy from London bought it and made it habitable, only to rent it out, of course – never lives there himself. You see, they say it's haunted … especially at Christmas.'

Emma suppressed the urge to laugh out loud; she

didn't believe in anything remotely ghostlike. But she would not miss a moment of drama. 'Well, nothing like a spooky Yuletide thrill – tell me more.'

The landlord now spoke in a low whisper. 'Back during the First World War, Christmas of 1914, the pretty young woman who lived at Lane's End was expecting her soldier husband to return on leave. Fine man – officer, he was. He'd sent a letter telling her he was coming and would be back on Christmas Eve but –' the man's wizened face darkened '– he never came. A blizzard blew in, and she waited and waited. She cooked the goose and hung the mistletoe. But the presents stayed unopened and the Christmas dinner grew cold. A few days later she received a letter telling her he'd been killed in No Man's Land just before setting off on leave. She didn't stay round here – she left and married someone else.'

'So is it her ghost which haunts the house?'

'Hers? Oh no, not hers.' He turned away. 'I'm closing early. Finish up.'

Far from her blood running cold, excitement instead coursed through Emma, compelling her to return quickly to the house. After throwing the rest of her wine down, she wished the men Merry Christmas – they didn't return the greeting – and hurried back. The snow was falling more thickly now, and forming a downy white covering on the freezing ground. She glanced up, letting the soft flakes land with feathery touches on her tingling skin.

She had left a light on and was glad of it; a blizzard was stirring. Emma rushed inside and leaned back against the closed door with a smile. *A haunted house at Christmas.* Better and better. She glanced around. The old building certainly had something intangible about it. But her fairy lights and tree gave it a cosiness which calmed and entranced her. She loved it. *If there is indeed a ghost, bring it on.*

Emma looked out at the snowstorm as it swirled pale against the dark of night. The wind railed around the isolated building and she shut the curtains against it. After locking the door, she put on her carols and nestled down on the sofa with a glass of wine and a book.

'This is the truth sent from above ...' The warming tones of the choir of King's College, Cambridge combined with the alcohol and lulled her. The wind continued to howl outside. Time slowed.

Bang! Bang!

Emma sat straight up, eyes wide, mind alert. Someone was knocking on the door. Surely not. She tried to ignore it. It must have been the wind.

Bang! Bang! Bang!

No. That was a knock, loud and insistent. *Shit.* Who the hell could it be? Should she answer? It could be one of the men from the pub; she cursed herself for telling the landlord where she was staying. But in this storm, someone may be in trouble. Picking up a fire iron for safety's sake, she walked to the door and, with a breath of resolve, unlocked it and opened it an inch.

There was indeed someone outside. Huddled against the cold with a large woollen coat clasped about him stood a man, tall, braced against the blizzard.

His eyes were the first thing she noticed. They shone out with depth and intensity, piercing through the stormy gloom. For a moment she was too dumbstruck to act. This was certainly no man from the pub; the person now standing before her was altogether much younger and immeasurably better looking. And, bestowing her with the most mesmerising smile, he spoke.

'I'm back. I've come home.'

And suddenly it was as if she was expecting him.

Losing her senses, Emma instinctively pulled open the door and let the fire iron fall from her grasp with a clatter. The man stepped in, his boot-clad feet stomping off the cold and snow.

Emma stared, immobile. Running his hands through thick, dark-blond hair and shaking out the snow, the visitor turned to face her. And then he too simply stared. He was searching her face, her own wonder reflected in his. His lips curled up into an intrigued smile and he took a step closer.

'Remarkable,' he murmured, his eyes still taking in every detail of her.

Emma felt her face flushing and a heat stirring in her belly. Did she know this man? *No.* Emma knew she had never before seen him until this moment and yet already a curious force seemed to connect them. It was as if she was meeting a long-lost friend. And now, still staring intently at her, he let his face break into another captivating smile. *God, he was gorgeous.* Emma drew in a deep breath. 'Sorry, but … who are you?'

His eyes sparkled with mirth. Holding his arms to the side, open and giving, he stated, 'I'm Harry. And this is my home.'

The owner of a property was allowed to inspect it, she supposed, although this seemed an odd time to do it. But this owner had a rich, honeyed voice, stunning eyes and a belly-churning smile. She wasn't complaining. Extending her hand, she said, 'And I'm Emma.'

His eyes closed, just for a moment, and he smiled to himself. 'Of course.'

'Excuse me?' Her brows creased in confusion.

'No, it's … Never mind.' Harry shook himself out of his reverie and took her hand in warm, strong fingers. 'Hello … Emma.'

She didn't want him to let go. The heat from his hand was flowing down to pulse unremittingly in her core, right between her legs.

'Perhaps we should close the door,' he smirked, finally withdrawing his hand.

With a laugh of embarrassment she did so quickly, shutting out the raging night.

Harry removed his coat with a sigh of relief. Underneath he wore a woollen suit with a rounded collar. The style struck Emma as being somewhat antiquated. Still, it suited him. Very much so. His height was matched by broad shoulders and a firm waist. Her eyes dropped further to glance between his legs. *Shit. She really should try not to do that.*

'A drink is in order, don't you agree?' His voice lilted with the mellow tones of a well-bred Englishman. Before she could answer, he strode across to a cupboard she hadn't noticed before and took out a bottle of brandy. Harry poured them both a glass and turned to offer her one. 'Sit down, Emma.' He smiled again. *Was it possible to come just from someone smiling at you?*

Harry drank long from his glass, sucking the amber liquid through his teeth and letting his head fall back. His eyes closed. 'Home at last. *At last.*'

'Don't you normally live here?'

He looked to her with a smirk. 'Not exactly.'

'Have you been away?'

'Something like that.'

'Whereabouts?'

'Oh … here and there.'

He joined her on the sofa. Again, she noted his clothes. They were made of fine cotton and wool but seemed to be hand-stitched and lacked any discernible brand labels, something she was unused to seeing. She recalled the words of the landlord: *'It's haunted ... especially at Christmas.'* She took a large gulp of brandy.

'So, er ... Harry ... what do you do for a living?'

He held her eyes but paused before answering, as if sensing her confusion, 'Army. I'm a captain in His Majesty's Royal Dragoons.'

His Majesty's? Her breath was held. *What was it the landlord had said?* The woman's husband had been due home on Christmas Eve but had been killed just before leaving and never made it back. Emma took an even larger swig of brandy.

She glanced over at him again. His cheekbones were high and his blue eyes alight. He had the smoothest skin she had seen on a man. And his handshake had been warm and strong and very real. She didn't believe in ghosts. *She really didn't.* And ghosts certainly didn't look like this. But whoever this man was, he was certainly real enough at this moment. She couldn't take her eyes off him.

Harry exhaled slowly. 'Christmas Eve.' His face was solemn now, etched with a deeper need. 'I've been away a very long time, Emma. A very long and lonely time.'

His head rested back on the sofa, emphasising his firm jawline and straight nose. He was unfeasibly good-looking. But beyond that – he was right to be here, here and now. Had they truly only just met? It was as if she had known him a lifetime, as if he had indeed returned, not only to his house, but to her. They sat contentedly, drinking brandy, barely talking, but a tranquility settled between them.

His hand was resting beside hers. She reached across and touched his little finger tenderly. 'No one should be alone at Christmas if they don't want to be.'

'I've been alone for many, many Christmases.'

She stroked his finger. 'You're not alone now.'

He smiled, softly this time, and then, his eyes not leaving her, he raised his hand and smoothed over her face. 'You are so very beautiful, Emma ...'

And with no hesitation, as if with a lover of many years standing, Emma turned her head and kissed his hand. 'Welcome home, Harry,' she breathed against it.

And it was sealed. He leaned in and kissed her. Immediately, she felt him energised and alive. Opening her mouth with his, he slipped in his tongue. She met it with hers and for a while they simply enjoyed the delicious intimacy of a long, deep kiss. But need asserted itself and, holding her head hard, he moved his mouth to her ear. 'I've waited so long, waited so long for you.'

If his words made little sense, she didn't notice or care.

'I'm here. I want you.' *And God yes, she did, more than anything.*

'If I start this, I can't stop,' he slurred as his hands moved to her buttons.

'Then don't stop.'

And he was kissing her again, devouring and desperate. Whoever he was, whatever he was, it didn't matter. Reason faded and Harry grew more and more real. Emma's shirt was soon off and, after a quick unhooking of her bra, her breasts were naked. With a moan of anticipation, he dropped his head and took a nipple hard in his mouth.

Oh, he was not going to go easy. He tugged and laved the nipple almost brutally as his fingers plied her breast. *Fuck, that was sweet.* Desperate to reveal his body, her fingers skittered over his clothes.

His mouth continued to assault one nipple, and his fingers tugged at the other, pulling and pinching. 'Oh God, that's good, that's so good,' she whimpered.

He broke away, dragging his mouth up over her neck.

212

'Do you like that? Tell me what you like. I want you. I want all of you, you beautiful, perfect creature.'

'Fuck, Harry, let me see you. I want your body on me, in me. Oh, fuck, hurry.'

By now, she was tearing at his clothes, and he chuckled as he stood up to strip them off. 'Interesting choice of words for a lady.'

'Oh, I'm only a lady when it matters. Hurry. I want your cock.'

He smirked, that same delicious smile which had sealed her lust as soon as she'd seen him, and unbuttoned his trousers. Before he had time to pull them down, she was on her knees, reaching in for his already rigid cock. It lurched out hard and high. *To hell with a sex-free Christmas.* She should have known it would be impossible, although she'd never imagined the opportunity would present itself quite this way. Giving him a teasing grin, she closed her mouth around the rock-hard shaft.

'Bloody hell!' Harry's face creased as he was racked with pleasure, prompting him to clasp his hands in her hair. Emma was already lost in his glorious cock; she feasted on it, her tongue twirling and licking long and hard before dipping into the slit to gather up the constant drip of clear salty pleasure. Warm, lust-driven saliva poured down the shaft; she gripped and pumped him as his leg muscles clenched in anticipation. But then she changed tack, opening her mouth and throat and sinking over him, deeper and deeper until her eyes watered.

'Damn it, that's incredible. Bloody incredible.'

With a gasp she pulled back at last, holding the man in her thrall, relishing the push of cock at the back of her throat. Still he held her head, watching with bleary eyes and ragged breath as she fucked him beautifully with her mouth. Emma continued, sometimes taking him so deep

213

that his balls bobbed on her chin, sometimes teasing with the very tip of her tongue. But, at length, she gave him his finish, holding his balls tight in one hand, gripping his length in the other, and sucking on his cockhead with hungry fervour.

'It's there, it's there. Move back or I'll come off in your mouth.'

She broke away only to demand, 'Do it.'

And so he did. With a slow grunt of pure release, he burst thick and long onto her tongue. After a lazy smile, she swallowed, relishing his taste as it slid warm into her.

Harry collapsed onto the sofa, utterly spent. 'Now, that is a homecoming.'

'Oh, I'm only just warming up. And to think that I vowed not to have sex this Christmas.'

'We can stop if you want,' he grinned.

'Don't you bloody dare.'

'In that case …' He stood, pulling her with him, and dragged her up the stairs to the bedroom, knowing exactly where to go. By the time they reached the room, the rest of their clothes had been shed.

Emma took a moment to absorb the impressive sight before her. *Weren't ghosts supposed to be translucent?* Whatever, this ghost had a fucking fine body, and right now it was approaching her. 'My turn,' he purred.

Before she knew it, Emma had been tossed onto the bed with her legs splayed wide, and Harry's head was poised between them. He parted her soaking pussy lips, exposing her clit for perfect precision, and brought his mouth down.

Who said sex was only invented in the 1960s? Emma's eyes glazed as she received the most outstanding pussy eating she could remember.

With two fingers hard up inside her, tapping with

blinding delirium on her g-spot, with his mouth sucking and lapping and delving at her clit and pussy, Emma was lost; her orgasm hurtled forward unstoppably. 'Fuck, I'm coming!' Pleasure shook her limbs, forcing out a wail.

He barely paused for breath. 'I'm taking you from behind. Kneel.'

If his dominance surprised her, she didn't question it. She wouldn't argue with this officer. Strong hands tugged her over and pushed her shoulders onto the bed, propelling her arse high in the air.

She could hear his breathing, rapid and fast behind her, and the slicking of his hand over his cock as he primed it for entry. 'It's going to be hard and fast this time, Emma. I can't hold back.'

'Just fuck me.'

Gripping her hips hard in his hands, Harry positioned his cock and thrust. The air was expelled from her with a grunt. He had filled her to the hilt in one go, forcing her into the pillows. 'Do it again.'

He did. Pulling back, almost falling out, he ploughed back into her with a primal moan. 'Hell, you're tight. Fuck! That is glorious!'

Emma grinned. Even if he was an Edwardian officer and a gentleman, she could still break his composure.

Harry now set about a steady fucking, ploughing his cock in and out of her hungry cunt with regular and certain conviction. He was big. She could feel her walls stretching with each push. But he moved in her perfectly, coaxing her g-spot with the ample head of his shaft. She reached back, slowing him to nudge it again. 'There. Just there.' And reading her body and her need perfectly, he eased his strokes and nuzzled her with his cockhead. Emma released a stifled sigh. When he reached under to stroke her clit, she was ready to come again.

He slowed his pace. 'Tell me.'

'Tell you what?' she moaned, so ready to shatter, so wanting it.

'Tell me when it happens. Tell me how you feel.'

'Oh fuck, Harry. Put it all in me again. Want your whole cock filling me. Hard, hard, *hard, please.*'

He inhaled violently through his nose and pulled out only to shove his entire length brutally up into her. 'Like that?' he hissed through gritted teeth.

'Yes!' It was a sob more than anything.

He went at her, a blur, deep and hard and long each time, his broad girth stretching the soaked flesh of her cunt. Out to leave her craving more, then in again, filling, cramming her with hard, hot man-flesh.

'Ooh …' If he was expecting words, he was to be disappointed. Her skin was cast with a conspiracy of heat and ice, so ready for another hard orgasm to grab and shake and leave her useless. That's what she wanted, to be fucked into oblivion. And so far, this man, sent from his own oblivion, was doing just that.

'Tell me,' he insisted.

With a supreme effort, she managed to voice her feelings. 'Cock – in me – so good, so close – your cock, full – oh fuck, *oh fuck.*' There it was. The rise before the fall. One more thrust, one more flick of her clit. 'Coming!' This time she screamed. Even if her declaration was lost in her cry, her orgasm squeezed his cock like nothing before. Harry laughed triumphantly as her flesh gripped him, tight and succulent. He carried on plucking her clit and managed to eke her come out so that she was left a juddering, blissful wreck.

'Oh, you are a beauty. Now take it. *Fuck!*' His head was thrown back, and, still driving into her with frantic determination and force, he exploded, filling her with come, each deep burst accompanied by a guttural groan.

They lay blearily afterwards, the intensity of their coupling staggering them both.

'Oh my God,' she panted, staring at the ceiling blindly. 'Bloody hell, Harry. I can't remember a Christmas Eve like this before.'

He turned to her with a smile, his face damp with perspiration, his breathing heavy. 'Don't you have a husband or a sweetheart?'

A sweetheart? The archaic term was ridiculously endearing. 'No. None of my – *sweethearts* – have proved to be very sweet or to have much heart.'

'I'm sorry.' He stroked her hair. 'Where do you live, Emma?'

'London. I'm an editor for a large publishing house.'

He raised his eyebrows, clearly impressed.

'What? Don't seem so surprised.'

'Forgive me. I forget that I have been a little ... removed from developments.' She didn't question his meaning.

'Have you always been in the army?'

He sighed ruefully. 'No. I was a writer. Quite successful. I moved up here for peace and inspiration.'

'There isn't much peace in the army.'

'No.' His face grew pale and distant, and Emma felt a sudden stabbing at her heart. Tears pricked her eyes and she turned away. Soon enough he was kissing over her arm, stroking her thigh, soothing away her grief. She allowed it and desire rapidly overcame her once more. 'Want you, want you here.'

'Yes, yes, my sweet, sweet Emma.' Their mouths met again, and, after a fearsome kiss, his eyes held a brutal certainty which almost unnerved her. But she had seen that look in a man's eyes before, and she knew to encourage it.

Reaching behind for the iron bars of the bedhead, she clasped them tight. 'Take me. Tie me.'

He needed no more. Harry stood quickly and paced around the room, gathering belts and ties.

Determination now darkened his handsome face as he reached up and coiled his tie around her wrists and the iron posts, tying her fast. She tugged against it, only to cause her cunt to throb.

'You're mine. You're tied to me here. Know it.' His smooth voice was laced with sinister intent.

'Yes, oh fuck, you're making me drip for you, Harry. God, I want it all.'

He slipped down the bed and took hold of her right ankle, tying it to the bottom right bedpost before repeating his actions on the left. Her legs were splayed and her sex exposed. Bound tight, Emma could only moan; her cunt was alight, desperate for touch, desperate for fingers, mouth, cock, anything he'd give her.

Three fingers were soon inside. He leaned over and took a nipple in his mouth while his hand pumped her pussy. If he had been rough before he was even more so now. After sucking the taut flesh so that it was red and hard and long she felt a sharper pang. She glanced down; his teeth were closing on her nipple amidst a wicked grin. Emma cried out, prompted by pain but propelled by pleasure. Her head thrashed from side to side and she demanded him. 'God, that's too fucking good. Fuck me now. Please, please, you bastard, give me your cock.'

'Oh no ... if I learned one thing from that bloody war it was patience. Something you can clearly learn now.' He took a silk scarf and fastened it around her mouth, gagging her. A moan of need was muffled thick in it.

Restraining her desire as surely as her bonds restrained

her body, she let him do as he would. She lay there, God knows how long, while his tongue and lips and teeth and hands explored and prodded and stroked and plucked and bit and licked and adored her. Sometimes as soft as a feather, tickling and teasing, sometimes hard and sharp to send gorgeous shards of pain to prick at her. He held her constantly on the brink of orgasm until her body was not her own. She lived simply to come, and when she did, she wondered if she would survive it.

Finally, he leaned over her, his cock dripping unstoppably onto her taut belly, and readied himself. Harry, close and hot, whispered, 'I'm coming home, Emma. Release me.'

And he eased in. She was so wet that at first he slid through with barely any resistance, but his tremendous size soon registered as she stretched to accommodate him again. A low groan of deepest satisfaction caught in her gag.

He moved almost tenderly now, low over her, and when he noted her eyes flaring and her breath coming in ragged pulls, he released the gag and let her come. Emma wailed, bucking and straining against her bonds futilely; they only reinforced the pleasure which ripped through her, feeding off the hard cock impaled in her. Only then did Harry release, come shooting hard into her in long, explosive bursts.

Their bodies limp, he untied her bindings silently, curled his limbs around her, and together they fell asleep.

Emma awoke to distant church bells. Christmas Day. At first her mind tricked her. Perhaps she had dreamed the whole thing. Perhaps she would turn and find him gone, a mere figment of her imagination. But then a strong arm curled around her, and she smiled. *No.* Still here.

Emma turned and planted a kiss on his lips. 'Happy

Christmas.'

'And to you.'

'Do you want to do anything special? Go out?'

Harry smiled softly. 'I can't leave this house.'

She nodded, understanding. They spent the morning in bed, their bodies constantly touching and joining. At noon she managed to tear herself away; she'd brought a small turkey joint to roast and enjoyed preparing Christmas lunch her way.

It was the loveliest Christmas meal she could remember, shared with a long-dead soldier in a snowbound Yorkshire house. Harry was content – beyond content, she could see that – but there was a shift as the day progressed. They returned to bed, but their lovemaking was now contemplative.

As midnight approached, he turned to her, his face serious, his eyes fading. 'I have to go now.' With a soft smile, she nodded. Harry pushed himself heavily from the bed and began to dress.

'But you'll be back next year?'

He smiled remorsefully. 'No, Emma. I have waited so long for this – for *you*. And you have released me. You let me in. After so long, I came home. Now I can move on – I *must* move on. And, as much as it pains me, you cannot come where I have to go.'

Tears formed in her eyes, hot and heavy, as she got up and moved to him. 'Harry, I won't forget you. I won't ever forget you.'

'Go and live, Emma. Promise me that.'

She nodded. He kissed her so passionately she had to cling to him not to stumble. Then he turned and paced quickly downstairs. Emma followed. The blizzard had slackened, but there was still a thick white fog which hung about the house. Harry opened the door and looked out. Turning back, he took her head in his hands and bent for the sweetest final kiss before whispering against her lips, 'Goodbye, Emma. It could only be you. Thank you.'

She could barely speak. 'Goodbye.'

And after one last smile, he walked out and was swallowed up into the fog.

The weather cleared almost immediately. Despite missing him, Emma was content. *Perhaps she did believe in ghosts. Just a little.*

The next day, Boxing Day, she ventured into the village. This time the pub was full of people in festive mood. Even the morose landlord managed a smile. 'You survived, then?'

'Apparently so. Dry white, please.'

He reached for the bottle. 'Anything go bump in the night?'

'Only things I wanted to go bump in the night,' she smirked. 'Did you survive the blizzard?'

He looked at her shiftily. 'What blizzard?'

'From Christmas Eve until last night – there was a terrible snowstorm. Couldn't go outside.'

He frowned. 'Apart from a bit of light snow, the weather here's been fine.' He turned to a man sitting near them at the bar and, gesturing at Emma, chuckled, 'Sounds like someone's been enjoying the mulled wine!'

'But I –' She stopped herself and instead took a drink. Nothing surprised her now. 'What did the soldier who lived in Lane's End House do before the war?'

'Author – he was a writer of some kind. Waste of talent when he was killed, like so many. The story's been passed down to us all. Apparently, he comes home every Christmas Eve to his wife, but as she buggered off after his death, there's no one to let him in, and so his ghost wanders around outside, a lost soul at Christmas.'

'Can you remember his name?'

'Captain Henry Hawkesford. But he was always known as Harry.'

Emma's stomach tightened. 'And what was his wife called?'

'What was it again? Can't think off-hand. There's a picture of her in the village hall. Looked a fair bit like you, come to think of it.'

Smiling softly to herself, Emma headed for a table. 'Don't worry about the name.'

'Hang on. I've got it now. His wife's name was Emma.'

Her smile deepened. 'I thought it might be. Oh, and … I don't think the house is haunted – not any more.'

A Christmas Confession
by Tinker Crowley

Dear Santa Claus,

I hope you are well and getting plenty of rest in the run-up to what promises to be the "hardest" night of the year. Fingers crossed all of your little helpers are busy beavering away, so that on Christmas morning there'll be a satisfied smile on everyone's face.

But Santa, I have a confession to make.

I know you said that I must try to be better this year, and that you'll be watching in case I do anything that's too naughty to deserve even an inkling of the pleasure that you share. But I'm afraid temptation has been far too testing for me since you last came, and at times, I fear, I have been a very, very, very, bad girl.

It's hard to pinpoint every single fall from grace but I know you saw at least one of my indiscretions. I felt you watching me. I knew then that it was wrong, but as you witnessed, I was unable to resist the lure of his rigid length.

I didn't intend to, Santa – I *promise* I didn't – but it was as if just his glance alone was enough to juice me up to the point of premature climax. The blueness of his eyes penetrated me; they plunged and probed just as hard and

223

as deep as the long, thick girth of his fingers in my pussy. It was as if he had me hypnotised. I was engulfed by the desire to feel him inside me – every single inch of him.

I had started off so well that day too. My assignment on *Romeo and Juliet* was due to be handed in the following week, and I was determined to please my college professor with the thoroughness of my analysis.

That's how I came to be sitting across the library from *him*. It was creeping towards the early hours of the morning. You know how I love to study at that time of night. Nine times out of ten no one is there but me and the night clerk. That night was the exception, of course.

There has always been the appeal of the silence and isolation that such a place at that hour brings with it; the smell of the wooden benches, worn smooth from the generations of scholars that had sat, studying in solitude, before me. The faint aroma of dust from the rows of anthologies, books and journals that line the darkened avenues, bound in leather. The dim glow from the individual desk lamps like tiny flickers of candlelight illuminating the pages before me. My brunette hair was piled high on top of my head in a tumbled twist. Loose tendrils tickled the back of my neck and the dark rims of my spectacles were perched, just slightly, toward the end of my nose. I was frowning in deep concentration, sucking absent-mindedly on the end of my pen when I sensed his gaze scan over me, seemingly assessing every curve and every gesture I made.

I stiffened as I dared to meet his stare. It was unlike anything that I had ever experienced before. With one look he had me mesmerised. His eyes were on me, watching me intently. His perfect lips were set in the slightest of smiles and the tip of his tongue occasionally moistened their very corner, teasingly gentle. I wanted to look away. His attention unsettled me and yet I was powerless.

Your words of caution rang in my ear. 'I'm gonna find out who's naughty and nice, Roxy!' But their meaning was momentarily lost as I felt the telltale heat of my moistening underwear begin to betray me.

The bare skin around my neck and cleavage began to flush crimson as he drew me deeper and deeper into his sapphire glare. Then I noticed his hands. He was using one of them – well, one finger – to stroke the sensitive area of skin below his mouth with featherlike intimacy – in just the way I knew he would slowly encircle the hood of my clit and the smoothness of my wetness if given the chance. The other was hidden from view, but I knew at once where it was as I saw the subtle movement of his upper arm rising and falling rhythmically as he held my attention. I remained unresponsive, or so I thought at first, but it soon became clear from his sudden, toothy flash of a smile that he knew I'd clocked him … and it pleased him.

I know I should have been appalled, Santa. I know that I should have been disgusted, that I should have raised the alarm at what this beast was enticing me into. My body and brain, however, seemed to react in the very opposite way, as if they had been programmed to do so. Instead of being outraged by his actions, I was overwhelmed with the desire to take him, all of him, inside me right then and there and in any way he chose. In any hole, Santa.

You saw this in me didn't you? I could sense you there spectating, courting free will. You saw me fight the compulsion to reach down beneath my skirt and caress the slickened folds of my tight, eager pussy. You witnessed from afar my inability to break away from him. I wanted him, despite the fact that I didn't know who he was or why he had homed in on me, and I'm ashamed to say it, Santa, but for that moment, I didn't care.

Don't get me wrong, I'm no nympho. If it had been some dirty old man illicitly rubbing himself publicly over the sight of a vulnerable-looking me, I would have been sickened to my core; but this guy was different. He was the clichéd epitome of every fantasy I had ever had, all that and more personified. A part of me suspected I had fallen asleep and his presence was merely some horny dream, but alas it was not. His rugged complexion, the two-day growth of stubble that subtly masked his strong jawline, his tanned, toned arms, the tousled waves of his hair, they all pulled together into some sort of delectable, sexual jigsaw that I was impassioned to complete.

In the split second that followed, I seemed to compose myself, momentarily at least. In one sudden movement I stood up, but in my attempt to break the inappropriate tension between us, I clumsily knocked several reference books onto the floor. Instinctively, without thinking, I dropped to my knees to retrieve them, flustered. It was then that I saw it for the first time.

Under the table, I could view his actions more clearly. His cock was fully exposed. It was as impressive in girth as it was in length. I could tell he was throbbing for me from the shine of his skin, stretched taut by the inrush of blood beneath its surface, and by the broadness from his base to his glistening purple helmet. His veins jutted out like three-dimensional scribbles – scribbles that I wished to trace with the very tip of my tongue before devouring him deep into the back of my throat …

But, Santa, I didn't do it. I resisted. Believe me, Santa, I resisted. I wrenched myself away and tried not to acknowledge his laugh as I turned and walked determinedly towards the back of the library to hide from his obvious intentions. You see, I tried to be good. I wanted to please you. You'd always said that naughty girls wouldn't get what they wanted – my fear was that if I had stayed beneath that table, then what I "wanted" would not necessarily be something that could be wrapped in shimmering paper and adorned with a bow of ribbon.

My heart was racing. I could feel the deep burn of forbidden desire drilling the walls of my all-too-willing foo, but I found myself begging to ignore it. I put my forehead to the coolness of the shelves and inhaled deeply, scenting the musky undertones. I bit down hard on my bottom lip in an attempt to induce a contrasting pain that would divert the explosive feelings of longing in my loins. For a moment, it seemed to work. My breathing slowed and those internal fires mellowed. My nipples retracted from the softness of my bra and my inner stirrings momentarily ceased. I peeked through a gap in the woodwork to the station where we had been sitting, and saw that it was now completely vacant. He had gone.

In truth I was relieved, Santa; of course I was, but I feel I should also admit that a part of me *was* a little disappointed. You see, just because I *try* to be a good girl it doesn't mean that the minx inside me is forever completely at rest. She's my alter ego. A pest. She hides behind my timid, studious alias like some sort of sexual superhero. For the most part, she manages to lie low, usually for long enough to lull me into a false sense of my own restraint and decorum. Sometimes this continues for months at a time. But she never goes away all together. She lies in wait of a target she deems worthy then she is unleashed, for the purpose of temporary satisfaction, to settle her most primal of needs – to fuck.

With an element of calm restored, I straightened up and turned on my heel. I was set on leaving the library, Santa, I was going to head for the exit straight away, before the allure of what the stranger had been silently suggesting corrupted me further – but it was too late. He had followed me to my secluded spot.

I swiftly glanced around to see if anyone else was close by, if anyone else was aware of the predator advancing upon his submissive prey – me. I couldn't help it. I was pleased he had found me. Had my previous suspicion that he had disappeared proven to be true, I may have had a chance – I could have driven home at speed, squirming in the juices that had by now saturated every surface of my ripening peach. I could have hurriedly wrestled with my door key then, once inside my flat, have dropped onto the mat like a delivered letter. There I would have sought out the throbbing swell of my clitoris and pried apart the lips of my wetness, in order to rub and caress my sex to the point of toe-curling climax. But this stranger had other plans, and as a flexible girl, I was more than happy to adjust my schedule accordingly.

He smiled at me. 'Did you like what you saw?'

I could barely muster a nod. My eyes had already made their journey down from his muscular shoulders, to his ripped torso, to the bulbous swell barely restrained by his now buttoned flies. Please trust me, Santa, I had always believed that my willpower was impenetrable, but with this man in front of me, that belief was now in tatters and I was insistent that penetration was absolutely going to be permitted. Little Miss Minx was out!

'I thought you had run away,' I purred. 'I suspected that you were a man who just took matters "in hand" rather than follow them through with the actual goods.'

He smirked, then growled, 'Now how would that make me look?' As he spoke, his voice low, he backed me into the corner and reached for the sheer lapels of my blouse as his lips and tongue found mine. His confidence excited me. My breasts felt firm under his grasp as if they were challenging him to grope them harder through the material. He used the flats of his palms to circle them, moving the satin of my bra aside to free the hard brown nipples it had enclosed.

I reached for them too, unbuttoning myself to create as much access for him as possible. I took hold of his hands and guided them to my wanton flesh. He scooped my tits out of the cups and pushed them together, tweaking at the puckered nodules at the same time. His tongue slid down and lapped at their peaks, making me run my own over my lips. hoping to mirror what he would do to the quivering ache between my thighs. I could feel his erection against my pelvis. It was still under wraps, but his grinding conjured up a multitude of phallic pleasures in my mind's eye. As you will remember, Santa baby, I'm a sucker for a big dick, and this man was not going to disappoint – of that I was sure.

His hands began to travel south, towards my skirt, the hem of which had worked its way upwards to reveal the scant material that was scarcely sheathing my heat. His fingers gently worked at the elastic, threatening to delve frantically underneath and plunge into the hot pool of silken desire that lay in wait; but Little Minx wasn't ready to be finger-fucked just yet – not before she'd had a taste of what he had to offer.

I pushed him away, gasping. He stumbled against the opposite bookshelf but I was quick to steady him by targeting the buttons of his jeans. His flies parted under my sleight of hand and his cock sprang forth, his foreskin already pulled back as it struggled to contain his swollen helmet. Fast as a whippet, I was down on my knees sucking on him. It was obvious that his earlier fumblings had brought him very close to orgasm, as the sweet taste of precome glazed the head of his dick like a marinade of lust. However, the mere fact that he'd got a head start didn't mean I was going to let him finish first. He may have instigated the situation but I wasn't in the mood for playing the prissy little innocent he had singled me out to be. Choosy I might have been but I was no virgin.

I continued to work him until I could sense he was coming to a shuddering conclusion. His breath was now more audible and erratic and he seemed to be pulling away from me a little in an attempt to relieve the sensitivity that was threatening to prematurely end our unplanned clandestine liaison. I waited until I could feel him clench in readiness to ejaculate, then immediately straightened up, let go, and began to walk away, severing all contact. His eyes looked wild but needy. With one desperate glance, I could see that he was devastated that I had stopped, but intrigued that I was obviously still game.

Like a lust-struck puppy, he followed me to a desk that was hidden from the view of any late-night visitors who might happen along. Slowly, I bent over to peel off my panties and then hopped onto the polished wood. Invitingly, I spread my legs to exhibit the glistening folds of my juiced-up pussy – now there for his taking. I reclined onto my elbows so that I could maintain eye contact with him as he enthusiastically approached. His cock was still proud and hard, but he knew how to tease too; he could sense that I wanted him inside me but now that he'd found somebody willing to play, he was keen to stick to my rules as well as his own.

In a flash, he was down on me, licking my wetness in slow, firm strokes. It was obvious from his technique and the muffled groans that rumbled in his throat that he was a man who loved to dine out on cunt. He put his thumb on my clit and stretched me lengthways in order to extend and expose every inch of me, to tenderly lap at my sex, all the while circling the protruding nub that was crying out to be taken between his lips and sucked. His touch was electrifying. All too often, I'd had head delivered to me as if it was being performed with a sense of obligation, a tediously necessary milestone of foreplay before the giver would be permitted to ram home the headline act, but this was in another league altogether.

What he was doing to the exterior of my pussy had sent me into delectable throes of ecstasy – and now he added an internal pleasure-pain to the mix by sliding two fingers inside me. He curled them upwards to massage my g-spot, twisting them to make contact with every part of my inner dome. I cried out as his tongue finally reached my special place – I hadn't quite come but the feeling was so exquisite that the sound was spontaneous and unexpected. I had no control.

It was then that he withdrew his digits and thrust his cock into me with rough abandon. His thickness overwhelmed me, stretching me wider than I had ever experienced before. In truth, it hurt, but it was the kind of pain I get off on. I wanted to feel all that he had to give. His hands moved around to the cheeks of my arse and drew me closer to him, as if he were trying to drill beyond where any man had gone before. His mouth sought my heaving breasts, nuzzling and biting, kissing and licking.

We rutted together, fighting against each other's deliberately contrasting rhythms, composing our own erotic orchestral movement. All the while each of us kept to our own beat, slightly out of time with the other's, but we both knew we were building up to the most rousing of crescendos.

I threw my head back, thrusting myself even harder against him, impaling myself on the slick shaft of his pulsating member. My pussy continued to milk him in its vicelike grip, sliding effortlessly back and forth as he ploughed into me. We didn't care. The night clerk was still on shift but neither of us paid him any regard – in fact, I'll admit that I *hoped* that he could see us. Hear us. Even wish he was with us …

Indeed, for a split second I let myself imagine just that. I allowed myself to fantasise about how it would feel to have the rigid cock of this stranger fuck me from behind while the searching tongue of the library assistant lapped at my clit from the front. I felt my orgasm begin to rumble in my toes. Instinctively, I clenched in order to steady myself against his hardness as I felt the waves ripple and tease me to the brink of losing control.

As if sensing my imminent explosion, he deftly managed to withdraw, flip me over and re-enter me again. He was skilled, I couldn't deny that. His rhythm slowed but the depth of his thrusts remained. He pressed his right hand against the throb of my clit grinding it in circular rotations timed to the thrusts of his cock.

The feeling was electric. I moved against him and felt the climax resonate throughout my body in a deep, low, gasping moan which seemed to last an eternity. Every nerve ending seemed to spark into life, firing at me, varying in intensity and reducing me to the most primal of reactions. As I continued to come hard and wet, he too began to lose control – and, as he peaked he pulled back, took his cock in hand and shot his hot jets of jizz against my engorged button, rubbing his shaft against it, using my toned, slender thighs to wank himself, empty himself, sap himself of every drop of come he had to give.

At last, He slumped on top of me, spooning my back as our feet remained firmly on the floor, both of us bent over the desk like masochistic submissives anticipating a good, firm spanking. Neither of us moved save for the occasional butterfly kiss he dropped on the nape of my neck. We breathed in sync, drinking in every last second of our fiery union – and that was the very moment at which I thought of you, Santa.

I hoped you were watching. I hoped you could see. I wanted you to know that your good girl didn't want to make the choice between being naughty or nice – because being both was far more thrilling that any gift you could leave for me under my Christmas tree. I was performing for you, because I know your game. You're a voyeur. And you've embraced your role as the overseer of good and bad behaviour so that you can watch. Don't worry, I'm not judging you – I like to watch too. Let'd just say it's a perk of your job, shall we …?

And so, Santa, I guess there'll be nothing from your sack for me again this year. I do so wish I could have been good … But something tells me neither of us would want that – after all, with such a talent for being naughty, it would be such a shame for me to put all of that wickedness to waste!

Until next year – Merry Christmas!

Much love,

R

XXX

234